P9-DEC-190

# notes from ghost town

# notes from ghost town

kate ellison

EGMONT
USA
new york

*Notes from Ghost Town* is a work of fiction that takes place in Miami. Names, characters, landmarks, and neighborhoods are entirely of the author's own invention or are used fictitiously.

EGMONT

*We bring stories to life*

First published by Egmont USA, 2013
443 Park Avenue South, Suite 806
New York, NY 10016



1 3 5 7 9 8 6 4 2

www.egmontusa.com
www.kateellison.com

Library of Congress Cataloging-in-Publication Data

Ellison, Kate.
Notes from Ghost Town / Kate Ellison.
p. cm.
Summary: Young artist Olivia Tithe struggles to keep her sanity as she unravels the mystery of her first love's death through his ghostly visits
ISBN 978-1-60684-264-5 (hardback) — ISBN 978-1-60684-407-6 (electronic book) [1. Love—Fiction. 2. Death—Fiction. 3. Schizophrenia—Fiction. 4. Ghosts—Fiction. 5. Murder—Fiction. 6. Remarriage—Fiction. 7. Mystery and detective stories.] I. Title.
PZ7.E476485Not 2013
[Fic]—dc23
2012024616

Printed in the United States of America

To Adley and Rece,
the sweetest boys who live.

# prologue

Think about a moment, a little centimeter of time you'd happily exist in forever, if time could be laid out along the spine of a ruler. Maybe it haunts you in that blue inch of half consciousness just before you're fully awake.

Here is mine: Miami, me and Stern. One week before I was supposed to go back to art school.

If I could stay there, in that moment before everything changed, I would stay there forever.

I'd see him standing before me, spun out, golden, suspended in light that looks like honey. The thick black curls of his hair, how wide his eyes get, blazing electric in the sun. The slender gap between his front teeth he always tries to hide with his hands when he smiles.

We'd be in the old shed behind Oh Susannah, the bright purple house my parents built before I was born. Stern named the house when he was four years old—the year he began taking piano lessons with my mom. It's the first song Mom taught him to play when he was a Tiny. He came to associate the house with the song.

*Oh Susannah, don't you cry for me*. He sings it as soon as the house comes into view. I hear him singing it, and I see him approach.

And right there, I'd press the *freeze* button.

His smile would be spread across his whole damn god-awful glorious face. Silence. Nothing would have begun yet, nothing would have begun to end. *Freeze.*

I could stand here at the door to the splintery shed with that vibration of anticipation between us, staring at his god-awful glorious face forever. And we would never have to do anything but this.

And we would never have to change.

And he would never have to go away.

# one

U*nfreeze.*

But only because there is no other way to tell this story.

"It's too hot for manual labor, Liv," Stern complains, as we lift a giant painting I made over the summer—a seascape, the sky bleeding aqua into the deep green waves—from a fat stack of other paintings inside the little storage shed behind Oh Susannah. My best friend's voice is husky and smooth, not like it was when we were kids.

He heaves the canvas above his head, while I stoop to the dusty ground and lift a different painting—blackbirds, nestled between the thick leaves of palm trees. Stern and I both pause in the dark of the shed, still not willing to move back out under the sun. The cotton of my tank top sticks to every inch of my skin.

I notice the way Stern's muscles twitch as he shifts his grip on the canvas, and I realize I'm twitching, too, just looking at him. And this scares me a little bit, but also thrills me.

"We'd better move now," Stern says, tapping his big, neon Nike sandal-clad foot against the concrete floor of the shed. A cloud of dust rises. My eyes water. "Or we're going to die like this."

Stern moves toward Jasper, my rusted-up, old, frog green Capri, so-named because it reminded Stern of the color of the swamp frogs he's always called by the same name.

Mom and Dad will drive me (and Jasper) back to school tomorrow, all the way from sea to shining lake. They will suffer the presence of each other in cramped-car-quarters one last time, for my sake. Then they will leave us—Jasper and me—to the mercy of Michigan and I will cross my fingers for an Indian summer before all the snow comes while they jet back home, where it is eternally hot. Mom will call to tell me they've arrived safely. What she'll probably spare me is all of the details of what's to follow once I leave: Dad's departure (they decided he wouldn't actually move out until I was out of the house), deciding who gets what, packing boxes piled up in the living room, and those Styrofoam popcorn things I used to love to pinch between my fingers, scattered across the hardwood floor.

They've been separated for three months already, divorced for one week. Mom knows the divorce is still too fresh for it to seem like anything but a momentary sickness to me. An open wound capable of being stitched back together.

"Come on, Liver!" Stern calls back, when he notices I've fallen behind.

"Slave driver!" I grunt, beginning to move backward out of the shed and to the trunk of the rusted-up old Capri at the top of the driveway.

Through a window, I see Dad inside, preparing dinner. Biscuit flour sifts through the clear of the window like softly falling snow. I didn't even know what snow looked like until last winter. We don't get much of the stuff in Miami. Stern made me Skype with him the first time it snowed, and position the computer outside the window so he could watch it with me.

We finally make it outside of the shed. We settle both paintings gently inside my trunk, our fingers slick with sweat.

"Nice," I say with a sigh. "Okay. Can we stop now?" I smile huge, tucking my top lip under so my gums show.

He sticks his tongue out at me, wipes his hands off on his shorts, and starts walking back into the shed. I follow him. "We can stop when we're finished," he says. Then he stops, sighing. "I can't believe you're leaving already." He fishes for something in the pocket of his shorts. "Oh, by the way—I made you something to remember me by on those lonely, lonely Michigan nights. A going-away gift." He hands me a CD marked *L. STERN, PIANO GOD* (subtitled in very tiny red letters, *Lucas Stern vs. Juilliard: Practice sessions of our nation's foremost musical savant*).

I grip the CD in one hand, bringing it dramatically to my

heart. "Wow. What an honor, L. Stern, piano god. Because I was just thinking that listening to you practice the same audition piece with my mom hundreds and hundreds of times just wasn't enough."

He grins. "I know, right? Don't you wish you could be there at the recital to see the piano god himself, in real time? Especially in case he screws it all up and needs someone to make him feel less shitty about it afterward."

A fresh bead of sweat trickles down my back. "There's no chance of the piano god screwing it up," I say. "And you know I'd be there if my stupid trimester didn't start so early."

"Now, his next great challenge: eating two separate dinners with your parents, alone, every night while you're gone."

"Well," I start, laying the CD safely atop a box marked *LIV: MICHIGAN* in dad's chicken scratch as my jaw tightens, "you've still got a couple of single-dinner days before Dad moves in with Heather." I take a deep breath and shoot Stern a pitiful glance. "Wish there was a CD to remedy that. . . ."

He swivels the tip of one sandaled foot into the concrete ground. "I'm sorry, Liver," he says softly, "I didn't mean to bring it up again." His basketball shorts begin to dip down his hips a bit and he tugs them up a little higher before bending to lift the next painting. I see the line of dark hair that snakes down from his belly button, the flat of his belly where once there was little-boy chub.

The length, the height of him. The flush of his skin. The red swell of his lips.

"Well, they're practically your parents, too," I say, quickly, hoping words will shut out the unexpected buzzing feeling he's sending through my body. "I mean, you've definitely hung out with my mom way more than I have this summer."

"I wouldn't exactly call drilling the same piece for a Juilliard audition until my fingers go numb 'hanging out,'" he says, hugging one of my half-assed paintings into his chest. "Though your mom is way cooler than mine ever will be."

"Aside from the whole schizophrenia thing, you mean?" I say it as a joke, but the word—*schizophrenia*—brings a weird taste to my mouth.

Some days, she's still fine. Better than fine: brilliant. Stern still takes lessons from her, when she's actually taking her meds, (when she's not so preoccupied with how they *dull her creative spirit*), when she's safe—when her fingers glide across the keys and what results is the kind of music that makes you stop just where you are and notice every beautiful thing around you.

*His* fingers can do this, too. I listen to his music as I paint sometimes, up in my hardwood triangle of a room.

Now, as I watch his long, beautiful fingers curled around the edge of my canvas, I feel a weird, sudden thrill, like being buckled into the swaying plastic seat of a roller coaster, just before it rockets downward. This feeling has been building in me for a long, long time—a thing I still don't quite know how to define.

Until this past year, I never even looked at him like a *boy*. I know everything about him: that his first *real* kiss was with Marisol Fuentes, in eighth grade, in Marisol's mom's hot tub. I know that, as a little kid, he used to like to play dress-up in his mother's clothes, complete with headbands and clip-on earrings. I know that his biggest fear is getting in an accident and losing his hands.

But none of this ever helped me to realize that one day something would change without either of us quite understanding How or What. Stern—my funny, chubby, nerdy little Stern—suddenly became this other *being* with stubble and a little chin cleft that gets even deeper when he smiles.

I can't deny it, no matter how hard I try. And I do try. But Stern is undeniably and unquestionably hot. How did I not notice before?

I meet his eye for a second and there's a glint there—like he knows, too, that something has . . . shifted. We squat down and wrap our fingers around the next frame, an oversized piece, and—eyes on each other—haul ass back into the double-balls-hot outdoors. I watch some lopped-off power lines wriggle in the breeze. The heat's dizzying, the palm trees quiet and still, heavy leaves drooping. Devil sun.

We're near the end of the stack of paintings, and I'm leaning against the hot metal side of the car, probably singeing holes into my tank top. Stern's got a funny smile—one that makes his face look sort of monkeyish—as he walks toward me, carrying one of the final paintings. "I found my favorite one," he tells me, raising his eyebrows.

"I don't believe I asked you to select one, Sterny. . . ." And then he flips it around so I can see it: my self-portrait. My *naked* self-portrait. Boobs. Fire crotch. I painted it last year for an assignment. One of those art-class-bonding things. We all had to do it. Mine was a major fail. *Disproportionate*, Mrs. Webb had commented as the other students nodded their agreement. When I came back home that summer, I made sure to hide it way back in the shed so I'd never have to think of it again, which I haven't, until right now.

"Nice . . . um, *work*, Liv," Stern says, barely managing to stop himself from laughing. "You've got really nice . . . brushstrokes."

I try to wrestle it from his hands, but his grip is strong. "Let go, asshole!" I cry, leaning into him, wrapping my arms around his waist, trying to tickle him. He lifts the painting over his head, moving his weight into me. We topple over onto the hot, dusty side yard just next to the driveway, pushing and pulling, the canvas sliding from his fingers, face up, onto the gravel. I grip my thighs around the outsides of his legs and roll into him until he's panting beneath me. But before I have an opportunity to reach for the painting, he rolls me under him again, leg rooted between my thighs, and presses my wrists together above my head so I can't even wriggle them an inch. I gaze up at him, sun gold-white behind his head, grunting, sweating.

"Stop freaking out," he says, gazing down at me, a little crack in his deep voice. "I meant it: I think your painting is beautiful, Olivia." I realize by the heat in my cheeks that I'm blushing like crazy. And so is he. Cheeks vibrant pink, almost electric. He's moving his big hazel eyes over me like he's never seen me before. We stay like this, heat pressing against us from all sides. And then, tentatively, he moves his hand to my cheek and draws me toward him, touching his lips to mine, so soft. I feel his fingers through my hair, his big hand cradling the back of my head; a hot rush, a pulse, fills my whole body as I press into him, kissing him back. I let my eyes shut as he presses even closer into me, and I stop noticing the heat. I stop noticing anything but a vague, vibrating dizziness pulsing through me—my body melting and trembling into his. *Stern. This is Stern.*

He pulls away for a moment and when I open my eyes to look at him my stomach drops out from beneath me, hard, like on a roller coaster. His eyes.

His hazel eyes have turned gray.

I scuttle back, dizzy, blinking hard—his eyes won't change back. We kissed and now his eyes won't change back. The world seems to tip, pulling me with it. I can't get steady, can't make sense of it. His skin isn't tan anymore; it's the color of old newspaper.

Suddenly—like the flash of a photograph—the sky loses

its blue, goes heavy-looking. I blink several times, but it's still the same: dim, gray, disorienting, like I've stepped into a black-and-white dream.

*No.* I'm shaking my head. *No.* Panic floors me. I cannot move. *The Gray Space.* The place Mom told me about: the dead place, without music, without color. Is *this* the Gray Space?

It's happening. I'm going crazy. Like Mom.

Stern looks deflated. "That was—that was a mistake," he mumbles. "I didn't . . . I wasn't thinking. It just happened." He bites his lip. "I hope it doesn't . . . I don't want this to mess things up for us. As friends."

*No.* "Stern—" My chest is tight, voice weak—I don't know how to explain what's happening without seeming totally *nuts.* I can't get anything out at all. I can't tell him that I don't regret it, that I would never regret it. That I wanted it. So I just sit there. Mute. Terrified. He stands up, avoiding my eyes.

"I—I have to get to work. . . ." He slaps the dust from the back of his basketball shorts. "Forgot I was covering Lupe's shift. . . . Look, I'll see you soon, okay?"

And that's that.

Moments later, still frozen there in the dirt, I watch him—shirt back on—speed walk back out to his now-gray Toyota without even a wave good-bye. I watch the gray exhaust snake through the gray sky.

Gray. Gray. Gray. *The Gray Space.* The dead space. Mom's hands, lingering on the piano keys as she described it to me. *As long as I have music, as long as I am healthy, the Gray Space stays away.*

I bang the back of my head against the wood, trying to knock out whatever has gone off. But it sticks. The horrible, sickening gray. Everywhere.

And beneath the gray heaviness, a sharp, jabbing concern: why didn't I fully realize until this instant that I *want* Stern? I want him like *that*. I want to wrestle with him in the dark dirt and kiss his lips and run my fingers through his thick black hair and hold his hand at parties. He was always the best part of coming home, on break from school, and I'd hardly even realized it.

Stern. I want to feel him press against me, spin me under him again.

But he said it was a mistake. It didn't mean anything. So why did he do it?

My head won't stop spinning. The world still looks stone gray.

The first time mom's brain "went funny" on her, or at least the first time I really heard about it, was when I was almost twelve. She was sure she'd seen snakes, pressing up through the keys of her piano. She stood hovering over the instrument with a butcher knife, preparing to stab clear through to their hearts. Later, after Dad calmed her down and her eyes cleared up, she said: *Something's happening to me. It isn't right. I'm scared.*

*Boom.* Thunder shudders through a dark gray sky, warm raindrops spatter to my skin—I guess my eyes aren't totally wrong. A storm is coming. I lift myself from the ground to my car, slam my trunk shut, lean against the hot metal, and let the rain take the dirt from my skin.

Tomorrow, I'll drive clear through the heat and swaying palm, far away. I'll give it a few days, settle into my new dorm room, finish my paintings. If Stern doesn't call within a week, I will break down, and I will call him.

I will tell him I love him. There will be tearful confessions on his part, and we'll be in love. And my eyes will flood back with color, instantly returning to normal.

I'm not worried.

Except that there is one tiny little snag in my plan.

In one week, Stern will be dead.

And Mom will be taken in the middle of the night and stuffed behind the bars of Broadwaithe Jail, accused of murdering him.

# two

"A little less than a year," I tell Dr. Levine, my ophthalmologist, face planted against a heavy metal contraption as I stare at shapes projected against the wall in colors I can't distinguish.

I've been completely color-blind for ten months. Ten months since the kiss; ten months since the last moments I ever spent with Stern. Ten months since he died. I can't help but wonder what the Fourth of July fireworks will look like tonight, shooting through the sky in shades of gray.

I'm starting to forget what color ever looked like. Since I've stopped painting, other things have started to mute themselves, too: how a brush felt in my hand, the feel of the palette knife, the smell of charcoal and turpentine. I miss leaning toward the mystery of what would appear on the canvas. I could trust my art. I could depend on it.

But that's gone now. That trust has disappeared, along with my mother's freedom, the most important friendship of my life, and my relationship with Dad.

Now, all that's left is to wait for the inevitable.

Nine days. Nine days until her hearing. Nine days until they tell us, officially, she's gone for good.

Dr. Levine was nice enough to take an appointment on a holiday. Maybe, like me, he doesn't have anything better to do. He moves the machine to the side and turns the light back on, swiveling a chair up beside me. He's tested me for the past hour—quick bursts of air to each cornea, a too-bright light so he can see straight through to the back of my skull, pieces of paper filled with dotted numbers, rising from similarly dotted backgrounds.

"Olivia," he begins gently, "There's no evidence of retinal damage in your eyes. Actually, your grayscale contrasts are surprisingly high."

"So? What does that mean?" I shift forward in the big leather chair.

He pushes his glasses up the bridge of his nose. "Cerebral achromatopsia, which seems to be what you're complaining of, is almost unheard of. It's an *extremely* rare condition—almost always a result of some kind of damage to the occipital lobe on both hemispheres of the brain, which is why it's so unlikely that you have it."

I can feel my face flushing. "I—I can't even paint anymore." My voice catches and I try to clear my throat.

"I'm not saying that it's not a big deal, or that I don't believe you, Olivia," Dr. Levine says, resting his hand softly on my shoulder, like he's speaking to a four-year-old—he's spoken this way to me *since* I was four, in fact, never bothering to alter his tone. "What I'm saying is . . . I don't think there's a *physical* reason for what's going on."

I look up at him, narrowing my eyes. "Then why is this happening to me?"

He clears his throat, pulls a pen out from behind his ear, and replaces it absently. "Maybe you ought to think of talking to someone—someone professional. I know some really excellent people. I think it would be very good for you."

He tries to put his hand on my shoulder again, but I instantly recoil.

"What are you saying?"

He opens both hands, palms up. "There's nothing shameful about it. I've seen a therapist for decades. It's very normal."

The room goes suddenly morgue-cold. I know this path: my mother went down the same one, and he knows it. "You think I'm crazy."

"No." He shakes his fuzzy white-gray head. "I'm saying you've been through a lot lately . . . more than your fair share."

More than my fair share. He doesn't know the half of it.

I don't respond, just scoot quickly out of the deep-set chair. He sighs as I make my way to the door. I don't want to talk about all I've *been through* with him or with anyone.

I tried therapy for the first time when I was twelve. That was the first year Mom's patchwork craziness crept in full-quilt-swing. Dr. Adley Nolan, an old dude with a long, horsey face, told me after two measly sessions that crazy was in my genes. All I had to do was wait.

Dad never made me go back to therapy after that. I think he felt guilty about how much that traumatized me. Also, Dad doesn't really know how bad things have gotten.

No one does.

Dr. Levine opens the door, ushers me into the lobby, stopping me just before I can scoot the hell out of there. "Olivia. Look—I've known you since you were a little kid. I've listened to your parents go on and on about you. I know how important your artwork is to you. How important it's *always* been."

In my head I'm going, *yeah. So?* I stare at my chipped black fingernail polish—last year, I would have been able to see that it was plum.

"Keep sketching—just stick to black and white for now," he says. "The colors will be there for you when you're ready for them, don't worry about that. You'll see—everything will turn out fine. I know it will." He fixes me with the kind of condescending grin reserved for babies and nutjobs. "You're young; that won't last forever. Try to relax, for me, huh? Can you do that?"

I sit in my car for a while, forehead against the searing-hot steering wheel, not caring that the air's so stiff it's almost impossible to breathe. A group of middle school kids amble through the dry lawn in front of the parking lot, obviously on their way to the beach. They wear string bikinis over their little tadpole chests, barely-there booty shorts high up on their brown legs.

*Brown* only because they're a darker gray than my own.

I've become good at such guesswork—distinguishing things like blue from red from brown. I memorize the particular hue and texture of things like postal boxes and stop signs, trying to place them again in things like T-shirts and lip gloss and sand. It's hard: relearning the colored world in shades of gray.

The girls push one another into the hairless boys in front of them, giggle, and cartwheel.

I turn the engine on and blast the AC, finally, to block out their sounds. They remind me of a time that only makes me sad now—before I left, before Mom started seeing things in droves that weren't there, before Dad decided he couldn't handle it anymore, before Stern and I ever had the notion that we'd be anything to each other but BFFs for life. Before we knew that we were not permanent, and that a good, easy life is not something the universe is contractually obligated to grant you.

I inch out of my parking spot, pull through the manicured complex of boxy, brick doctors' offices, lines of plumeria trees stooped in heat—all of it, to my eyes, the same smudgy, dull gray color. I keep wondering when my mind will get even worse: when I'll start imagining things that aren't there, when I won't be able to hide it anymore, when everyone will know.

It all started for Mom in her freshman year of college, those first insidious signs: lights suddenly seeming overwhelmingly bright, snippets of other people's voices heard alone, in the dark.

I've read that schizoisms usually start creeping in between the ages of fifteen and twenty-five, often set off by trauma or an unexpected event *(check)*.

*It's starting*, a small voice jabs at the backs of my ears. *Now's when it starts.*

My phone vibrates in the pocket of my favorite old cutoffs, badly frayed at the bottom and covered in paint. Maybe it's Raina. Calling to beg me to come to her uncle's boat to watch the fireworks, like we used to do every year with Stern.

This year, I'm being forced to attend my father's awful business party, and Raina's already offered up my spot—and Stern's—to *Tif and Hilary, from the swim team.* I wonder sometimes if she's bragging—like we're keeping secret tally of new friends made. Olivia—minus one; Raina—gain two. But maybe—by some miracle—she wants to ditch the whole thing to pregame in the parking lot with me, then stumble drunk into that stuffy ballroom arm in arm. I check my phone at the next stop sign with shaking hands, but it's only Dad: *Darlin! Don't 4get about the party 2nite!!!*

My heart drops like a weight. *The party 2nite*—I hate the way parents text. My dad obviously thinks I'm *excited* to spend my Fourth of July at some lame business event with rich real-estate execs and their boob-jobbed housewives. Of course, he doesn't know much about what excites me anymore. He hasn't been around a lot recently; he divides his time between his soon-to-be-wife Heather and his creepy, soon-to-be-condo-complex for rich people, Elysian Fields. His Texas doesn't drip out anymore when Heather's around. It gets squinched in, flattened into something else.

A few months ago, when I found out Dad was going to marry Heather—literally, the most boring, Hallmark-card woman on earth—I couldn't believe it. They'd only been dating a little over a year—met at some support group for people with "loved ones afflicted by emotional instability," back before the divorce was even official yet. I didn't even know he'd been a part of the group in the first place.

He and Mom had been separated less than three months and already he and Dingbat were busy falling in love. And then he proposed to her. He called me up on the phone on a Monday morning in January, right before first period—art history—and broke the news in a soft voice, like that would make it easier to take. I had to hang up so I could puke. Until then, I'd still been holding on to this idea that Heather was just a placeholder, a temporary fixture in Dad's life while he figured out that he could never love anyone but Mom.

My colors were gone at that point anyway, so I stopped painting entirely, shoved all of my art supplies into a big army bag so I wouldn't have to look at them. Instead of doing homework, I went to parties and made out with too many angsty art boys to count, before I let myself fail out of school entirely and returned home to Miami. I've been back a month and a half; it's amazing how slow time has gotten, like clocks themselves have learned to work less quickly.

I still haven't even told Dad about the Gray Space, the color blindness. I keep thinking maybe if I don't talk about it, the color will come back.

*Honnnnnk*. The Mercedes behind me blares its horn. The light in front of me must have turned green several seconds ago. I toss my cell phone onto the coffee-stained passenger seat and put my foot on the gas. "I'm going!" I yell—to myself, to the cloudless, ash-colored sky, to my rearview mirror. "I'm going."

Heather's sipping iced tea at the kitchen table when I get home. "Oh, good, you're back!" she says, her pointy features harnessed upward toward her tight, blond ponytail. She looks almost albino to me—both her hair and skin this mute light gray. "Dave was starting to worry you'd forgotten about tonight. Did you have a good—"

"—yeah. Great." I mutter, cutting her off as I race upstairs. I hate that she calls my father Dave. Just *Dave,* as though it's some private club she's now become a member of.

Back in my room, I try to select my outfit for the night. Dad's voice runs through my head as I thumb through my messy dresser drawers, dresses half-cocked off hangers in my closet: *please, Liv, try to tone it down a little for the party, okay? For me.*

This is new, too. This idea Dad's suddenly developed that I have qualities that need "toning down." Mom would have defended me—she always encouraged my style. Heather, on the other hand, wouldn't know creativity if it bit her hard in the ass. What she knows is what other people tell her: saltwater pearls, creamy pastels from Ann Taylor, Coach handbags.

The only good thing to come out of that woman is Wynn, her five-year-old daughter—still, thankfully, too young to be tainted by her mother's obscene blandness. Wynn's the only reason I can get dressed and not look like a total fool. A couple of weeks ago, she helped me separate my clothes by color, thinking it was a game. She loved every minute of it, grinning half-toothless as each pile grew. *And what color is* this, *Wynn?* I'd ask as she looked shyly down at the pile. *Blue! It's blue, Livie!*

And, that's why I've got twelve different color labels written out in a five-year-old's messy scrawl, scotch-taped to the base of each divided section of my closet and dresser. I poke my head out of my doorway and call to her: "Panda! Come help me pick out what to wear tonight." I hear the rush of her padded footsteps on the carpet as she runs to me and wraps herself around my legs.

"Gwizzly!" She squeals, hugging me tighter. Last time I was home, we discussed what kind of bears we would be if, one day, aliens landed in South Florida and changed everyone into bears. I'm pretty sure she picked *panda* based solely on my childhood stuffed animal, which I passed on to her over Christmas—Stern gave it to *me* after I got my appendix out in second grade. There was no point in staring at it every night; it only made me feel hollow and alone.

She ballerina-twirls into my room and picks out a clingy strapless dress from the "dark perple" pile, lace-up-the-ankle leather sandals from the "tan" pile, and a necklace of sandalwood beads that used to be Mom's.

"What are you doing tonight, little bear?" I ask her, studying my reflection in the mirror above my dresser, running my fingers through my wavy auburn hair (now a muddled, murky version of gray), making pouty model faces at my reflection. Wynn imitates alongside me, swishing her ballerina skirt side to side.

"Going to see the firelights with Lisa. But can I come with you instead? Pleeease?" She zips her lips up and stands soldier-straight, eyes wide and pleading.

I pick her up and hug her to me, planting a kiss on her freckled nose before setting her back down. "You know what, Panda? I wish I could come with *you*. You're going to have so much fun seeing the firelights. I know it."

I shoo her back to her room so I can finish getting ready, and watch her swish happily down the hallway.

A few minutes later, Heather calls to me from downstairs. "Olivia?" When I don't respond, she just keeps talking. "I'm going to drop Wynn at the Jeffreys' and head over to the party. Your Dad's already there." *Duh.* "So I'll see you over there in a few minutes?" I hear her sigh, imagine her just standing there, hands on narrow hips, staring up into emptiness, waiting.

"Yes," I finally shout. "I'll see you there."

I give myself a final go-over: push my boobs together in my dress, run mascara over my lashes, spread clear gloss over my full-petal lips.

There'll be private school boys there tonight—the sons of Elysian Fields' monstrously rich investors, no doubt—in full-on rich-boy boat-shoed glory. And even if they're all dick-brains, I still want them to think I'm pretty. I hardly want anything anymore. But I still want that.

The scent of plumeria mingles with other heady, floral smells—white ginger, calla lily, sage—as I shoot my way down less traffic-y side streets to Dad's party on my bike, trying not to go too fast, not wanting to get sweaty: a difficult task during a South Florida summer. The ocean *whurr-whurr*s as I draw closer to it.

I ride into the parking lot of Elysian Fields only moderately soaked and my heart shimmies into my stomach. Elysian Fields is Dad's first venture into the wild world of Commercial Real Estate. Raina and I call this place Ghost Town—from the first time we stepped foot on the grounds, something about it set us both shivering.

They started construction about four months before Stern died and Mom was locked up, bail posted at one million dollars, obviously way more than my dad could cough up. Every time I came home from school, I saw more and more of Elysian Fields, and less and less of Mom. That's all it makes me think of—that sick feeling that hollowed my stomach every time I'd drive past it. The irony is that Elysian Fields is a mere fifteen-minute walk down the beach from our perfect old purple house. Seeing it complete, now, is just that final punch-in-the-gut reminder of how completely gone Mom is from me, from all of us—like it's actually *her* beneath the grounds. Dad built something huge and ugly and expensive on top of it to obscure her.

Ghost Town, any way you slice it.

My throat aches. If I was with Raina and Stern right now, we'd be listening to Bob Dylan and drinking Miller High Life on the deck of her Uncle Peter's boat.

*Stern.* His name pounds through me like a second heartbeat as I lock up my bike and drag myself toward the spotless glass Ghost Town lobby doors. I miss him. Bad.

I never told Raina about our kiss, almost a whole year ago, even though I tell her everything. But all I've wanted to do is make it go away; telling her about it would make the loss somehow bigger.

As soon as I enter Elysian Fields's Oceanus Ballroom, that new-kid-on-the-first-day-of-school feeling rushes cold through my body. Ghost Town is grand and show-offy inside—all shine, and crystal chandelier, and mute gray walls. To everyone else, I'm guessing they're cream-colored.

The foyer is flooded with light. Huge, gleaming windows face the gravel drudge of the parking lot. If only they faced the ocean instead. If only the ocean were on this side of the building, or all sides of the building. If only the ocean would leap up and suck this whole bad juju-ed structure in with it. I run my fingertips along the surface of the baby grand piano they've got displayed, uselessly, next to the cushy deep-gray (red?) couches on the other side of the room.

If Mom were here she'd open the lid, and the second her fingers found the notes, this stuffy rich-person parade would abandon their prime rib to crowd behind her and listen, transfixed. Pure magic. *They all want to leave the Gray Space, Liv,* she'd tell me. *They don't realize they're dead until they remember what it sounds like to be alive.*

I spot Dad near the buffet with Ted Oakley—a family friend who fronted the money for this whole shining-new mess, and dragged Dad into it all in the first place when Dad's work as a builder dried up in tandem with the Miami housing market. I zigzag my way toward them through rows of pristinely set tables and high-backed chairs, tailored business men in near-identical button-ups, arm in arm with their spray-tanned, pulled-and-pinched wives.

I half trip over an errant dinner napkin, balled up on the floor, and catch Bryce Gregorhoff smirking at me from a table nearby, where he is sitting with Austin Morse—Ted Oakley's double-douche-bag stepson.

One glance tells me they've been talking about me. Olivia Tithe: daughter of a murderer. Art school dropout. General deviant. Several other Finnegan Prep boys look briefly over at me, too, giving me the once-over and turning around.

Bryce and Raina hooked up at a private school party a couple of months back. She called me the same night, wincing, saying he shoved his hands down her pants for about ten seconds, during which time Raina just felt like a couch he was scouring for loose change. I turn my back to their table, pulling out my phone to text her: *Edward Crotchhands is here. He wants you to come visit.*

The biggest, loneliest part of me hopes she'll respond with something like: *Miss you, Liv! This really sucks without you.*

But when my phone buzzes in my hand, her text says: *Nooooo! The twat-mangler!!! Told Tif and Hil all about it and they're dying.* Now that Raina's on the swim team, the "cool kids" have started noticing her. She's got new things to think about that don't involve me. Like Tif, and Hilary.

Dad spots me and hollers across the room from his table: "Olivia Jane! We're over here!" Which makes the boys look back at me again and laugh. I shoot them a *fuck off* look, walking quickly away, heels clicking on the shined-up parquet.

Ted Oakley stands from the table, smiling broadly.

"Olivia. It's so good to have you back home. You look great." He pulls me in for an over-long hug. He smells good, in a comforting, old-man way—like expensive aftershave and even more expensive booze.

"She looks *skinny*, is what," Dad says. "Take my plate, and then get seconds. I mean it!" he says, pushing it gently toward me as I sit down beside him. That's another thing that's happened since the world went gray: food tastes different. I didn't even realize how much better the sun-bright yellow of a pepper made it taste, or the vermillion of a tomato sauce on ravioli, which now looks washed-out and disgusting.

I push the plate away. "I'm not hungry, Dad. Ate a huge sandwich for lunch." I feel my face flush again as I say it. I can't tell him that the Gray Space affects everything, takes away my hunger, my senses. I want to tell someone, badly. But I can't risk it. Can't risk Dad thinking that his only daughter is on the road to Crazy-Town, that same road his own ex-wife walked down.

Would he ditch me, too, if he knew? Send me away somewhere?

No. He can't know.

He and Ted share a glance—that silent *oh, teenagers!* exchange that's somehow infuriating and reassuring at the same time.

"You know, Austin's somewhere around here. . . ." Ted says, scanning the crowd. "Have you two gotten a chance to touch base yet?"

"No, I haven't seen him," I lie, forcing a forkful of arugula (stone-colored, to me) into my mouth so as to spare him the awful truth: we are not two people who "touch base."

Austin's always been somewhere in my life, floating just beyond reach. We played as little kids, but by the time we were in elementary school, he'd already started at an expensive prep school while I stayed put at the public one. Our differences have always been abundant and clear: he's a spoiled, self-involved dickbag whose mom and stepdad are richer than god, and I'm a weird art-chick whose mother went bat-shit and murdered her piano prodigy student.

Never gonna happen.

I spot Heather pushing toward our table with her pointy Chihuahua grin, blond hair bouncing.

"Well, that's my cue," I say, not caring how rude I sound. I scoot out of my chair just as she reaches us.

"Olivia! Where are you off to in such a rush?" Heather asks, adjusting her probably-pink shirtdress nervously as she watches me pull away.

"Bathroom," I chirp, brushing swiftly past her and finding my way to the bar instead.

I twist a thin plastic straw around in my mouth while I wait my turn. I glance back at Dad's table—he's rubbing Heather's shoulders, giving her little kisses on her ears. I turn back to the bar so quick I practically give myself whiplash.

The bartender looks young. I think he might be a little

stoned; he kind of looks it. I order a Stella when it's my turn, hoping he's too mentally hazy to ask for ID.

"You are twenty-one?" he asks with a Cuban accent.

"I'm twenty-two, actually," I tell him, remembering Raina's no-fail dictum: *fake it 'til you make it.*

After a pause, he shrugs. "Okay, Mami, whatever you say." He turns to grab a glass and starts pouring. I reach for a couple dollars from my wallet, float them into his tip jar like I do this all the time.

"*Gracias.*" I smile at him. His eyes drop briefly to my chest.

"*Ahem.*" Someone clears his throat behind me, taps my shoulder. My spine goes rigid.

I spin slowly around, expecting the disappointed stare-down of Dad, or Heather.

But it's Austin Morse.

His eyes tick down toward my glass and he smirks. "Go slow, kiddo, okay? Don't want to have to hold your hair back later."

Every single thing about Austin Morse is tinged with the kind of condescension that says, *I've always been better than you*—from his thick dark blond hair that seems perfectly tousled to his square jaw to his perfect teeth and, as my mother used to say, his *Herculean* build. Six foot two, captain of the swim and lacrosse teams. A bratty, tiresome jerk in the body of a Greek god. It's amazing that he was raised for most of his life by Ted Oakley, who married Austin's mother when Austin was an infant. Ted Oakley has been nothing short of amazing to my family ever since Mom got locked up, and I can't imagine why some of his goodness didn't rub off on his stepson.

"I've been drinking since I was fourteen, actually," I say.

"Oh, really?" he asks, looking me over. "I heard about some other things you've been doing since you were fourteen, too. . . ."

I shouldn't take his bait, but I do. "Like what?"

"Oh, you know. I seem to remember hearing about some epic game of truth and dare . . . when you gave Heath Pratt an HJ in his parents' basement."

I take a long swig from my beer, hoping the liquid will cool the blush off my cheeks. "Heath Pratt *wishes*. I wouldn't get close to him with someone *else's* hand."

"So you're a prude, then?" he whispers, right up close to my ear, grabbing the drink, suddenly, from my hand and taking a drawn-out chug. He hands me back the empty glass, a wicked smile on his face. "That's disappointing."

I *really* want to punch him. "I'm not a prude," I say.

He laughs. "Care to prove it?"

I see him exchange a look with the rest of Finnegan Prep conglomerate across the room—Bryce quickly sets the steak knife he'd been holding to Mitch's neck back on the table when he catches me looking.

Suddenly, I can't bear to be in this room a single second longer, everyone's gaze flitting on and off me, trying not to look, unable to resist—like I'm a roadside accident and they're slowing down traffic just to see how ruined I am.

I wait until the bartender's looking the other way and then reach behind the bar to swipe a full bottle of the first thing that comes into sight: Grey Goose. I turn on my heels and start walking away.

"Hey—Prudie. We were in the middle of a conversation," Austin calls out.

I pause, turn briefly back to him. "I'm going to the beach."

"Oh. Really?" He sounds disappointed.

"Follow me if you want." I don't know why I even offer; I don't care whether he comes. I don't care whether he *drowns*.

He hesitates.

"And you call me the prude?" I say. Then I turn back around and slip through the entranceway, back outside, into the thick heat.

Seconds later, the doors *whoosh* open again and he's standing on the concrete beside me.

# three

Where's the freaking fire?" Austin calls. He's walking several feet behind me along the shore.

I don't answer. Austin Morse deserves to suffer a girl's silence once in a while, as far as I'm concerned. The farther out we walk, the more the fist-like lump in my throat grows. We're getting close to my rickety old house—the one Dad built himself, which Mom painted vibrant purple—raised on stilts like some awkward, discolored pelican. Oh Susannah.

"Do you know where we're going?" he asks. I glance back at him but don't answer. "It seems kinda sketchy over here."

"Trust me," I say, "I know this place better than you think." Ghost Town is so close. So freaking close to Oh Susannah it kills me. Before it was erected, we had a clean-sweep view of the city. Afterward, just shadows cast long off its massive face.

The bottle is cool beneath my armpit, the vodka a sloshy whisper against my ribs. I can't tell if it's schizo-tendencies or what, but I swear I can *hear* her—Mom—in the *hush-hush* of the ocean. The waves, rising, receding, are her long, bony fingers, crashing along the keys, lifting briefly as though to take in another breath.

"Let's sit here," I finally announce, throwing down my purse and plopping myself on the cool sand in front of the stretch of abandoned piers that have, for years, been deemed unsafe and off limits. The wood is salt-eaten and rough, slick with algae and studded with rusty nails. One old pier snapped in half when I was in sixth grade and a couple standing on it ended up with spinal cord injuries that left them waist-down paralyzed.

Austin squats beside me. "Pretty dead out here," he notes, sifting the sand through his fingers and eyeing the bottle between us. He raises his eyebrows. "No chaser?"

"Don't need a chaser," I answer as I grab the bottle up from the sand, tug the smooth cork from its mouth, and take a long-ass swig. It burns, hard, leaving my esophagus and belly buzzing and warm.

He stares at me, stunned. "Man. I've never seen a girl do that before." He sounds genuinely impressed. Boys like Austin are always impressed when they meet girls like me—girls who didn't come from money, girls raised skipping shoeless through sand and swampland. He adds, "I don't think I've seen many guys do it, either. Except for me, of course." He smiles, reaching for the bottle and tilting a clear stream of vodka back into his mouth. He swallows and then starts coughing, grimacing as he shakes his soft gray (blond) head. "Man. That's . . . good."

"I'd only steal the *best* for you, Austin Morse," I say, taking another long swig, listening to the waves play out my mother's sonatas, the achy piers creaking and moaning. I take one more sip before he reaches for it back. I'm already beginning to feel softer around the edges, warm. It's working: memories of Mom, of Stern, going fuzzy and distant. Unimportant.

"I get the feeling you're being sarcastic, Olivia," he says, drawing little *x*'s in the sand with his pinkie finger.

"We never learned about sarcasm in public school," I answer sweetly. "That costs extra."

"Weren't you in, like, some art school for awhile?" He takes another swig, lifting the bottom of his shirt to wipe his mouth with, so I can see the tan cut of his stomach, the line of white (blond) hair leading down into his soft gray (khaki?) shorts. I'm surprised he even realized I'd been gone; I didn't think I was on his radar.

"Yeah . . . *was*." I drop my palms behind me in the sand, recalling my brief stint of freedom, away from here. "And weren't you at Ransom Everglades," I ask, "before you got expelled for doing drugs and your Dad got you transferred to Finnegan?"

"Yeah, *was*," he answers, smiling like all the shit he gets away with on account of his being the stepson of a bazillionaire is no big deal. When my friend Chris was arrested, during the same bust, he didn't get to go back to school. He got a stint at juvie and a job at Taco Bell. "So . . . how was Michigan?" Austin asks, obviously trying to change the subject.

"Boring," I answer, rising back up. "Midwestern. Lots of fat people."

"At your school? I thought artists were all supposed to be starving." He hiccups and makes a face. I laugh, walking my fingers through the sand, back to the Grey Goose. The fact that he has human bodily functions, like hiccupping, is surprising for some reason and makes me weirdly happy.

"Nope. They just sat around eating Velveeta all day. No one even painted." I pull my shoes off, leap up from the sand, and start cartwheeling around, warm all over, a wild, reckless feeling soaring through my whole body. Nothing matters right now and I don't care what Austin Morse or anyone in Miami, or Michigan, or anywhere, thinks of me. *Nothing matters*.

A few moments of silence, and then: "Bryce told me he hooked up with Raina," says Austin, hauling himself to his feet, picking a loose shell from the sand and tossing it across one of the piers and into the water.

"Yeah," I giggle, finding my own shell and chucking it. "You'd better tell him to wear gloves the next time he hooks up with one of my friends."

"Well you'd better tell her to wear a mouth guard." Ooh. *Burn*.

I push him a little, playfully. "Whatever. My girl *knows* what she's doing. Trust me."

"In that case," he says, pushing back, "could you give me her number?"

I walk further ahead, ignoring his comment—*am I actually* flirting *with Austin Stevenson Morse right now?*—digging my feet into the sand, watching the line of ocean foam slink back from the shore.

The satisfying thing about talking to Austin Morse is that he's just sort of easy. He's filler. Fluff. Eye candy. I'm an alien creature to him—a puzzle to slot together. But there's something exciting about having power over a person like him. It's the power that comes from being a girl, from having nothing to lose.

When I catch him staring at me, something swirls through my chest, sharp and fizzy as champagne.

"So . . . what do you think of the new condos?" He stands up and comes toward me, offering me the bottle again. "Sweet, right?"

I take another long swill and the world begins to spin a little. I frown at him. "Elysian Fields can suck it," I say, and realize I'm starting to slur. "Raina and I. We call it Ghost Town, you know? But don't tell your daddy, 'cause he paid for it!" I hiccup, stumbling over a rock before I can manage to turn another cartwheel.

"Whoa girl," he says, catching me before I face-plant into the sand. "Maybe we need to take the vodka away from you."

"Hold on hold on hold on." I put my finger up, move it to his lips. "Listen up, Aus-*tine*. No one puts *Livie* in the corner." I crack up, twirling around again. "You've seen that movie, right? I mean, I know it's like *old* but it's soooo gooood." Something inside me unlatches, and a wild fluttering feeling breaks free from its cage. I grab the bottle back, put it to my mouth for one more sip. "So, we gonna go for a swim or *what*?"

"I don't think that's such a good—"

I don't let him finish. "Shhh. It's a great idea." I skip closer to the waves, inching my dress down to reveal the lacy black bra I bought from a French lingerie maker on Etsy. He freezes, watching me. I feel like the Sirens that Mom used to read me stories about from the *Odyssey*, like I've got some mystical hold over Austin Morse right now, as I inch the dress further down, past my ribs, past my belly button, over my hips, and thighs, and calves. I can tell that he's breathing differently—slower, deeper—as I step fully out of it, standing now in bra and underwear, tossing the dress toward him.

A shiver runs up my thighs.

"You're next," I announce. "It's about time I get to see you with your shirt off."

"But my bra's not as sexy as yours," he jokes, unbuttoning a single button so his chest shows just an inch. He steps even closer. Suddenly, a *whoop-whoop* sounds from down the beach, bright lights flashing wide against Austin's back. *The cops*.

Austin whips his head around, his eyes going huge, terrified. For a second, he just freezes. "Shit. Get dressed,

Olivia. We gotta go." He throws my dress to me across the sand. I watch it arc through the air and land at my feet.

I snatch it up, suddenly confused, afraid. No more screw-ups. Dad will kill me. "We have to *hide*."

"*Hide?* No way." He comes to me, scoops up the dress, presses it into my hands. "Come on, Liv. Let's move."

The cops are getting closer. I back away from him—drunk, desperate. "*You* go."

He shakes his head, like he can't believe anyone could be so dumb, and starts jogging back toward the party. "Come on!" he calls over his shoulder, one last time. But then the cop lights come too close and he starts running faster. I wrestle my dress over my head and watch his body disappear into the shadows, still frozen, fear beating a path through the haze in my mind. The *whoop-whooping* grows closer and, too late to do anything else, I fling myself into the shadows beneath the closest dock. I press myself into the dark, adrenaline making my whole body wild-hot and prickly. It smells down here—like something fishy and sharp.

The car stops. I hold my breath and grow stock-still as a flashlight beams closer and closer, an officer clucking his tongue, like he's trying to summon chickens instead of teenagers. I can't let them find me—Dad's overprotective enough as it is, especially since I flunked out of art school.

*Craack*—something snaps behind me. Footsteps. Someone else's breath. *Oh, shit.* My breath goes rigid again, and I'm so startled, I almost pee.

"You got a cigarette?" asks a harsh, ragged voice.

Medusa, the local, crazy homeless lady, stands behind me holding a ratty, tooth-marked comb. "I give you this. Free, for a cigarette," she says.

"No," I whisper, still shaky, realizing it's true—my purse is up there, where the cops are still patrolling with their flashlight beams. Double shit. "Nothing."

"Nothing *chica*? Nada?" she asks, gazing at me through dark cloudy eyes.

"Nothing," I whisper. "Please—please be quiet."

"Over here, Tom!" That's one of the cops. As the flashlights sweep in our direction, some barely submerged instinct to *run* bubbles to the surface and I do—straight into the water. I slosh into the angry waves, a shock of cold drumming through my whole body; I put my head under and swim.

When I surface, I'm fifty feet from the shore. I cough out salty water as the waves rise, wondering how long it'll be until the cops go away. The surf is rough tonight; the ocean ink-black. One cop's voice reaches me like a faraway gurgle and when I see his flashlight shining toward me in the waves, I duck back under, swim even further out, holding my breath underwater until the very last second.

Bursting, needing badly to breathe, I lift my head and try for air. But as soon as I do, the tide surges, waves rising over my head. Salty water fills my mouth, my lungs; I spit and cough and try to lift my head back up but the current pulls me back, lassoing me beneath the surface. Dragging harder.

I kick against the water, try to lift even my lips above it, my nostrils, anything. Anything. My body begins to weaken as I thrash, exhausted, fighting for a single second of air. All I hear is the punch of my own heart against the crush of water as it devours me. It's big, so big, and I can't stop it now. And Stern pops into my head right then: that suspended, honeyed version of him in the light from the shed. His mouth, his lips, his tongue forming the words he'd sing. *Oh! Susannah I froze to death Susannah don't you cry don't you cry.*

It occurs to me just then in my vodka haze: Stern died here. Right around here. Where his body was dumped. The ocean took him; it will take me. It *is* taking me. No point in fighting. Can't stop it. Can't stop. Can't . . .

*I froze to death Susannah froze to death don't you cry don't you cry for me.*

And then, out of the tug and tumble of the water, something grips me: arms, around my waist. Drag me. Pull me up. My heart clicks back on—air—I'm lifted above the waves, coughing the water from my lungs, everything burning. I don't struggle, don't question. I'm not sure if I'm coming back to life or on my way out.

Moments later, these arms lay me out on the shore, while I gasp and sob, figuring out how to breathe again. Everything feels raw, painful. Finally, I open my eyes, squint at the figure beside me through the fog of my tears.

A *boy.*

I try to make out his features, silhouetted against the bright of the moon. But I'm still so dizzy and blurry and I can't see anything until the high beams of a passing motorboat sweep across us as it turns, flashing momentarily bright on his face.

And the world goes still, deathly quiet.

*No. No.*

*Impossible.*

My heart does a triple-flip in my chest. My whole body turns to ice. I'm going to faint.

When he finally turns to me, a smile spreads across his face—that brilliant, honeyed smile of his that always made me smile back.

*Stern.*

# four

I can't take my eyes off him—his deep black curls, the cream of his skin, the little cleft in the chin. My Stern. I have to be dreaming. I clench my eyes shut, feeling the cool wet sand against the back of my neck. *Wake up, Olivia. Wake UP.* I pinch myself, hard, and blink several times, but nothing changes.

Okay. Not dreaming. Dead, then. Must be.

*The Gray Space.* Mom's words skip sharp across my skull. *The place of the dead.*

My breath comes in short, shallow bursts and my head feels so light when I finally manage to gasp: "Stern."

To say his name out loud makes all of my insides feel suddenly pummeled by heavy stones.

"Liver."

There it is: the familiar curve of his lips as he says this word—this nickname that sits in a locked box inside me. There they are: his perfect, very soft lips inches from my face, forming this word. I am dreaming. I am dreaming of something magnificent, terrifying, and impossible.

"You're not here." I must confront it. This is fact.

"Really?" He stares at his long, white hands, the skin of his arms beneath his rolled-up flannel. "Where am I?" he asks.

"You're dead." This, too, is fact. Stern is dead. Stern is dead, because my mother killed him.

Stern frowns. "I guess the two aren't mutually exclusive then, are they?"

"Yes. They are. They are *definitely* mutually exclusive." I rub my head, trying slowly to sit up.

"Evidently not."

"Evidently *yes*." Dead, dreaming, or crazy. One of the three. "You cannot English me into believing something that I know is not possible."

"Admit it: what's both impossible and true *isn't* impossible." He covers his mouth when he smiles. As he always did. To hide that little gap between his teeth. He shifts closer to me in the sand, his hand only inches from mine.

But when he does, the parts of him closest to me—right hand, arm, then the whole right side of his body—go unsolid again. Like he's made of water, but just half of him. He winces like he's in pain and shifts away.

He closes his eyes. "I *felt* you, Liver. I felt you come close to me. And I reached for you, and I ended up back here. On this beach. In front of Oh Susannah. And you were here." He shakes his head, opens his eyes, staring ahead beyond the pier and the dunes to my old crumbling purple house. It's still unlived in, even after ten months. Can't sell it. Dad says it's *the damned market*, but I suspect it's the murder that happened just yards away. The blood soaked invisibly into the sand, creeping back toward it like thorny vines. He lowers his voice to a whisper. "I drowned, didn't I? I remember that. Nothing else. Just the water."

"Yes." My throat is squeezing up. I shiver beside him—there's a coldness radiating from him, from his fingertips—like how it feels to poke your hand into the freezer on a very hot day.

"I remember," he says, quietly. "Oh Susannah was the last thing I saw. The only thing I remember." He looks right at me, the whites of his eyes seeming to glow.

Dead. He's dead. A dream, or a *ghost*. The word tunnels to some back part of my brain, *ping*ing some invisible button that makes everything suddenly seem very real and very unreal all at once. An in-between, a teetering between worlds.

*The Gray Space.* Am I trapped somehow in this otherworldly dimension, without color, inhabited by the dead?

*No. She* invented *it. It's not a real place, not a real thing.* Mom made up the Gray Space, the place of anti-art, antifeeling, the cold dark place that *felt* like death. It was just her zany way of describing the place she went when she felt most depressed, when making music at all became impossible.

It isn't real.

I'm shaking all over, clutching my arms over my chest. I have to stay calm. I have to think logically. "I'm dreaming." Saying the words out loud makes them feel more true. "I'm dreaming of you because I miss you, because you're always in my head. We learned about that last year in psych, when we had a lucid dreaming unit." I pound at my head, trying to wake myself up.

"Liver. Stop. Listen to me." Stern's voice is urgent.

I open my eyes.

His basketball shorts fall just above his knees and seem more solid than his entire body, the new height he'd cultivated going on seventeen that summer, last summer, the summer he died. He's wearing a plaid shirt. Stop-sign-red gray. Sleeves rolled up.

I try to grip onto the sand for support, but it whittles away between my fingers.

We'd found that flannel together at the mall, over Christmas break. He'd tried on at least ten others before finding this one; he wore it almost every night it was cold enough to wear a flannel. Stop-sign-red and cut-grass-green gray. White between the blocks of color I cannot see.

Stern was cremated, after his body was hauled from the ocean, bloated and foreign. His body is ash. Stern's body is ash. Stern doesn't have a body. Stern does not exist anymore. I'm staring at a boy made of ash. No.

"You have to help me, Liver," he says in a cut-up voice—a voice that puts an instant lump in my throat. Hearing the ghost of my best friend in pain—even if it's all in my own head—is horrible. "I'm stuck. I'm in a place I'm not supposed to be. You have to help unstick me. I think I'm here now, with *you*, for a reason."

"I can't help you. You—you aren't real." I'm freezing. My dress is wet, plastered to my skin, the back of it coated in sand. I refuse to meet his eye, though all I really want to do is look right at him and have him be real and living and wrapped around me, with cheap beer in our hands and a fire and a surfboard at our side. I pinch myself again, harder than ever. *Why can't I just wake up?*

He frowns. "You're so stubborn when you think you're right." He shakes his head, his thick, dark curls swaying along. His skin shines. "You were always so stubborn."

*Boom!* Fireworks explode suddenly above us. I always loved fireworks—just last year, Stern and Raina and I would have been lying on the deck of Uncle P's boat now, staring up at them, opening our mouths to the sky like they might land on our tongues and melt down our throats like sugar. They look like ash to me now. I try to stand. My stomach churns, and when I bend my chest into my knees, I gag up a stream of saltwater.

*It's happening. You're turning. Schizo schizo schizo.*

I straighten up. I can't bear to look back again to see if he's there or not, if he was ever there, as I grab my purse and race away through the sand.

"Liv!" I hear his voice in the distance, though it somehow feels like a whisper in my ear at the same time.

His voice fades as the hopeful part of my brain keeps saying: *this isn't real. It'll be over soon. Dreams always feel long, and then they end. They* end. *You're not crazy. You're dreaming. Just dreaming.*

But another part of my brain says:

*The Gray Space. Maybe it* is *real. How did it find me?*

I run, dizzy, along the empty stretch of beach, past the rotted piers, flanks of sand kicking up behind me, spattering the backs of my calves. My breath is fast and short, chest dry-heaving. I feel the final blur of vodka-drunk melt away.

Drunk. I was drunk. Wasted. I hadn't eaten much of anything, and I was upset, and scared, and so I had a little vodka-dream about my dead BFF rising to save me. I probably wasn't as far out as I thought I was, must have been thrust back onshore by an incoming current.

I press my palm firmly into my forehead like I'm trying to keep my brain from frothing out, staring into the headlights spearing the dark road before me. *I'm not crazy. I'm not crazy. I'm not crazy. I'm not crazy.*

I repeat this mantra over and over again as my breathing calms. I retrieve my bike from the parking lot of Elysian Fields. I put my feet back on the pedals, inch slowly home on sidewalks, off the main roads, trying to keep my eyes focused, trying to shut off my brain.

Plumeria cloaks the streets and the sidewalk starts to even out before me, even as my heart pounds, ticking out the words I will continue to repeat inside my head until I believe them.

Ghosts aren't real.

*I'm not crazy. I'm not crazy. I'm not crazy. I'm not crazy. I'm not crazy. I'm not crazy.*

# five

They're not real. I know this for a fact," Raina says, leaning closer to me, her dark hair in its trademark braid down her back, her big eyes glinting in the sunlight. "Cassidy ended junior year president of the Itty Bitty Titty Committee, and now she's got, like, *jugs*. It's so obvious. Something like this—" she says, making mountainous circle-arcs from the top of her chest to the bottom of her ribcage—"doesn't just happen overnight."

Raina continues to judge Cassidy's inflated side-profile from several hundred feet away. Cassidy, along with several other girls I knew in middle school, sit on a blanket in the grass, smoking clove cigarettes. I can smell the bittersweet bite of them from here. Raina and I were close, weekly-sleepover-type friends with Cassidy in sixth grade, before she dumped us for a "cooler" group of friends who take pills and razor-shave shapes into the sides of their heads. Raina's competitive streak has been in hyper mode ever since.

Sometimes I even think Raina's competing with me:

to be cooler, funnier, more unique. I don't know why she bothers. There's no contest. Raina's effortlessly cool. Her mother's Cuban, Dad's Minnesotan, and wherever she goes, and whatever she does, people stare at her. She's a hard person to disagree with; when she says something, it sticks.

A spurt of hyena laughter explodes from their circle.

"Silicone, right?" My head throbs when I speak. Every sound—Raina's voice, the achy creak of the swing set, the thrum-buzz of insects—feels like a little knife blade to the back of my skull. The tiniest vibrations make me feel a little bit like hurling.

Eight days until Mom's sentencing. Eight days until she leaves the holding cell where she's been caged for the past ten months like some snarling animal. Eight days until she pleads insanity before the judge and she's shuffled off to the coldness of a different cage.

I scan the park, keeping an eye out for people who might try for a free ride on the carousel I've been charged with monitoring. Most of the kids who hang around here try at least once—leap right past me and onto one of the ancient porcelain horses hoping I won't notice they're freeloading. It's my sole job this summer—collecting the two-dollar-and-fifty-cent charge, ripping tickets, and yelling at people who violate the Miami-Dade Parks and Rec rules. That should have been the job description when Dad encouraged me to apply: *Carousel Bitch.*

I hug my knees into my chest. The fray of my cutoffs stick

to my thighs and my dumb Parks and Rec T-shirt seems to choke me, the neck so tight, so high-cut. Annoyed, sick, sticky, I pull the rubber band from around my wrist and move my hair off my neck and into a messy bun.

"You okay, babygirl?" Raina asks. "You look a little pale." Raina, like Dad, like pretty much everyone, doesn't know about my eyes. After Dr. Levine's knee-jerk *see-a-psychiatrist-you-nutjob* reaction, I can't risk having anyone else know, too. So, I'll hide it—as best I can, as long as I can.

I don't know how to respond. All I can think about is last night—alone on the beach, the cold radiating from his fingertips across the sand, from Stern's fingertips. Why did he seem so *real*?

"I'm just . . ." Before I can think of a way to complete the sentence, two guys I recognize from some beach parties over the past couple of summers—major burners, always reeking of weed—leap onto the carousel without paying and start pretending to ride separate horses, smacking their sides and groaning, porn-star style. Disgusting.

"Ooh! Go get 'em, girl!" Raina says, thumping me on the back.

I stand up from the bench. The pounding in my head is getting worse. "You have to buy a ticket first!" I call out. "Or you have to get off. Not my rules." It's pretty much the same dumb lines every time.

Thankfully, they don't resist. One of them—short, stocky, greasy-haired, Bob Marley T-shirted—squints at me over his sunglasses. "Olivia, right?" he asks, wiping the sweat from his forehead onto his baggy shorts. "You party sometimes at Beast Beach, right?"

I nod. "Yeah. I used to."

"Thought you moved or something." He pauses. "Did you come back because of your . . . ?"

The other guy coughs; Bob Marley Wannabe abruptly trails off. Mom. He knows. They both know. And it almost seems to give me some weird kind of authority or something: when a girl with a murderer mom asks you to do something, you do it. No questions asked.

"My what?"

"Um. I—I was thinking of something else, sorry . . . " he answers, his cheeks darkening. Blushing, obviously—it's good to know I can still tell.

"Enjoy the rest of your visit today, here at beautiful Dovedale Park." I paste a big fake smile on my face.

They're still looking at me with a mixture of fascination and fear, like I might suddenly lunge for their throats. "See you around," the other dude—tall, slouchy, acne-ed—says, and then they turn and hurry away.

The good thing about Michigan was that most people didn't know about Mom. I told my closer friends—Ty, Ruby, Amanda— but only the bare minimum. I had to admit why I missed two weeks of school, for the funeral, for the grief that came afterward. And when I went a little crazy back at school—oscillating between sudden crying jags, total numbness, and drunken binges that kept me out of school for days—they treated me with gentle indifference. Lots of encouragement to eat chocolate and cry in bed watching rom-coms.

They had their own lives to focus on, assignments I couldn't be bothered to do, classes I was too deep-dark-down to attend. Ruby made an entire oil painting of me over the course of a week that I knew nothing about. I was mostly sleeping.

I'd wake up next to boys I'd passed in the halls before whose names I didn't know. Sometimes, I didn't remember how they'd come to wind up in my dorm room in the first place, or what we'd done. How far I'd let them go, though I was pretty sure I hadn't actually gone all the way. Some crazy part of myself was saving it, though who knows why. I knew the only person I wanted to go all the way with was gone forever.

I just didn't want to think. There wasn't room to think. Starting that machine meant it would never turn off again, meant it would spin so fast and loud it would just blow up inside my skull.

I move back to Raina, steadying myself beside her on the bench. I feel wobbly.

"Job well done," she says, patting me on the shoulder. "It's hard work you do, Olivia Jane Tithe, and there's no one who does it quite like you." She leans back on the bench, finishing off her Mountain Dew with an intentionally loud burp. Even her belches are cool. It's annoying.

"So, did you have fun last night?" Raina asks. "Did you talk to dickbrain Bryce?" She lifts her head suddenly;

her eyes light up, go saucer-wide. "Wait a second . . . did you hook *up* with someone? Is that why you're being so weird?"

I groan, stare at my gray hands in my gray lap. My brain continues to shudder painfully in my skull. "No. Ew. Definitely not. Austin Morse was there, and we were drinking on the beach together, but the cops came. . . . He ran off. I had to hide by myself. . . . Whatever. It's—it doesn't even matter."

"He ran *off* on you?"

I don't have the energy to tell Raina that I *told* him to. She leans in toward me, planting both hands on my knees. "Well you be sure to let him know—let *all* those dumb-ass private school boys know—they can't just mess with you and not suffer the consequences."

"It wasn't a big deal. For real. I basically told him to go. But then, later . . ." I hesitate. Saying any of this out loud, to another person, will make me officially crazy. Raina will call Dad once she leaves the park today. Dad will call the hospital. I'll go home to find a small army of orderlies standing just behind my bedroom door with a straight-jacket. They'll load me into a van, lock me in a padded room in the psych ward. And then they'll all find out that the world's gone gray and never let me out. Ever again.

"Later . . . ?" She prompts, blinking into the sun.

I inhale deeply, stare at the empty carousel. "Rain, do you believe in ghosts?"

"Uh . . . random," she laughs, swatting at a mosquito on

her arm. "What does that have to do with anything?"

"I don't know. . . . I just had a weird dream last night," I lie, crossing my arms in front of my stomach, gulping back the lump in my throat. The way she has of dismissing me makes my blood boil up a little beneath my skin. My head feels all swimmy for a second, so I take a deep breath to push it away and keep going. "This weird dream that I can't stop thinking about." Full of nervous energy, I pull the rubber band out of my hair, redo the bun; it's even messier this time, pieces falling out over my shoulders, sticking immediately to my sweaty neck.

"You know what you need? A *sexy* dream. Maybe tonight you'll dream that I'm making passionate love with Jonah Twist in the middle of the soccer field. Then you'll forget all about your nightmare."

"Ugh. *That* sounds like a nightmare," I try to joke, but there's a knot, twisted around my intestines now, and every second I feel it grip a little bit tighter. "Plus, Jonah Twist definitely peaked in seventh grade. He's been on a downward slope ever since." I sigh. "It's very sad. He had such potential once."

"To each their own," Raina says. She shrugs and smiles in the wicked way that only beautiful girls can get away with. She stretches in front of me and a few boys I don't recognize watch her hawk-eyed as she moves; she stares them down and they look away. "So," she says, looking back to me, lifting one of her ankles behind her head. "Stern's unveiling is next week . . ."

My stomach flops down to my toes, bringing my heart with it. "Right," I mumble.

"It's some Jewish thing they do at the gravesite. Everyone comes and they say some prayers and—"

"I know what it is," I say too sharply.

Raina doesn't react. "So are you going to go? I mean, I know it's weird, because of . . ." She trails off.

"You can say it, Rain."

Raina sighs, standing normally now. "Because of your mom."

"I think I have to work." My throat's all clenched-up, and my words come out like they've been pressed between two heavy iron slats. I haven't seen Stern's parents since the funeral. I don't want to see the way they look at me, because I am my mother's daughter. They blame me. I know that they do.

She nods, but she looks unconvinced. "Yeah. Okay. Work is . . . important."

I check the time on my cell phone: 4:30. A short wash of relief. "Sure is," I say. "But it's over now! Time to head out."

"You want to come over and watch a movie or something? Make ice-cream sundaes? Old-fashioned sleepover style?" She lifts her big canvas bag onto her shoulder.

I hug her, because she's still my closest (living) friend. "Can't. I told my dad I'd run some errands for him. Ghost Town bullshit."

"Bummer," she says. She shoots a final, spiteful glance at Cassidy and her circle. "You want me to come with?"

"I do, but you can't," I heave my book bag from the dirt onto my shoulders. "Dad's been weird about me bringing other people around when he's not there, and he's already pissed at me because I ran out on the party early without saying anything." I look away from her in case she can tell I'm lying. "Call you later?"

"Sure," she says, as I walk to the small booth to shut the carousel down. The rows of pale lights overhead blink off all at once; the horses go darker beneath them, duller. After I lock the (mostly empty) cashbox inside the booth, I motion for Raina to follow, and we walk to the outside of the fence surrounding the carousel grounds and lock it up, so no one can even try to go inside without my expert ticket-taker supervision. My final end-of-day task.

I finish securing the u-lock in the gate and Raina walks me out to the parking lot where my banana-seat road bike is locked to a stop sign.

"Oh, shit," she says, looking at her phone. "I forgot Parker's parents are out of town tonight; he might be having people over. So definitely text me later, okay?" She pulls me into a tight hug before we split mid-lot en route to our separate vehicles. "Miss you already!"

"You, too," I say, watching her turn her key in the lock, wincing as she ducks—all that dark, slender height—inside her hot car (deep-dark blue—only a memory now, too difficult for me to distinguish from straight black), long velvety braid snaked down her back.

*Thunk-thunk-thunk* goes the hammer inside my skull.

* * *

*Eight days.* My heart pounds as I ride up the long lily-lined drive that leads to Ghost Town, my book bag accumulating little lakes of moisture where it presses against my back. I stand up to pedal as the hill goes steeper, sweat rivering down my arms and forehead and neck. *Eight days.* I wonder what she does all day long in that cell. I wonder if she's angry we couldn't come up with the million dollars in cash required to bail her out while she waits to go right back in again, though I can't imagine her expecting us to have even a hundred grand lying around for a bond.

I lock my bike to a lamppost in the parking lot, lift the accordion file, full of receipts, from my book bag, various mind-numbing legal contracts, account statements—I stopped snooping quickly after I discovered that everything inside interested me about as much as the Pythagorean theorem—and hug it into my chest, walking toward the gleaming entranceway.

I reach for the keys inside the side pocket of my woven purse, turn the lock open, walk inside.

"Dad?" I call out—I'm supposed to meet him here with the files, help arrange his office for a meeting he's got in an hour, and set up drinks. No answer. The air-conditioning gusts and my skin pricks up with gooseflesh as I walk to stand in the center of the lobby. It smells like new construction, that over-cold insulation smell that some basements carry, though the light pouring in from those huge square windows makes everything slightly more inviting. I hurry forward, turning left down a short hallway that leads to Dad and Ted Oakley's administrative office, wondering if I'll find one of them inside, immersed in work. I knock softly. Silence.

I don't have the key to his office, so I lay the files outside his door.

My phone buzzes in my pocket; a text from Dad: *Still in a meeting with the caterer. Sorry, darlin'. Be there soon and we can start setting up!*

Typical. Dad is caught up in more wedding preparations with his bride-to-be, while his own flesh and blood waits it out in a place he knows she hates. But Heather's his priority now, not me.

I walk back into the lobby. If I have to wait, at least there's AC. It's the one thing this place has going for it, as far as I can see.

I notice a folded up piece of paper by the entrance. I pick it up—it's crisp, lightweight—and unfold it once my butt is planted on the cold floor, my back pressing comfortably against the wall just left of the entrance. It's a computer printout, some kind of CAD architectural plan.

I smooth out the creases with the side of my palm, running my fingers over the straight lines, the angles that make up the hulking, hideous structure, the complex of brick and mortar and faceless glass before me. It's all I have now to glom onto—shapes and angles. Structure. I stare at the curves of the piping system, snaking through the walls, along the ceilings of each room, little rectangles drawn around the places they intersect.

Snaking through the walls. Snakes in the walls.

Something catches in my throat. Impulsively, I reach for a pencil, and quickly begin sketching, eager to change the pipes into something else. I surround them with looping, wiry vines, big, heavy, drooping flowers, petals, bird's wings, spiny feathers.

My body seems to disappear beneath me. The pain in my head slinks away and, with it, all the things mucked up inside. I'm breathing fully again. My hand sweeps and licks and dances of its own accord.

Freedom. Just a lick of it, but, still. I can almost smell Mom's version of the sea, feel the vapory gods she always told stories about descend from the heavens and cradle me up inside their arms. And then Stern creeps up again from somewhere inside of my head. I see the smile on his face, the ocean swelling beyond us. How we used to swim together, late nights. His body next to mine. The way I'd always know he was there before I even saw him coming: *don't you cry for me, I come from Alabama with a banjo on my kneeee.*

"Man, that's so beautiful." The voice startles me and rolls my stomach back into knots.

I don't get a chance to turn around to see who it is, because, the next time I blink, he's moved, crouched right beside me on the marble floor.

Stern.

He's back.

# six

Liv. Stop ignoring me. Look at me." The invented ghost plants himself in front of me on the shiny floor. He's wearing the same clothes he was wearing yesterday—same basketball shorts he wore pretty much every day he was alive, same painstakingly selected flannel shirt.

I don't look at him because he's not real. And I know that because I'm not crazy. I'm a rational person, waiting for her father, sketching on top of the blueprints for an ugly building.

"Hey. Come on. You need to look at me. I don't know how long I can stay." His voice breaks when he says it; I glance briefly over at him: he's watching me, so intense, so focused. "Liver, you have to listen to me. Your mom didn't kill me, Liver. I wanted to tell you last night, but you ran away, and . . ."

I start humming to myself, blocking out the words. *Just ignore him.* I will myself to keep breathing, though my air supply feels short and strained again. *He isn't real. If you ignore him, he'll go away. You're not crazy.*

*You're* not *crazy. You can choose to make this go away.*

"She didn't do it, okay? I know that. That might be the *only* thing I know for sure. That's what I wanted to tell you."

I'm startled to see the paper blurring in front of me, feel the burn of tears behind my eyes. *Wish fulfillment*: A Freudian theory; unconscious aspirations that come out in dreams, hysterical fantasies. I'd paid attention that day in psych class. It resonated with me, even then. I bored pencil into paper, digging lines across it, just shapes now, nothing concrete.

"Did you hear what I just said?" He moves to squat right in front of me now, hands on his knees, leaning only inches from my face. Weirdly, he smells like firewood. "Do you understand? She's innocent. You can *help* her. You can help *me*."

I'm starting to shake, my own terrible hopes squeezing my insides like mutant weeds. "Stop. Just stop." I want to stand up, I want to run, but I don't trust my legs to hold me.

He sits down now, still in front of me, quiet for a moment. For a while, he says nothing. He stares out the wide, glass lobby doors, over the parking lot.

"What was here before?" he asks abruptly. He looks around, at the sparse, light-flooded lobby and the darkened hallway beyond it, at the highway visible just beyond the gates. "It was Shepherd's Field, wasn't it? We used to have Little League games here! Oh, man . . . that's one of the first memories I've had since . . . since being wherever I am now. It feels so good."

"Raina and I call it Ghost Town," I say cautiously, quietly, conscious that I am having a conversation with someone who doesn't exist. "She says it's got some major bad energy."

"She's right. It does—I can feel it." He cocks his head to the side. His dark curls stick up from his head. He could never control them. He won't stop looking at me. "Do you hear that?"

"Hear what?"

He closes his eyes, presumably to better listen. "Someone's crying. . . . Can you hear it?"

I shake my head—I can't. I can't hear anything but the sway of thick palm leaves, knocking occasionally against the big glass doors, the distant swish of cars along the highway.

I decide that I will not wait for my father any longer. I need to get away from this—from this moment, this insane, imaginary, hysterical moment. I refold the architectural plan and slip it into my purse.

"Where are you going?" he asks.

"Home," I answer, sharply. "You're not here, Stern." I look him square in the eye. "I invented you."

As soon as I say it, he shivers violently, and then disappears. *Poof.* Like that. I shake my head, heartbeat quickening, skin hot, tingly. I'm losing it. I'm really losing it.

I throw my purse into my bag, sling it over my shoulders, and push through the lobby doors to my bike. The humidity's so thick it practically chokes me. My hands shake as I twist the key into the chain lock, and leap onto the broad, hot seat, weaving quickly down the long gravel drive and down Sparrow Street to the boardwalk.

The road blurs behind me as I ride. My tires bump against the up-and-down of the boardwalk slats, and images flash into my head, memories unbidden, unwanted.

When Mom's paranoia got bad, she couldn't leave the house anymore without a baseball bat; the doctor upped her meds so high she could barely move, let alone go anywhere. She said the pills dulled her brain, that even if she lived half the day in fear of death-by-rattlesnake, she'd rather that than the alternative: sitting at her piano and finding her brain blank of all inspiration, her fingers unable to remember the intricate symphonies they'd had down cold before.

One of her sonatas, one that always made me think of Dad—steady and comforting, cowboy boots clicking through a rainy street—plays through my head as I ride.

Back home, the air-conditioning is on full blast. I pull my shoes off and rest them in the cool-tiled foyer, peek my head quickly into the dark kitchen, and see a lizard scurrying across the far wall over the pantry. I lean my bike against the wall and pad quickly up to my room, locking the door as soon as I step inside, waiting for my heartbeat to slow.

This room still feels foreign to me. I miss the room I grew up in—wood floors, Turkish rugs, Mom's old childhood furniture we repainted together when I was a kid.

Only my bed is the same, and now I can't wait to crawl under the covers. Sleep long, deep—maybe forever. Like him. I wonder if there's singing where he is, in Nowhere. If there are lullabies. Maybe I'll put him in my head as I fall to sleep. Maybe I'll have him sing to me. *I had a dream the other night when everything was still I thought I saw Susannah a'comin down the hill. Don't you cry, oh don't you cry, Susannah, don't you cry for me.*

I turn around, prepared to jump under my covers, and freeze: Stern. Sitting patiently at my desk, leaning forward on his knees, staring at me.

"You know," he says, smiling in a way that still looks pained, "you've always biked like a girl."

I have an impulse to scream, wrestle him to the ground, and claw his face off. Instead, I shut my eyes, place my hands over my ears, and start chanting, "I can't hear you I can't hear you I can't hear you," and: "I'm not crazy I'm not crazy I'm not crazy . . ."

Stern stands up and crosses to me. "You're not crazy," he says. And as he says it, I feel his hands over my own—like a shiver where he touches me.

My eyes shoot open; he's so close, so cold. "Why is this happening?" I whisper.

"Look." His voice is steady—so reassuring and familiar, it makes something break inside of me. That rational boy I grew up with my whole life, the boy who always knew how to bring me back down to earth when I was scared, nervous, upset, anything. The boy who anchored me. "I realize this must *seem* crazy to you, but, in the simplest terms, I'm telling you: the person who killed me is still out there. Walking around. Free. And this light I keep seeing, from wherever I am—when I reach for it—it sends me back to you. And not just because you're my best friend. Not because we said we'd be best friends forever, okay?" His voice turns pleading. "You're supposed to *help* me. You have to help me. We have to figure this out. Solve it. End it."

I stare at him, hard. "I can't help you, Stern. The murderer isn't free. She's in jail. She's my *mother*."

He shakes his head. "She didn't do it."

I'm shivering all over now, furious, full of fire. "Are you insane? There's *evidence*. They *found* her with you—with your body. It took a long time to deal with it, but now we are, or we're starting to, and I just need to come to terms with it. Okay?" I blink hard, unable to keep the shake from my voice. "Dad wanted to stay in Oh Susannah, to have Heather come live there. For me. But we couldn't. People egged our house every day. They painted—they painted horrible things on our door. They made sure we would never, ever forget." I take a deep breath, try to collect myself. *You're speaking to a person who isn't real. He's not real. He doesn't exist.* I keep having to remind myself of this. "I'm sorry," I say, turning to face him. "It's really strange to fight with a person who isn't even here. Especially one who wears his Christmas flannel in the middle of summer."

"It's always cold where I am," he says, honestly and simply. There's a pause, and then he says, "Is any of your mom's piano stuff here?"

I'm too tired to wonder about the nonsense logic of my hallucinations. "Just a few boxes that I wouldn't let Dad put into storage," I say, rubbing my eyes. "Sheet music and notebooks and other random stuff. Why?"

At that, he sweeps past me—more shivers—toward my bedroom door. "Take me to them," he says, and I hear excitement in his voice. "I'm going to prove to you that I'm real."

"They're right here." I walk toward my closet. The cardboard boxes have been buried here, underneath my shoes and old scarves, since Dad moved all my things from the old house, but I haven't looked at them once. After I've dragged them out of the closet, I stand there just staring at them.

"Open them," Stern urges.

I tear slowly at the packing tape merging the edges of the box together. Once opened, stacks and stacks of papers are revealed. Now the tears are practically impossible to keep back: this is my mother's music. I turn away from Stern for a moment, embarrassed. "Well," I finally get out, "is this what you're looking for? Sheet music?"

"No. There's a small black wooden box with white music notes along the sides."

"I never saw Mom with a box like that." I reach tentatively into the first cardboard box, rifling through dog-eared papers slowly, carefully, as though they'll disintegrate at my touch—like she does now, in my nightmares.

"Try the next box. It's not in there. Next one," he continues urging. "C'mon."

I've stopped fighting his voice. I push the first box aside and start on the next. This one's got a few old photo albums on top, and beneath them: a small black box. White music notes dotted across the sides. A chill creeps along my arms. I've never seen the box before. I'm sure of it. So how could I have made it up?

Stern kneels next to me and I shiver as he inches closer. "That's it," he says, excitement piped through his voice. "Open it. There's a little top layer you have to remove, and beneath that, there're Goetze's Caramel Creams. She always gave them to me after piano lessons. She knew they were my favorite. And she told me once that she hid them in here so you and your Dad couldn't get to them."

Feeling as though my hand belongs to someone else, I lift the lid to find another wooden layer beneath it, as Stern told me there would be. I remove the thin slat of wood slowly from the box: Goetze's Caramel Creams, layered two-deep inside the small box. I stare at him.

"Jesus . . ." I feel my pulse rapidly quickening, a duel sense of relief and terror surging through my bloodstream. He *is* real. He must be.

He nods. "Yeah."

Questions fire suddenly through brain, out my lips. "Do you remember what happened? How you were killed?" I choke a little on the words. Stern. My Stern—here. Real and yet not real. Still not back, and still not mine.

Stern rubs his forehead, looking troubled. "No."

"Then how can you be so sure my mom is innocent? How come you can remember where she hid her *caramels*, but you can't remember what happened the night you were killed?"

Stern's mouth flattens. "That night is just . . . dark. Almost *all* of my memories are dark. But I just . . . *know*. I can still, I don't know, *feel* certain things. I can feel you. And I can feel that there's something wrong about my death. It must be why I'm here, right? Unfinished business. The memories I have are sort of random—I don't know where they come from. I don't know why I get some and not others. Nothing makes a lot of sense right now, but I think that's part of it—of dying. Of pushing your way back in, when you're not really supposed to. I can't access most of it. It's slipping away."

He lifts his eyes to mine, and for a moment we stare at each other.

I take a deep breath. *Let's just play along for a second. Let's just see where this goes.* "Okay . . . let's start with the basics. What *do* you remember?" I ask.

My door flies open just as he opens his mouth to respond.

Dad.

I turn instinctively back to my best friend, to my love, to my Stern, but he's gone. Disappeared. I don't know why

I'm so shocked—he's a ghost. A real ghost, with weird ghost powers.

I don't know why I feel so empty, too.

"Christ," Dad says, breathing air hard through his nostrils. "I was worried sick. You could have been dead, or *kidnapped*, or something." He puts a hand to his head, shuts his eyes for a moment, still catching his breath. "I told you to *wait* for me. What happened? Did you forget to tell me you had better things to do?" Sweat beads against the ridge of his salt-and-pepper hairline; he pats it off with the hanky in the pocket of his suit jacket he always carries around. Mom always called him old-fashioned because of it.

I stare back up at him, defiant, even though he's right: I blew him off, bolted when Stern showed up. "You didn't leave me the key to your office so I just left the files." Thankfully, lying is a skill of mine. "Sorry, but I wasn't just going to wait around for you and Heather to finish up meeting with wedding caterer number 973."

"I cancelled my meeting with Mr. Pomeroy. I told him I had to make sure you weren't lying in some ditch in Liberty City. He drove all the way from *Key West* for the meeting, and I had to send him back during rush hour." He sighs, fiddling with his old fashioned hanky. "You can't *do* that, Liv. I'm trying to get a business started up here. You might have cost me a client."

"You didn't *have* to cancel." I scratch at a hard spot in the carpet, trying to push back a guilty feeling. "It's not my fault you freaked out. I'm not some defenseless two-year-old, okay? So, just stop worrying. Focus on your clients and your blushing bride . . . I'm fine. I'm *golden.*"

"I know you're not fine," he says, quietly. "The hearing's coming up, and I know you're damn scared about it, and so am I. So don't you pull that crap with me, Olivia. You're *sixteen*, and even if you think that makes you old and wise, you're still my baby," he says. He re-pockets his hanky, his gaze softening. "You will always be more important to me than any client. You know that, don't you?"

I nod. "I know." But the truth is: I don't. Not lately, at least.

He starts to duck back out into the hallway, pausing first, turning back to face me. "By the way, who were you talking to?"

I stare at him blankly, and he prompts: "Just now. Before I came in."

"Raina," I answer quickly, moving my gaze to the boxes full of Mom's things, still exposed on my carpet. Dad hasn't mentioned them. He won't. "We were Skyping."

He shakes his head, gives me his *I know you're lying and it only disappoints me more* look. "I know what you're up to, you know," he says with a sigh. "And it's not going to work."

Dad probably thinks I'm plotting ways to prevent him from marrying Heather. But I gave that up as soon as he told me they were engaged. He was in too deep already.

He shuts my door behind him with a soft click. Without meaning to, I snatch a pillow off my bed and hurl it against the closed door. It thuds softly to the ground. Then I sit on the floor next to mom's boxes, drawing my knees to my chest.

I take a caramel from Mom's secret box of treats. *Poor Dad. He's got a nutso ex-wife, and a nutso daughter now, too.*

But . . . if Stern's real, and if he's right, then there's a chance I'm *not* going crazy. That I'm fine. Sane—at least for now.

I haven't had caramel in forever. It tastes good.

Every year, on my birthday, Mom would spend hours making my cake from scratch, trying out new recipes, new combinations. I'd watch her stir smooth icing in a big ceramic bowl, rapt; *come over here, Livie. Tell me what this needs,* she'd say, letting me taste off a long silver spoon. She'd dye it pink with beet juice, or sapphire with blueberries, ice it all over in colorful peaks and valleys.

And I know: if there's even the smallest chance in hell that what Stern says is true, I'll listen, I'll help, I'll do anything.

I lean back against the edge of my bed for a second, trying to think what to do.

In the blankness of the ceiling, I see Mom, smiling above me from the middle of a white ocean.

*Let him be real.*

A current of panic snakes its way up my chest, and I

sit up stock-straight. If he's not real, if this is just how it starts—what happens next? How does it end?

*Please. Please, god—please anyone. Let him be real. Let him be* right.

He *has* to be.

I'll prove it.

# seven

I consider calling Raina for help, but only for a second. She won't understand. How could she?

The thing about Raina is: sometimes she gets on my nerves so badly I could scream. I love the girl, and I'd probably be dead in a ditch somewhere without her, but sometimes I think our friendship is just this other *thing* she's trying to win. Next week, she'll go to the unveiling, stand beside Stern's parents like *she* was his best friend, act the saint, while I, the capital-*A* Asshole, can't even face them.

And the award for *Most Compassionate Friend to Parents of Dead Kid* goes to . . .

Raina!

What kills me is that I introduced them in the first place. Raina was in my social studies class in sixth grade and she looked lonely—she'd just moved to Miami from Minneapolis—and I liked the streak of fake pink hair she'd clipped into her dark ponytail. So I invited her to sleep over. Stern, who always went to magnet schools that would help *foster his musical talents*, came over to eat a mushroom pizza from Stefano's and watch *The Sandlot*; it was the first night the three of us ever hung out.

We talked all night long, about Minneapolis, about how her dad just split town one night without a word and she and her mom and three sisters moved a month later because her mom got a job here, as a translator. She taught me how to put liquid eyeliner around my eyelids, real thick, and we snuck into Mom's closet and dressed up in her concert gowns, put pantyhose on our heads, and invented a fake band called "The Stockinghead Sisters." Stern acted as our manager, booking us fake gigs at all of the most influential venues across North America, Western Europe, and China.

We were pretty much inseparable after that.

But he was always mine first.

I inhale sharply: Stern. *Mom*. My heart hiccups a little in my chest, replaying again what he said: *she didn't do it; she's innocent*.

I stand and begin tearing off my sweaty work outfit, then turn to my color-categorized closet—throw on a clean "blue" tank top that buttons up the front, a pair of suede "beige" shorts, a holster-like belt with a ram's head engraved on the buckle, black doc martens with "pink" laces—all of it, just a dull wash of gray.

The end result is that I probably look like a cowboy-clown-mechanic-stripper mash-up. Which I'm fine with. I've got bigger fish to fry—like figuring out if my dead best friend's theories about Mom hold any truth. I need to find someone I can talk to—someone *alive*. Time is running out.

I haven't even *seen* her in six months—when I was last home for winter break—and it was through a thick pane of plastic. Dad forced me to go. I was angry with her, beyond angry, even though I never thought she'd *meant* to do what she did. She was on one of those off-meds kicks while working on a new series of compositions. In the past, she'd go off every once in a while to do this—it had always been fine before, for the most part—just little blips of paranoia, the occasional manic jag. But this time, her brain spun her a new reality and she got tangled in it; by the time she became untangled, Stern's blood was already all over her hands.

I heard the talk, the gossip buzz, traveling like a thick swarm of Florida-grade mosquitoes around me wherever I went: the divorce pushed her over the edge.

But she shouldn't have gone off her meds in the first place. She should have known. She should have been better. That part *was* her fault. And I couldn't forgive her for it. Can't forgive her. Can't even face her.

Unless . . .

*Unless she didn't do it.*

My stomach groans but I ignore it, heading out to the porch with my laptop. I type the name of Mom's lawyer into the browser: *Cole, lawyer, Miami.* I don't remember her first name. Maybe I never knew it. In any case, ______ Cole spent hours and hours with her, digging, delving. If

Mom didn't actually do anything, the woman would have doubts, would have noticed inconsistencies in the case.

But when I type in her name, about a hundred different Coles come up, and when I go through the task of clicking on each and every one, none seem to be lawyers. I must have my information wrong, or misplaced, or misspelled.

I take a deep breath. I can't tell Dad what I'm doing. I won't. He's made it perfectly clear that he's ready to move on, and forget all about mom. Who else would know where I can find her?

The drive to the Oakley estate isn't long, but the division between neighborhoods is massive. The lush, winding, palm-lined path leading to their Coral Gables mansion makes Dad and Heather's condo—by far the most expensive place I've ever called home—look like a halfway house for dwarves.

My stomach goes queasy as I pull my dinky old junker up to the Oakley's four-car garage, right beside Ted's BMW. It's just starting to get dark, shadows stretching long as the sun dips toward the ocean. I walk up the shaded walkway to the door of their palace—a mammoth beast of a house that never fails to make my head spin by its sheer hugeness, completely white. It has zillions of wide-paneled windows, a Spanish-tiled roof, French doors, verandahs, intricately carved porticos, and marble decks.

I wipe my sweaty palms against my skirt and ring the buzzer twice before Clare Oakley swings it open, smiling broadly with her botox-plumped lips. "Olivia, sweetie. It's so good to see you! I'm so glad you called." She pulls me in for a muscular hug. "You came at the perfect time. My trainer just left, and Ted's all finished with his swim." She leads me down the gleaming marble hallway, her golden bob swishing at her chin, asking about *the new condo* and *isn't Heather just a lovely woman* and *oh, will you be starting back up at the* public *school this fall?* and *will you know anyone there, will your credits transfer from that* art *school?*

I nod and smile and answer *oh, yes* to every question, whether or not it's true.

"Ted?" She says, leaning her mouth toward the little intercom at the end of the hallway as she presses a small white button beside it. Ted's voice reaches us, crisply, through the speaker: "In my office, honey. You need something?"

Clare places one deep-tanned hand on my shoulder and guides me to the door of Ted's office, knocking gently. "Olivia is here. Are you decent?" She giggles, squeezing my shoulder. I hear Ted's chair scoot back against the wood floor.

"Olivia! Come in, come in," he says, flinging open the door. He puts a meaty hand on my shoulder and ushers me inside—the bumpy slope of his nose especially prominent in the office's shadowy light. He's wearing a dark

Harvard T-shirt and well-tailored medium-gray pants that I'm guessing by the shade and cut of them are khaki. His office smells like cedar and cologne—or maybe it's just cologne made to smell like wood. "Do you need anything, sweetheart? Some ice water? Tea? Coffee?" Ted offers me a seat on the other side of his dark-wood desk.

"Oh, and we've got a fabulous quiche Marjolie made us if you'd like some of that," Clare pipes in from the doorway; I didn't realize she was still there. The hand on her hip sparkles with a rock the size of Texas. With the other hand, she fiddles with the strand of pearls around her neck. "Leeks and Gruyère. You're welcome to stay for dinner, of course!"

"I'm okay," I say, running my finger through the deep, tribal-looking carvings along the arms of my chair. "I ate before I got here. And I promised I'd have dinner at home tonight."

"Make sure you say good-bye before you leave, sweetheart." Clare flashes me a dazzling white smile and steps back into the hall. I fiddle with the chair arms some more. Ted leans back in his swivel chair and runs a hand through his thinning hair.

"It really is good to see you, Olivia. We've missed you around here. I know your dad misses you, too."

I try to hide my disbelief. "He's busy with wedding stuff. . . ." I knock my feet together softly.

"Trust me," Ted says. "He's working hard right now, but he loves you like crazy. He talks about you all the time."

He leans forward, and rests his forearms on the desk. "So—to what do I owe the pleasure, little miss?"

I clear my throat, inhale deep. "It's—it's actually about Mom."

"Your mom?" He's obviously startled. "I don't know if I'll be of much help, but I can try. Go ahead and shoot." He moves a pen from the top of his desk into a drawer in front of him, rests his hands on top of one another.

"I just wanted to know how to get in touch with her lawyer . . . Cole. Something Cole."

"Carol?"

*Yes. Carol. There we go.* "I—I have some questions I want to ask her about Mom's case." I fight the urge to cross my arms. Even speaking the words into this vast office makes them feel hopeless.

"What kind of questions?" he asks, watching me steadily.

I hesitate, look at the shine and shadow of the desk. "Well, the hearing's next week . . . so, I guess I just want to hear a little more about what she's going to say, and, you know, what she—what Carol—thinks is going to happen. If there's any new evidence that . . . that something might change." I look back up at Ted. Radiating from his eyes is pity so full and thick I feel immediately stupid.

He rubs his chin, shifts in his king-sized chair, picks up his Blackberry and consults it, then scribbles something on a bit of paper and slides it across the desk to me. *Carol Kohl.* I had the name spelled wrong. "Here's Carol's phone number and address." he says, "But—I don't want you to get your hopes up too much, Liv. This is painful stuff you're digging into. I'd really hate to see you disappointed." He sighs heavily. "We all miss Miriam, and wish all of this would just go away, but that's not how it works." He puts his hand forward, reaching for mine. I let him take it. "I'm sorry, honey. You've been through so much. If I thought there was anything else I could do to help your family, I'd do it in a heartbeat. You know I would."

The giant room seems to get closer and closer in until I feel the walls press my body paper-flat and near-breathless. I take his piece of paper, fold it up, and put it in my back pocket. Then another thought occurs to me. "What about the other lawyer?" I blurt. "Mom's first lawyer, the one who quit on her. Greg Foster, right?"

Ted looks momentarily shocked, straight-backed now in his chair like someone's just snapped his spine straight. He was just as horrified as we were when Foster quit on us.

"Look," I say. "I know you don't think it'll make a difference, but I'd still like to talk to him. Just in case."

He opens both hands, palms up, on the desk. "I don't actually have any information for Mr. Foster. He may have moved. Did you ask your dad?"

"No," I say quickly. "And I'd appreciate—I'd appreciate it if you didn't tell him I was here."

"I understand." Ted nods, his face softening into a smile again. "I really am sorry, Olivia. I know how badly you must want to fix this." He stands from his chair and I do the same. "But the best thing you can do is try and move on." He comes around the desk to give me a fatherly hug. "Come back anytime, okay? Maybe dinner some time soon, with the family?"

I manage to mumble something noncommittal; then, as Ted returns to his desk, I make my way back through the long, chandelier-lit hallway.

I remember my promise to say good-bye to Clare. I find her outside, watering plants on the deck in the fading daylight. "Come back soon," she tells me as we hug a brief good-bye. "And say hello to Austin on your way out. Aus!" she yells, down toward the pool. I freeze—I forgot, somehow, that he might even be here.

"What?" He calls out from somewhere below the deck. His voice is muffled. There's a splashing sound.

"He'll get such a kick out of seeing you, I'm sure," Clare says, sotto voce, to me. If only sweet, BOTOXed Clare knew of our sandy little tête-à-tête on the beach.

I suppress the urge to let slip that he *has* seen me . . . a lot of me, as well as my French-inspired lingerie. Unless he was too drunk that night to remember.

"What, Mom?" Austin calls out again. Clare nudges me forward, down the stone stairs to the pool, where Austin makes easy backstrokes through the glassy water.

I can practically feel Clare's eyes on me from above. There's no way I'll be able to make a sneak exit, although for a moment I consider bolting for the back gate. Instead I suck in a deep breath, wait for his head to emerge from the water at my end of the pool, and force myself to say: "Hi, Austin."

He whips around, beads of water spiraling off his hair. "Whoa. Olivia Tithe. Hey." He sounds oddly pleased to see me. The bad girl. The poor girl. The girl who gets so drunk she takes her shirt off for boys on the beach. He moves a few feet forward and rests his forearms on the smooth concrete lip of the pool. "What are you doing here?" He grins. "Did you miss me?"

Something about being in the presence of such sheer *boy*-brain loosens the knots in my stomach. It's like watching the same romantic comedy remake again and again. It's so easy to know what's coming and how it will end.

"I came here to see your dad, so, don't get too excited," I say, watching the water ripple around his body with every small movement. "Working on your sunset tan?"

"You could say that, Tithe." He hoists himself up to the deck, grabbing a towel from the beach chair beside me and shimmying the wet from his slender torso, his legs, his shoulders. He's got a lot of freckles I hadn't noticed before, when I still saw in color, a little bit of hair around his flat, dark, penny-sized nipples. He moves a little bit closer, all six foot two of him, suddenly towering over me.

"Look." He says, and his perfect face grows perfect-serious. "I wanted to apologize for ditching you the other night. . . . I was way more drunk than I thought." He grins. "It's not every day a girl can outdrink me."

I look away. The way he's staring at me makes my

body feel hot. "Yeah, okay," I mumble. "I was pretty drunk, too."

"Well, hey." His voice drops: "Nothing to get your purple panties in a bunch about." Ugh. So he does remember. Everything. I bite hard into my bottom lip. A lick of wind sweeps more ripples across the face of the pool.

I check my phone for missed calls or text messages that don't exist, and announce in a tight voice: "Shit. My best friend's having a crisis. I gotta go." I drop the cell phone back into my purse and wave him an awkward good-bye, walking as quickly as possible to the back gate to let myself out.

"Hey, Red," Austin calls out, right before I unlatch the little wedge of wrought iron from its resting place. I turn, cringing at the nickname. Not the most original, but better than Fire Crotch, which was the name I heard practically every day in seventh grade. He beckons me back. I hesitate for a second by the gate, hand still on the latch. "Come here for a second. Just a second."

I walk slowly back over to him. "What?" I ask, annoyed now.

He leans close, pressing his lips almost directly to my ear. "I just wanted you to know," he whispers, "purple is my favorite color."

I don't even want to know what color my face must be right now.

# eight

I call Carol Kohl first thing before work Friday morning, but all I get is the drone of her voice on the machine. *This is the office of Carol Kohl. Attorney at Law. Office hours are Monday through Friday, nine AM until five PM; please leave a detailed message with your number and the time you called and we'll get back to you shortly. Thank you.*

*Seven days*. The number lodges into me, an uncomfortable knot in my throat.

A long beep. My words tumble out: "Hi. My name's, um, Olivia. Tithe. I'm—I need to speak to Carol, I mean, Mrs. Kohl. To Carol Kohl. Concerning my mother, Miriam Tithe. Please call me back as soon as you can. It's important." I pause, correct myself: "No. Urgent. It's urgent. Thank you."

Work is impossible.

The only paying customers for the carousel, all day, are a mother and her bouncy pigtailed daughter. I take their five dollars and watch them go slowly round and round, the little girl shrieking. The ride seems to last forever.

After they leave, I check my phone every minute—waiting for a call back, fingers working nervously at the edge of my Parks and Rec T-shirt—driving myself crazy. *Seven days.*

And the whole time, though I'm sure no one's paying me even a lick of attention, I swear I feel *eyes* on me, boring into the back of my head. But, every time I whip around to catch whoever is there, I realize I'm just as alone as I ever was.

I plunk my cell phone into the pocket of my purse, fingers brushing against my sketchbook. I pull it out, open it onto my lap—an action that brings back the singing realization of how easy it all used to be, how art just flowed from me. I start to sketch a teenage couple, entwined on the swing set across the park, hungrily making out. But I keep seeing Stern. All I can see is Stern. His lips, his teeth. His hands. The black of his hair in every shadow, in every fractured angle of sunlight. It's always him.

*Stop it, Olivia. Stop it.* I start to sketch the sprawl of banyan trees mid-park instead, wild roots licoriced through the dirt. But Stern's face keeps returning to me, everywhere I look—how different he is in death. The dark smudged now beneath his wide hazel eyes.

A storm rolls in around three-thirty—huge, pregnant clouds—and then the mother lode of thunder erupts from the sky. Everyone rushes away to the shelter of their cars before the rain starts, except for a boy, Carlos, whom I recognize vaguely from the neighborhood, and his crew of dipshit friends. They start to hoot, slide in the grass with their shoes off. A homeless person is rooting through a trash can near the water fountains, oblivious to the storm.

I decide to cut out of work an hour early, so I can go to Carol Kohl's office before it closes. I do a scan for boss man and, seeing that he's not around, quickly complete my end-of-day duties, powering down the creaky carousel before locking up the ticket booth and fence outside of the carousel grounds.

Carlos and his friends are still roughhousing in the dirt, and I'll have to pass them on my way out of the park. Weirdly self-conscious—*why do I even care?*—I pull the sweaty Parks District shirt over my head, revealing the even sweatier paint-smattered tank top I wore underneath it, zip my sketchbook into my bag before it gets too drenched, and re-ponytail my hair, prepared now to cross their path en route to my car.

As I approach, the boys have started on a new game: crumpling up their wet, empty, greasy potato-chip bags and cans of orange Slice and Coke and throwing them at the homeless woman, hunched, still digging through a trash can several feet ahead of them. The woman turns briefly to face the source of her bombardment, a wad of sodden tissues clenched proudly in her fist. I recognize her as I come closer: Medusa. Her three remaining teeth nub over her bottom lip as she frowns, turning back to her task, wild wet hair plastered to the sides of her face.

"Get outta here, you crazy bitch," Carlos shouts, nailing her right ear with a soda can. She swats at her ear and keeps digging, undeterred, like she's lost something precious that she'll stop at nothing to find. She drops her treasures into the plastic bag at her feet: empty cigarette boxes, a broken flip-flop, dirt-encrusted latex gloves. Carlos's friends crack up and ping her with more shit, nailing her in the small of the back, the bony right shoulder, the edge of her other ear. She hunches more, but keeps digging.

Carlos approaches her, a sharp stick in his hand, which he uses to start poking at the center of her back. Like she's a piece of trash on the side of a highway. His crew cackles from the sidelines.

With a hot rush of horror, I march over to him, knock the stick out of his hand. "Get the hell out of here." My voice is a contained growl. "Right now. I'll call my boss. I'll call the *cops*."

"Jesus. Okay, okay. We were just messing around." Carlos raises both hands, still laughing.

"I'll have you kicked out, or you can *get* out. Up to you." I squeeze my fists into balls.

"Come on. She doesn't know the difference. See?" He motions to her. Medusa has her back to us again. Carlos's crew echoes their approval, and look up at me like I'm some unreasonable teacher who's just given them three weeks of detention for chewing gum in class.

Something snaps in me then, some twig-dam in the

center of my heart. "You think because someone's different you can throw your *trash* at them?" I say,

"Oh, shit, I forgot." Carlos smirks. "You got a crazy mom. You know," he smiles sideways as he licks his lips, real slow; "you look a lot sexier when you're not yelling at people."

I see him wink at me again and then: *whoosh*—everything inside of me, once contained, surges forward. "Out. *Now*," I shout, louder than I mean to. "What the fuck are you waiting for?"

The boys look to Carlos for the verdict. He shrugs before signaling the others to move out. As they start walking away through the rain, he shouts to me over his shoulder: "Guess crazy runs in the family."

"Guess asshole runs in yours," I shout back. Rage bubbles up inside of me. I free my right hand, grab a crushed soda can, and hurl it at the back of his head. "*Dicks,*" I scream. The four of them take off running, laughing.

I'm still standing there, staring after them, trying to catch my breath, when Medusa hobbles over to me. She stretches a clenched palm toward me and says, "*tu mano,*" in her deep, cigarette-ash voice, pointing to my hand with shaking ash-colored fingers.

"What do you want me to do?" I ask, confused, cringing slightly at the rotten smell of her.

"*Abrete*," she says. "Open." I open my hand to her and she drops a small, dirty coin in my palm; it has a small hole poked through the top, like something that has once been worn on a necklace. "Tank you." She cups her palm over mine and smiles, walking slowly back toward her trash can, where she resumes her digging, undisturbed.

I turn the coin over in my fingers again, trying to make out the design on the front—it looks engraved, but I can't make out the initials beneath the crust of dirt—before slipping it into the pocket of my shorts and racing through the park gates, just as the storm redoubles its force, and the skies open up like they're bleeding.

# nine

B*uzzzzzz*. The secretary (wo)manning the lobby of Carol Kohl's office peers through the glass at me, and I see her hand feeling for a switch beneath her wooden desk. I've had that same *watched* feeling ever since I left the park. Maybe it's residual ghost-sensitivity. I expect to find Stern, secreted away in every molecule of air, and at every turn. The lock to the door clicks, and I push through into a shocking wave of air-conditioning, my still-damp cutoff shorts sticking to my thighs.

The walls are a drab gray, lighter than the carpet, darker than the secretary's pinned-back hair and lipstick. The furniture in the waiting area is ultra-modern, expensive-looking. All right angles, sharp-looking edges. A small plastic sign next to the secretary's computer says *Jeanette*; a giant Monet reproduction—smeary, blurry grays—decorates the wall behind her desk.

"Hi. I'm looking for Carol Kohl?" I try not to fidget too much with my hands, but, momentarily overcome with self-consciousness at how wet and raggedy I must look in this neat, gleaming office, I try and stealthily smooth out the wrinkles in my wet tank top and reconfigure my ratty ponytail into a smooth(ish) bun.

Without looking up, *Jeanette* jiggles the mouse along the mouse pad, peering at the computer screen. "I see a four-fifteen . . ." She consults the clock, frowns, and glances up at me. "Was she expecting you?"

"No. Well, I don't know. But it's urgent." I tug at the bottom of my tank top, tighten the rubber band around my ponytail, feel the words start to pool beneath my tongue. Her eyes are warm. She wants to listen. "My mom's hearing is coming up really soon . . ." I trail off, shaking my head. "I just really need to see her. Mrs. Kohl. I'll wait all night, I don't care."

"Let me see what we can do," she says softly. The flesh of her arms jiggles as she picks up the phone and presses a square button on the console. She examines her long, tricked-out fingernails as she speaks, low, into the phone. "Someone here to see you. Olivia Tithe . . .?" She looks to me for confirmation. I nod. She writes something down on a notepad, nibbles on the pen cap after; her molars carve new shadows into the plastic. "Yes. Well, okay. Uh-huh. And did you want me to move your— No. Okay then. " She hangs up, stands from her chair and crosses behind her desk to the edge of the hallway. "Come on, *bonita*," she says, cocking her head toward the offices. "Let's go."

I follow her, my rain-drenched shoes squishing noisily in the quiet of the building. At the end of the hall, Jeanette directs me to *turn left at the dolphin sculpture*. When I do, I find myself standing in front of a wide glass-paneled room.

I peer quickly inside and see Carol perched at her desk, typing furiously. I've only met her a couple of times. I hadn't realized before how birdlike she looks: sharp-beaked with small, piercing black eyes; close-cropped blond-streaked hair emerging light and feathery from her scalp.

I clear my throat, knock lightly on the open door. She raises her long twig of a neck. "Olivia," she calls—commands, more like, her voice deep, sharp as her nose. "How are you." It's not a question. "Come in. Come in. Sit down. Would you mind shutting the door behind you? I'd absolutely appreciate it." She shuffles some files on her desk, moves a pen from behind her ear to a square penholder on her desk, which feels miles wide between us.

"I'm sorry I just showed up," I start, throat swollen with a ferocious kind of anticipation. "But I called—"

"Yes. I know. Things have been absolutely crazy around here. I feel awful, Olivia, I really do; glad you came by." She peers at the slim gold watch on her wrist. "We don't have a lot of time—I've got a meeting in a few minutes. But we'll make it work, yes?" She nods, answering her own question. "Yes."

My thighs feel sticky against the leather chair even though it's arctic-cold. My stomach is burning, a fire climbing up my torso and throat, out my mouth. "I wanted to ask you some questions about—"

"—about your mother. Yes." She nods her head, vigorously, like she already knows exactly what I'm going to say. "About her upcoming hearing, I assume? You want to know how things will proceed? What's going to happen next? Well, Olivia, I don't want to get your hopes up. I'll say that right off the bat." The paintings on her wall seem to shake as she says it. I blink, wait for it to go away. "Are you thirsty? Would you like some water? I can buzz Jeanette."

"No. I'm fine," I say, louder than I intended. *Another early schizo-symptom: inability to control the volume of one's voice*. I think I remember reading that on Wikipedia. "I don't want any water. I just want to know if you're—you're completely sure." I inhale deep. "Do you have any doubts at all? I mean—are you completely sure?"

Carol shifts in her chair, interlaces her fingers on top her desk. "I'm going to tell you again, Olivia, because holding on to false hope really isn't serving you," she says after a moment. "There is no doubt in my mind whatsoever that your mother killed Lucas Stern. The circumstantial evidence was tremendous. She had the kid's DNA under her fingernails, for one. But I am also quite certain that her *reasons* for doing so weren't malicious. She was under duress, suffering a particularly potent schizophrenic episode—we have solid medical testimonial to back that up. We even have brain scans. That's the silver lining we're working with here."

"But, then, why has she just been *sitting* there for ten months?"

"Ten months was the absolute soonest I could get the sentencing hearing, Olivia," Carol says. "I know you know that. As it is, we're lucky to have gotten a date less than a year after the arraignment."

There's a fire between my ears. A sharp, hot light. Suddenly, all I want to do is fight back. "Couldn't his DNA have ended up on her after he was dead? If she just handled the body for some reason, by accident . . . and . . ." I pause, starting to lose steam, gripping at the chair's studded edges.

She purses her lips. "That's true, Olivia, and it certainly might have been *possible* that your mom didn't do it—that she handled the boy's body postmortem," Carol Kohl says, in a voice too low and firm for her delicate songbird face, "except for one small thing."

"What?"

"She confessed."

I stare at her in disbelief, feeling all the blood drain from my face. I spent so much time distracting myself from the details of mom's hearing and Stern's death, drifting through a haze of pot smoke and drunken hook-ups, that this detail somehow escaped me. "Confessed?"

"She understood what she'd done. She understood that her sentence would be more forgiving if she took responsibility."

"But doesn't she deserve to stand up for herself, at least? She's my *mom*; she must have some reason, some explanation?"

"I arranged for your mother to have two separate medical evaluations. *Both* determined that she was unfit for trial." Carol frowns at me, pity thick in her eyes. "Our only hope here is to plead insanity. At least this way, she'll be placed in a psychiatric facility, where she can be treated. Cared for."

The room seems to swirl around me, like I've just closed my eyes after having too much to drink. "And that's just that? That makes it over?"

"Yes," she says, in a slightly gentler voice. "That makes it over." She looks at her watch, frowns. "Four-fifteen," she says. "Can I walk you out?"

I don't let her. I walk alone down the long corridor of Carol's office, feeling stupid, shrunken, and cold. How could I let my head—the stupid, ghost-inventions of my head—light a new flame of hope in me?

I hug myself hard as I move back to the elevator. Jeanette's turned the other way, phone pressed to her ear, which means, thankfully, I don't have to worry about speaking with her. I want to go home, huddle beneath my covers in the dark. There's just no point anymore. Nothing to fight for. How did my mother become officially, legally insane? So insane she can't even *appear* in a courtroom, before a judge and jury, and stand trial?

None of it makes sense. And yet, every step I take echoes the same stubborn conclusion: *She confessed.* And as I wait for the elevator, watching the floor numbers ding as it rises to collect me, they, too, ding the same bleak truth: *you're crazy, too.*

*You're crazy. You're crazy.*

The doors whoosh open.

Ted Oakley steps out of the elevator.

He looks startled. "Olivia—so you *did* come to see Carol—I didn't expect to see you." He steps out and pats me quickly on the back, briefcase gripped hard in one hand like it's full of something very heavy.

"Yeah." I blink a few times. "She told me—"

He cuts me off. "I'm sorry, honey. I'm running late." He glances at his wrist. "Stop by the house again soon!" He speeds down the hallway, and I take his place in the elevator, feeling weirdly off-kilter. I had forgotten Carol was Ted Oakley's lawyer, too. But of course, he was the one who found Carol after Mom's first lawyer punked mid-hearing.

I pass Ted's sleek BMW in the parking lot and walk slowly to my eyesore junker, parked just feet away. I turn my key in the car door, opening it and sliding into the hell-hot seat. I turn the key in the ignition, blasting the radio so it obscures the whine of tree frogs. My throat still feels like there's a rock lodged in it.

I flip through radio stations as I pull out of the parking lot; burn past the top-forty, alt rock, and then freeze when I hear it—*sun so hot, I froze to death, Susannah, don't you cry.* Suddenly, Stern's face is all I can see, his face across the dunes, those words off his tongue.

I can hear him . . . swear I can hear him, like he's right here.

*Oh! Susannah, don't you cry for me, I come from Alabama with a banjo on my kneeee.* The funny Southern accent he'd do. I hear it. Like it's right here. Like he's singing right beside me.

Then I realize: he *is* singing right beside me.

I jump, and nearly swerve into the other lane. "Jesus! Stern . . . Jesus." I straighten the wheel, focus on keeping the car on the road.

"'I froze to death, Susannah, don't you cry, don't you cry for me.'" His hair is wilder than I've ever seen it.

"Stop singing. Just stop, please." I punch the music off. "It's over, Stern. Okay? My mother confessed. Miriam Tithe killed you. She's a certifiable lunatic. It's over." I feel the cold radiating from his skin beside me.

"Listen, Liver," he says, "ghosts don't just appear for no reason, right?"

I glance quickly over at him—his eyes glow, so intense. It's hard to look away. "You're here because I conjured you. It's called denial. Delusion." My voice breaks a little and I clear my throat.

"You know that's not true," he says softly. "Even if that's easier for you to believe right now. I'm here. I'm telling you the truth. Look at me, Liver."

I tighten my hands on the wheel. He sighs. "You were always stubborn. Weren't you?"

"I am *not* stubborn. I'm very open-minded. God—how

*dare* you ghost your way into my life just as I'm starting to try and deal with all of this shit and then tell *me* I'm stubborn?"

He laughs. "Ghost my way in. That's pretty funny." He leans over and nudges me and I swerve a little.

"You're gonna get me killed!" I press on the gas a little harder, focusing on the road ahead. Suddenly, I'm not sad anymore, just furious.

He's still sitting there beside me in the car, humming the tune to "Oh! Susannah" under his breath. "Didn't I recently *save your life*?"

I'd almost forgotten about the feeling of his arms around me—the strength of him hauling me out of the waves as I coughed up water. "Maybe you shouldn't have bothered."

"Careful what you wish for. Death is no picnic, Liver. At least I don't think so. I think my point of comparison is fading pretty fast; hard to remember what life was even like. . . ."

"Also not a picnic," I respond. "Trust me." It would be so easy: a quick swerve to the left. I've thought about it before. But something always stops me—some burning desire to live. I feel it pulse in me now, even as the other side—the Gray Space—creeps from the sidelines to tempt me.

We're silent a few moments. Then Stern clears his throat. "Does the name Elvira Madigan mean anything to you?"

"Elvira Madigan?" I rub my forehead. A dull pain is blooming between my eyes. "No. Why?"

"I'm not sure." His deep-dark eyes crinkle as he thinks. "The name just came back to me. One of those random memory-bursts. But it's fuzzy. A lot of things are just fuzzy. It might be important."

"Great. Another 'important' thing *I've* got to look into because you're too fucking dead to do *anything* but show up and make me feel like I'm totally *insane*." I thud my hand against the wheel. I haven't realized until now how angry I am with him. I guess I've been angry at him for a long time—for leaving, for being the whole sucking center of this mess. It feels good to yell at him.

But when I look over, triumphant, he's staring at me, eyes suddenly wide, afraid. His whole body is shaking, vibrating, vibrating so quickly.

"What's—what's happening?" Dread works its way through my chest. "I didn't mean that. Stern, I'm sorry." But it's too late.

He's gone.

Again.

"Stern," I speak his name out loud, into the buzzing silence of the car. Nothing. Immediately, my anger is replaced with regret and shame. I almost hope he'll come back, so he knows how badly I want to believe in him.

# ten

As soon as I come home, I plant myself in front of my MacBook. I can't get Stern's face out of my mind. I was terrible to him, angry and cruel.

Before I can talk myself out of it, I type *Elvira Madigan* into the search bar. Apparently she was a Danish circus performer who made a suicide pact with her boyfriend. A European director made a movie based on her life. What does a long-dead Danish circus performer have to do with my mom, or Stern's murder?

Still—it *has* to mean something; my brain couldn't have just *invented* the name. Could it?

I close out my fruitless search, and click my way to my news feed. Three friends from art school's stories pop up immediately.

*Roz Patel: is stoned, dude. Way stoned.* Typical.

*Mimi Barker: David Lynch Night part deux with Sammy baby.* David Lynch Night part eighty would be more like it. Mimi Barker has nothing but David Lynch nights, as far as I know.

*Rita Timmerman: Got accepted into senior independent studio with Mr. Moses!!!*

I stare at the update for a long time. I would have been in that class this year—or so my teachers led me to believe, before everything went to shit. Independent studio—the competitive senior art class that accepts only twelve students yearly.

While I'm torturing myself, I might as well take it one step further and look through every inch of Stern's old photo album—heart shriveling to the size of a walnut, breath high and tight in my throat the whole time.

My phone buzzes, persistent, in the pocket of my cutoffs: *Raina*. I hesitate. I want, badly, to talk to someone, to talk to my best girl friend in the world, but a part of me I can't hammer out also resents her: for hanging out with her cool new swim team friends; for having a normal life; for being able to go to Stern's unveiling.

But I pick up at the last second. I need a human voice. I need *her*. "Hi." My voice comes out exhausted.

"Babygirl. What are you doing right now?"

"I'm at home." I click off-line quickly, like she can see what I'm doing. "Where are you? It sounds really windy."

"I'm on my way to Parker's house. We're partying tonight. Rich-kid style."

"I'm actually in the middle of something, Rain—"

"Sorry, Liv. But it's already done. You don't even want to know what I had to do to get you on the guest list. So, now you have to show. Get dressed for fancy town and get your skinny ass over here!"

"Guest list? What kind of party has a guest list? Raina?"

Silence. She's hung up. I bang down my phone, frustrated, and it buzzes almost immediately with a text from Raina.

*You* know *you need to get out of the house . . . I'll meet you in front of P's house in fifteen. Please don't crap out tonight. Please. P.S. Hot trust-funders everywhere. For a limited time only.*

I sigh, staring for one more second at my now-blank computer screen. The Elvira Madigan search has turned up nothing of value anyway. I drag myself to my closet, dig my favorite dress out of the closet—dark, satiny blue that looks coal black to me now, a deep V-cut that shows just a little bit of cleavage. At the very least, a party will help take my mind off of Elvira Madigan. And art school. And Mom. And Stern.

"It's open bar, so just take what you want when you want it," Parker Rosen tells us, gesturing with a champagne flute. His other hand is seemingly molded to the lower back of some Playboy bunny wannabe in a silky bikini top and short skirt. Parker's rich, tubby, and super pretentious. He likes to wear golfing-style polos and carry on conversations about tax cuts for the wealthy despite the fact that he's not even old enough to vote yet, nor has ever (to my knowledge) held a job.

"Just don't touch anything in there"—Parker motions toward a pristine, antique-y looking room that could fit every room of my house inside of it—"and don't screw with the sound equipment, okay?"

He leads us to the back deck, thick with private school kids in various states of undress, dancing or milling or spinning in silky summer dresses and bikinis through the shallow end of the giant pool, glowing with dusk light and rippling with the sway of bodies. Raina grabs my hand and squeezes it as Parker and his blond bunny peel away, high-fiving their way into the middle of a group of shirtless boys in sport jackets, holding drinks in tall, sweaty glasses.

"*Ix-nay* on the *outey-pay ace-fay*," Raina says. Her long, silky black hair is parted in two braids today. "Let's just have some *fun*, okay?" She waltzes us over to the bar, still gripping my hand. She pours vodka into two glasses and fills the rest with alternating splashes of cranberry and orange juices, swirling the mixture with a pinkie finger. "These are called vodka sunrises. See? They're kind of the color of a sunrise, aren't they?"

I grip the drink in my hand, stare at what looks like dark gray sludge to me. "Yeah. Definitely."

She takes a sip of her drink and fights a gag. "You pour the next ones, 'kay?" She examines the crowd, sipping slowly at her drink with a permanent frown. "What do you think? Any guys worth talking to?"

"I doubt any of them will talk to *us*. They can probably smell our used cars from miles away." I scan the giant deck. A DJ is blasting a mixture of bass-y house and pop music, and the whole party looks like a scene from a black-and-white movie projected silent and huge.

The sun is setting over the ocean, a dark crack through the gray sheet of the sky. I feel a tap on my shoulder and spin around, jumping a little. Austin Morse.

"Didn't expect to see you here," he says, smiling.

"Raina dragged me. I don't know anyone," I answer sharply, taking a sip of my drink, trying to hide a grimace as I swallow. Part of me is pleased to see him. Maybe he'll whisper something in my ear, ask me what underwear I'm wearing tonight. I'll answer in a way that's just coy enough to keep him guessing.

It's all a game.

And yeah, sure, maybe I like the attention, too.

Raina fixes him with a menacing stare. She still thinks the fact he "ditched" me on the beach was jerky. "Oh, Austin, *so* nice of you to drop by, as always. Liv—I'm gonna go check out the bathroom—there's a fountain inside of it. You wanna come?"

"Um, I—no. I'm fine."

She looks at Austin, and then back at me, one hand cocked on her hip. "You sure?"

I nod. I want for her to leave us. I want, for once, to be the chosen one.

She turns to Austin, points a finger at him. "You treat my girl with respect, you got that?"

He does a fake boy scout salute. "Got it."

She spins on her heels and heads back into the house, drink sloshing in her hand. She has a habit of starving herself before parties so she can get drunk more easily—I guess a few sips did it tonight.

"You know me," Austin says.

"What?"

"You said you didn't know anyone here, before. But, you know me."

I narrow my eyes at him. "I guess."

"I was actually about to leave, but . . ." he says, taking a sip of some dark glass beer bottle with a fancy German-looking name.

"Now I have a reason to stay."

"And what's that, Austin Morse?"

His fingers brush mine as he reaches for my glass. "To try your drink, of course. I know you're an expert at this stuff." He swallows, coughs, and wipes his hand against his lips. "That's really awful."

"You can't handle the big girl drinks, can you?" I take the drink back from him. I feel his eyes brush over me, some blaze ignited behind them. *What does he want from me?* I wonder. And, more importantly: *what do I want from him?*

There's a loud splash from the pool—a bunch of girls, hand-in-hand, giggle as they float, half-naked in the deep end. But Austin doesn't even look. He keeps his blaze-eyes on me.

"You impress me, Olivia. You know that?"

"Why?" I watch his glass-gray (blue?) eyes continue to examine my face. "Because of my amazing tolerance for shitty drinks?"

"No. You impress me in general." He shifts his feet, coming millimeters closer to me.

I snort, glance at him sideways, stifling the desire to call him out on his staggeringly bad pickup lines—if that's what they even are. "How drunk *are* you, Austin Morse?"

"I'm sober, actually, Olivia Tithe." He leans closer to me and I can smell his citrusy cologne. "Will you go out with me? On a date?"

I almost choke on my drink, keep my face half-hidden behind the glass to avoid having to meet his eyes. *Go out with Austin Morse?* Austin Morse, the quintessential untouchably hot prep school boy—go out with *me*, the art girl from the killer-mom side of the tracks? I could see us, *maybe*, pressing our mouths drunkenly together in some secret place. But an actual date? An actual planned get-together where we might run into people we know?

My brain won't stop spinning out new reasons and anti-reasons. "Listen, I really don't—" I stop. I notice Raina step through the screen door, arm-in-arm with a tall boy in basketball shorts who looks so much like Stern, I blink. Not him. Just some random guy.

"Come on," Austin says, "Just one date, Red. You and me."

But I barely hear him then, my whole body flushing hot, heart jackrabbiting into my throat. Stern is lodged in my head now, the loss of him, and his ghost-presence, too.

A memory of our kiss flashes through my mind. I never got to tell him what I wanted. I never got to tell him I wanted everything from him: his smile, his laugh, his slow-easy speech, the warmth of his arms around me. His voice, singing full-lunged in the distance as he'd approach. *Oh! Susannah, don't you cry for me, I come from Alabama . . .*

Just as he looms huge in my mind, the now-familiar pins-and-needles chill comes over me and he's here. Stern, the real Stern, or the ghost Stern: all wavery and pale beside Austin's firm, tan solidity. *Shit.* I try not to stare at him, but it's hard to avoid.

*The Gray Space,* says the small voice between my ears.

"Something wrong?" Austin asks, squinting at me.

"What? Oh—I saw someone I know and—I was just—" I shake my head, smile up at him, firmly ignoring Stern. Obviously Austin can't see or hear him. "It's nothing."

"You sure? Everything alright?" Austin leans closer.

So does Stern. He comes to stand right beside me, his icy shoulder sending waves of chills through me before he pulls back slightly, wincing, clutching at his arm. "We gotta talk. Now," Stern insists.

"So, is it a plan?" Austin asks, at the same time.

I haven't had two boys aggressively vying for my attention since tenth grade, when I got drunk at my first off-campus party and played strip poker with a group of older painter boys. "No. I mean yes. I mean . . ."

Stern tugs at me; I shiver again. I smile awkwardly at Austin. "I'll—um—I'll be right back," I blurt out.

"Where you going?" he asks. Raina's no longer standing near the door, thankfully. I don't need her to try and loop me into a round of shots right now.

"Bathroom," I say quickly, already walking away. Stern sticks close to me.

"So, this is what cool rich kids like Austin Morse do?" Stern asks, headbanging to the awful electronica beat resounding through every part of the house, black curls flying. "Always knew it was a waste of time."

I don't respond. I can't be seen talking to thin air. I need privacy. We're walking down a long, open hallway on the second floor; the party is still visible from the massive windows that make up most of the back of the house, the torches glowing bright hot through the dark, the pool a giant glassy ripple.

"In here," I whisper. We step inside a bedroom and I fumble for a light switch: Parker's older brother's room, I'm guessing. He obviously hasn't spent much time here since he left for Stanford. A few Model Senate and academic awards are framed on the wall.

"You were thinking about me," he says softly. "I could feel it. From Nowhere, I could feel it."

"I was *trying* to have a normal night, actually. And *not* think about you."

"But you *were*, weren't you?"

I sigh. "Yeah. I was." I eye him, his stark height, his even starker beauty, the same Christmas flannel and funny shiny basketball shorts he'll wear for all of eternity now. "So, what?" I ask, taking a sip of my drink, which suddenly tastes even grosser than before. I set it down on a shiny shelf top, next to a shiny PlayStation beneath a giant flat screen TV. "Can you read my thoughts now that you're dead?" I cross my arms, hoping like hell that he can't.

"No." Stern stares at me intently. "But I can *feel* you. I felt you tonight. It's like I get sucked through a straw and spat back out beside you." He rubs his head.

"Stern, look." I have to put my foot down. "You shouldn't be here. You don't *belong* here. I need to have a life. Friends."

Stern raises an eyebrow. "Like Austin? You once said he was an 'overprivileged twat.'"

"He *is* an overprivileged twat, but he's also . . . I don't know . . ."

"Dreamy?"

"Alive." I'm suddenly exhausted. The mattress is hard, like everything in the house: hard-edged, new, all corners.

I wish he would go away.

No. Wrong. I wish he had never gone away in the first place; then we could return to the party together. We'd make fun of Parker and his stupid Playboy bunny friends, and he'd cannonball into the pool, and I'd laugh my ass off. And I wouldn't need Austin Morse and his so-cringe-worthy-it's-*almost*-cute lines. Wouldn't need anyone else at all.

"Is that really all it takes?" Stern asks quietly.

I look up at him, my throat squeezed practically shut. My secret still sits, burning, in the bottom of my belly—that I love him. That I will always love him. And everything I want from him is now impossible: A normal life. A normal relationship. Wrapping my arms around him whenever I want to. Not having to worry that at any moment he will evaporate.

"Maybe," I say. Stern sits next to me and a chill passes through my whole body, as though I've been plunged head first into ice-cold water. I stand up, and move to the wide-screen at the other end of the room, stoop to flip my fingers through the DVDs stacked in a neat pile on the shelf below the console, just trying to put distance between us.

"Anything good over there?"

"Tons," I answer, keeping my eyes on the stack of movies. "You know," I tell him, swallowing the lump in my throat, "there's an Elvira Madigan movie. Not here, I mean. But, in the world. I read about it online. Maybe we should watch it. Look for clues or something."

He moves suddenly from the bed and stoops beside me on the hardwood floor, peering over my shoulder. "Elvira Madigan . . ." He looks at me, eyes wide with excitement. "Of course—the soundtrack! A theme song!"

"What?"

"It's the piece of music I played for my recital, for . . ." He squints, like he's thinking, hard.

"For Juilliard," I remind him. "You practiced it, over and over again with my mom."

"Yeah. Of course. That's what it is. That must be why I remembered that name. . . ." He smiles, victorious, like everything's clear now.

The pointlessness of it all hits me, like a fist-drive in my stomach. "*This* was your big, important thing?" I straighten up, my hands starting to tremble. "A *music lesson*? Of course you remember a piece of music you played, what, like ten thousand times?"

"Do you really think I *want* this to keep happening? That I'm enjoying it?" Stern shakes his head, mouth tight. "The *only* good thing about all of this is that I get to see you." He looks right at me. Looks right *through* me.

I stare hard at my lap. If I look at him at this moment, something is going to burst. All that anxiety and emotion has to come out some way or another.

Wish I could touch him. Wish I had never met him. Wish I could hold him. Wish I could stop loving him. Wish I could pull his mouth to mine and never stop kissing him, ever ever ever. Wish I could forget about him.

Impossible. It's all impossible.

"Liv," he starts, gently. "I know you're scared."

"Of course I'm scared. I can't even *talk* to anyone about this because I'll just seem nuts. I don't want to realize one day I'm actually just like . . ." I trail off, terrified even to finish my thought.

"Look," he says, the quiet lilt of his voice like an arrow, finding its way to the center of me, "why don't you just talk to her?"

"Talk to who?"

"You know who," he says. A huge shiver runs through him.

"I—I don't—" The door creaks open and Stern disappears instantly. Austin stands in the doorway. I wonder how long he's been here . . . if he heard me talking to no one. If I'm angry for his interruption, or grateful.

"I was looking for you." He frowns, and sits down beside me on the bed. His skin radiates heat—so different from Stern's—and his body, in its well-muscled weight, sinks deeply into the bed. "What are you doing in here?"

"I didn't feel well. I thought lying down might help. But I think I might need some air instead." I still feel shivery from the conversation with Stern—like he picked the lock guarding some dark, dusty part of my brain and dug out all my secrets.

"You want me to walk you outside?" Austin stands up from the bed and takes my hand in his.

"Okay." I let him hold it and pull me upright. It feels good to be around someone alive, someone solid. "I think I should probably go home."

"Well, I'll walk you to your car, then."

"Bike," I correct him.

"Bike," he repeats. "That's cool. Your bike." He says it again, like it's something foreign, exotic. He moves his hand to my lower back—his heat vibrates through me and part of me wants to pull away but I don't because I like the feel of him, of his hand on me—as he leads me downstairs.

I look around briefly for Raina, to tell her I'm leaving, but I don't see her. I'll send her a text as soon as Austin leaves me.

The hot air plasters our skin as we weave through the spill of kids on the front deck—Raina's not out here, either—down to my humble little Schwinn, still sitting at the bottom of the driveway. I fumble for my keys and jiggle them in the slightly rusty u-lock, throwing it in my bike basket when I get it free.

"Cool ride," he says, putting one tan hand on my bike seat and the other on the left handlebar before I can hop on and ride away. He's looking at me like I'm some new, secret species he's discovered. "We're still on for that date, right?"

"Sure."

"Awesome." His eyes go soft as he leans toward me over the bike seat. He tilts his head slightly to one side.

He's going to kiss me. I let my face angle toward his, but when I look up—it's *Stern's* face I see, not Austin's. Terrified, I pull back before our lips meet. "Text me," I call out, hopping quickly on my bike—his face just beginning to register my rejection—peddling quickly out of Parker Rosen's driveway and onto the side streets that lead onto Fourty-second Avenue.

I keep hearing Stern's words, echoing through my head: *Why don't you just go visit her?*

*Talk to her.*

*You know who.*

# eleven

*Six days.*

I've only made the half-hour journey to visit Mom at Broadwaithe one, single, nightmare-inducing time before—six months ago—that made me never want to return again. Dad was with me. We didn't talk much as the roads curved beyond us, lush with color, transitioning to wide, flat swaths of farmland and then the monotonous tedium of highway that brought us to her.

It feels different today, on a musty white shuttle that blinks *BROADWAITHE* from the little window above the windshield. I'm playing hooky from work even though Saturdays are prime park-going days. I didn't even bother to call George and fake sick.

I stare out the filmy window as the Miami skyline—a trembling city in the scorching sunlight—disappears behind us. I peel my thighs off the sticky seat and pull my cotton dress further down to cover the backs of them. There's no air-conditioning. I close my eyes and try to think hard about Stern—I could use the shiver of him right now, the bone-chill he brings when he comes.

We're getting closer and closer now, and my stomach is all knots. All I want is to rush up to the bus driver and fake sick and make him pull over, but I know I can't—I have to see her, even if it terrifies me. I have to understand.

The shuttle veers off the highway and down a long gravel road. Then I see it, looming in the distance: Broadwaithe—the jail that's held her for the past ten months, as she's waited for her official sentence.

Everyone seems to go silent as we approach, as though sucked into the awful vortex of the place. I squeeze my eyes shut and I see Mom in the light-impression of a blink: long wavy hair streaming down her slender back, long legs as she ran with me into the surf, long fingers as she searched with me for seashells, the calcified bodies of starfish in the sand.

I don't want that Mom to be replaced by the Mom I find inside, the accused-killer Mom, peeling skin and dirty sweat suits, with no ocean in her hair.

"Oh, honey. Livie. It's you. You're here." Mom's voice is raw, cracked. Her sweat suit is way too big and her hair is short. Choppy. Like it was cut by someone trained to make her look as alien and crazy as possible. She looks tired, and old, and loopy.

Mom turns to the guard for the okay to hug me, and

when she gets it, she reaches for me and pulls me into her chest. I don't know why, but I go stiff in her arms. "Hi, Mom," I mumble—it's all I can manage to say before I surrender, let myself fall into her mom arms and hug her back, hug her so fiercely I'm afraid I might break her. My mom.

The guard watches every move we make from narrowed eyes. She's trained to be suspicious. Mom has to get permission for everything now—to go to the bathroom, to take a shower, to listen to music—in the three letters she's written me, she told me that every time; she also told me that her hands had started seizing up pretty badly sometimes and that it was hard for her to write and that there was no piano here so she couldn't even *dream* of playing. It would be too painful.

She smells different, too, as we stand, squeezing the air out of each other—not like sweet plumeria and ginger and ocean but like something stale and acidic and overly sanitized, like a hospital hallway.

The guard nods to her from near the door. "Why don't you two sit down now, Miss Tithe?"

"Come on, sweetheart," she says. Tears rim her eyes as she pulls away, taking my hand in hers—her skin still feels soft. "We'd better sit. Tisha doesn't mess around." She laughs a little at this.

"No, ma'am, I don't," Tisha responds, matter-of-factly. I can tell she likes Mom, though; I could never imagine anyone not liking Mom—even in jail, where prisoners are likened more to wild animals, or rotting garbage, than to actual living, breathing human beings.

Mom leads me to a wide, bland table, and we sit beside each other in cold plastic fold-out chairs in the cold white windowless room, empty of all decoration—a room devoid of color and music and light. In many ways, we are trapped in the same place.

She holds her hands over mine on top of the table. I still don't know what to say—how to start.

Mom speaks first. "How old are you now, Olivia? Are you still in high school?" she asks, her eyes still watery as she tries to focus them. She clears her throat, seems embarrassed. "They've got me on so many . . . so many medicines . . . I—I forget things so quickly. . . ." She forces a little laugh, examines my palm in hers.

"I'm going to be a senior next year," I tell her. My voice is wispy, lost in the broad drabness of the room. "A senior in high school," I add, just to clarify. "I flunked out of art school, Mom. Remember when I was in art school?"

"Oh, art school! Liv, I'm so excited for you. That's so, so . . . exciting." She struggles to get the words out.

"No, Mom, it's not exciting. I flunked out. They told me to leave."

She thinks about this for a moment, confused. "Well, I don't like that one bit, Olivia. Not one bit. How could they kick you out—you're so good at playing."

"Painting, Mom," I say, my frustration mounting. She was the one who made me a painter in the first place, who told me I was special, and good, and that making art was the most important thing in the world. "Not music. *You* play music." I stare at her hands. "You play really beautiful music. You won so many awards, Mom. Remember?"

She looks up at me, lips starting to quiver. "My hands—they cramp so badly. They won't give me medicine for it, either. Not even tiger balm. The stuff in that little glass jar that smells like menthol . . ."

"Maybe I can bring you some."

She shakes her head. "No. No, they wouldn't allow that." There're more lines on her face than before—around her lips, her eyes, her forehead—a slight droop around the corners of her mouth. "I just can't believe you're finally here. I miss you so badly." Her voice cracks, and she starts to cry. She was almost always on meds; they kept her even. When she wasn't on them, she was in her studio, composing. If she'd cried or sobbed or wailed in there, it would have been drowned out by the constant music. I wouldn't have known. "It's the worst part," she says, "and my hands." She holds them up to me and I watch them shake. "I can't even play, Livie. I can't do anything."

I want to tell her how much I've craved this, missed her voice, her music dancing up to me from the living room, her hand pressed to my forehead to check for fever, her mischievous smile in the middle of the night when we'd sneak out to the ocean to watch the waves crash huge on the shore. I want to tell her how little of all this I even understand.

"It'll be okay, Mom," I tell her, even though, of course, it won't. "We can work on it. We can make them better. I know we can. You always know how to make things better, Mommy." I scoot my chair around the table so it's next to hers, and wrap my arms tight around her neck. I miss her so bad, from the curled-up center of me. My mother.

Tisha clears her throat behind me, taps my shoulder. I raise my face to look at her and she shakes her head. "Sorry, miss, but I'm going to have to ask you to return to the other side of the table. It's for your own safety."

"But she's my mother," I protest, "I'm fine. What kind of a rule is that? She's my *mom*." Tisha glares at Mom and, obediently, Mom moves her chair away from mine.

"Miriam knows the rules around here," Tisha says, resuming her post by the door, still staring meaningfully at Mom. "And she knows what happens when she breaks them."

I take a deep breath and turn back to Mom. Time is running out. "Mom—I need to—I need to ask you something." I take her hands in mine and squeezes.

She clutches back, but shakes her head, confused. "What's wrong, honey?"

"Mom. Listen—the night you were found with Stern's body . . . you didn't take your medication that day, did you? Mom?"

"I don't—I don't know what you're asking me, Livie. I don't understand what my medication has to do with anything."

"When they found you, with Stern," I say, my voice low. "You were out of it, Mom. I don't think you remember what happened."

"Livie," she says, almost laughing. "Why are you whispering right now? What's the big secret?"

"Jesus, Mom." I pull my hands away from hers. "I'm talking about the boy they say you killed. My best friend. Your piano student."

"I don't know—I don't know what you're talking about." She glances around, seems to curl into herself a little, like a confused animal. "Do you need to use the bathroom?"

"What? No. Mom, look at me. You said you didn't remember what happened right before, right? Right? Mom?"

"No—I didn't. I don't," she says, her chin trembling.

"*Look* at me." She doesn't, she won't. I lean in closer. "Do you have any enemies? Anyone who would want to hurt you on purpose?"

"Enemies? Why would I have enemies? Why are you asking such strange—"

"Someone set you up, Mom." As soon as I blurt it out, I'm convinced it must be true. "You shouldn't be here," I go on, gripping her hands in mine, as I look around the cold, smelly, empty, blank-walled room, devoid of anything human, anything truly alive. She doesn't get it. Something isn't connecting. "You didn't kill someone—you couldn't have. You don't even kill bugs. Remember? Don't you remember anything at all? About anything?" My voice is starting to get shrill. Because as the words pour out of me, I know I'm right. I've got to be. "You wouldn't even let me kill spiders when they'd crawl across the walls even though I was so scared. You always taught me how everything has a soul, remember that? You believe that. You *couldn't* have killed someone. You couldn't have."

She pulls her hands away, stares at them hard. She starts to shake. "There was blood . . . there was blood on my hands—blood. Blood. There was blood. Blood on my hands," she says, softly at first and then louder, and louder, not even words any more, nothing I understand—rocking back and forth in her chair, covering her ears, pulling at her hair.

"Mom. Please stop. Look at me, just look at me." I try to pull her attention to me, to pull her out of her hole, her delusion.

She quiets for a minute, staring down with a faraway, hollow gaze before she rips her hands out from under mine again to grip at the edge of the table. She leans toward me and whispers: "biscaynebiscaynefiftysecond-biscaynefiftysecond," spitting as she does.

I shake my head and pull back. Her nonsense is freaking me out—and the way she's saying it with such importance. She keeps muttering her latest line of crazy—it's growing into a howl now, a scream, as her hands flail around her like giant twin moths—"BISCAYNEBISCAYNE BISCAYNEFIFTYSECONDBISCAYNEFIFTYSECOND—"

"Mom. What do you want? What do you need?" I cry, desperate, as Tisha rushes over from her guard post, pulls

Mom's hands from her ears, holding them roughly behind her back. "Miss Tithe. It's alright. It's going to be alright." She removes something like a baby monitor from the breast pocket of her uniform and speaks into it as I recoil in my chair.

Mom writhes and kicks, still screaming like an infant; Tisha tightens her hold.

I want to look away but I can't. Can't take my eyes off of her.

"You've got to calm down, Miss Tithe."

But Mom keeps at it, eyes wildly bugged as she fights, greasy hair sticking to the wet on her face, streaming from her eyes and her nostrils and her open mouth.

Two guards rush in. I watch as one helps Tisha restrain her, and the other flicks at a syringe, rolls up mom's sleeve, and jabs the needle into the flesh of her upper arm. I watch as her head lolls to one side, eyes rolling back, a string of saliva—like a spider's silk—rolling from her lips all the way down the front of her sweater.

And then, I bolt. Out of the waiting room. Down the cold dank halls that smell of urine and antiseptic. Through the metal detectors. Past the small army of armed guards at the front door. Through the heavy iron barbed-wire gates. To the empty lot where the bus waits to bear us all away from this place.

# twelve

I sleep—a lonely, heartsick sleep—the whole musty shuttle ride back to the city. Mom's in every black-and-white frame of my nightmare: her head lolled back, needles poking out of every inch of her face and arms, hands gone.

And then a memory creeps into my sleep: I'm a little kid, and she's beside me in bed, a glass of red wine in one hand, telling me the bedtime story I demanded she tell me almost every night. I can hear her in my dreams, just as it was. Just as we were then.

"Tell me again, Momma. Tell me how you used to live inside the ocean."

"Before I met your father, I was a mermaid. I floated along and I wished I could sing, but nothing came out of my mouth—"

"—nothing at all?"

"Nothing at all. Now close your eyes if you want me to finish," she'd tell me. "But I had a beautiful tail, fins the color of the bluest sky, and I slept on the pillowy parts of waves and waited for something good to happen. And then, one day, a god came to visit and said he had something important to give me."

"A piano?"

"Yes. A piano. I'd never seen a piano before that night. It was at the edge of the water and when I sat down before it, my fingers began to play. Then goddesses began to appear, their hair was the color of fire. Just like yours. So red. They got very excited and started dancing and everything changed."

"What happened?"

"My fins became legs, and my hair got very long, and when I opened my mouth, I could sing."

"And you couldn't live in the ocean ever again."

"That's true."

"But as long as you have the piano, and as long as you can make beautiful things, you'll be free."

"Yes, Olivia. And you are the most beautiful thing I've ever made."

"I am?"

"You are," she says, as the wine dips from her hand and my bed slips away and I slip away and the needles reappear.

I wake up with three mosquitoes rooting into my blood supply as the sweat-lodge of a shuttle sputters into the Sea & Shine shopping center parking lot.

The bus driver nods to me as I exit. He's a large, suspendered man whose features seem lost in the wide mallow of his face. It's the face of someone who has absorbed the psychic weight of so many journeys, back and forth between hellish dimensions.

A shiver runs through me as I walk to my car, that *watched* feeling creeping in again—the feeling of another person's eyes focused right on me, waiting for something. I whip my head around—there are people around, milling through the parking lot, but they're looking for their gas-guzzling sedans and beat-up pickups, not me.

I slide into the stupid-hot seat of my car and steer out of the parking lot—the wheel burning beneath my hands—trying not to think about Mom, about how she wigged out as soon as I mentioned Stern. It was like I flipped some switch that sent an electric shock of crazy straight through her. Bubbling and slurring and screaming—like the memory of it all was too much to bear.

"She did it, Stern," I say, as I wait at a red-gray light, aloud, angrily, like he might appear. I still can't understand why I can summon him when I'm not trying, but I can't when I really am—who's responsible? Who sends him to me? "Can you hear me? She did it. Okay? She's gone." I pound the rim of the wheel with my palm. "You're gone and she's been gone, too, since the night she killed you. You asshole. You dead asshole."

No answer. I look over and the boys in the car beside mine are pointing out the open window of their LeSabre, laughing at me—the crazy girl, screaming at herself, all alone. I roll my window down, hot and furious. "Mind your own damn business," I shout, honking for no good reason at all except that I feel like making noise. The cars in front of me move—the light must have changed—and I peel onto the highway, furious, eyes burning with rage.

I roll up my window and scream some more. No words—just pure, hot, wild sound, bursting from some busted-up pipe inside of me. I scream until my lungs burn, until I realize there are tears streaming down my cheeks and the salt I taste on my tongue is real and not imagined, as I worry now everything I see and experience is. And I keep screaming, and howling, and crying, until I pass a sign up ahead for a highway exit that makes me go instantly silent: *BISCAYNE BLVD, EXIT 12A.*

Something clicks in my brain. Biscayne. It's what Mom was mumbling. It wasn't nonsense at all.

It was an intersection.

I dart into the right lane as quickly as I can, ignoring the honking of other cars, and take the exit, my whole body humming. Biscayne and Fifty-second is an intersection on the edge of a long commercial strip in Little Haiti. *When would Mom have been here?* I look for a parking spot between the run-down laundromats and *botanicas* and car washes—I know she used to like to go into some of the *botanicas*, ask about ways to spurt her creativity when she was having trouble composing.

I turn the corner and find a spot on Forty-sixth Street, in a dusty rectangle behind a strip of sagging houses. A man wearing a wife-beater, several teeth missing, helps guide me safely between two hulking vans. Music with a heavy, steady drumbeat sounds from the handheld stereo of a man in a flowery button-up shirt, seated with a big pitcher of something several porches down.

In this corner of Little Haiti, there's less lushness and more mosquitoes, fat with blood feasts. There are no canopies of palm and gumbo limbo and banyan, stretched across the streets. Still, it's not awful—just isolated and eerily quiet, aside from the occasional man, hooting at me from an open window, usually things like *wouj*, on account of my hair, which Raina told me means *red* in Creole. Her mom used to have a Haitian boyfriend—he used to call me that, too, when I'd come over.

The strips of houses and grocery stores and *botanicas* are far apart, interspersed with dry patches of grass and weeds. Even though there's really no one around, my heart is beating wild—like walking through a dark house you know is haunted, waiting with held breath for the first impossibly terrifying thing to jump out and snatch you. The heat settles on my shoulders; flies buzz warnings in my ears.

The only thing on the corner of Fifty-second and Biscayne is a dentist's office. Confused, I start up the sidewalk, and climb the three creaky stairs to get a better look. Mom's dentist was *my* dentist—Dr. Fink—and he's in Brickell; no way in hell he'd ever set up shop in Little Haiti.

I ring the bell anyway and it *guzzzzzzzz*es open. Inside, it's lukewarm—the air-conditioner is clearly struggling in the window of the small (empty) waiting room. The single youngish receptionist lifts her head from the keyboard of her computer when I come in; a tiny spinning fan oscillates on her desk, blowing the few loose tendrils of her hair back.

"Sorry, miss, but we're closed," she tells me, unable to mask the yawn in her voice. She squints at me. "Office hours are Monday though Friday, eight to six, and Saturday to one." Her eyes are warm, almond-shaped—they remind me of Raina's, even in the flecked quality of their gray.

"You can call the office first thing Monday morning if you want an appointment."

"I don't need an appointment," I say. "I'm looking for information. About a crime."

Her head seems to tip back with the weight of her hair—piled about six inches off her head in a prom-ish up-do—as she turns quickly back to me, pursing her plush lips forward, swiveling her swivel chair right up flush with the edge of the counter, suddenly interested. She leans forward. "What are you talking about . . . like a break-in? The laundromat on Fifty-third got broken into last week, but we've been okay so far."

I shake my head, flushing pepper-hot, so embarrassed that I'm even here, that I actually took Mom's babbling to mean something. "No—I meant . . . it's about a murder." I can barely pronounce the word.

"Murder?" Her eyes go wide. "When?"

"A little under a year ago." I manage to say.

Immediately, her face falls. "Oh. Well, you won't have any

luck asking me, then," she says, moving the fan out a bit so I feel a stream of cool air. "We haven't even been here six months. You writing an article for school or something?"

"Yes. School," I say, finding it difficult to breath. Mom's words were nonsensical after all and I—the crazy daughter of crazy Miriam Tithe—was just hearing what I wanted to hear. "Well, thanks anyway."

As I turn to walk away, Big Hair says: "It was a lawyer's office before, if that helps any. Foster's, or something."

I freeze where I stand. A chill runs straight through me. I turn back to face her, the dark slate of her skin shining beneath bright overhead lights. "Greg Foster?" I ask, almost a whisper.

"That's the one." She beams, returning to her computer screen, tucking a loose tendril behind her ear. "Greg Foster."

I step closer to her, right up to the counter. "Did he leave any information? An address for his new office, anything?"

"Honey—I really don't—"

"Please," I say, my voice catching in my throat. "Could you just look for me? It's—it's really important. For the article."

"Will my name be in it?"

"Yes. Definitely." I answer. "I'll write you down as a contributor." Her gaze seems to warm one hundred degrees when I say it. She swivels her chair to a metal file cabinet on the other side of her desk.

I watch her rifle through a thick stack of papers,

humming under her breath. I stand on tiptoe and watch her fingers sift and separate. After a couple of minutes, she edges a sheet of paper out of the file and turns back to me. "It doesn't say whether this is a business address or what, but it's all I could find." She writes her name—*DEANDRA MENDEZ*—in big letters at the bottom of the paper before she hands it to me. The air-conditioner clicks its gray tongue from the corner window. "Good luck. And bring a copy of the article when it comes out, okay? I've always wanted to see my name in print." She laughs.

I grip the paper with Greg Foster's West Palm Beach address hard in my fist as I walk to my car, past the empty lots and weary grasses, past the half-bald palms striped along the medians, past the men on their sagging porches mumbling *wouj*, whistling beneath their breath. I nearly start skipping as I turn the corner at Forty-sixth and spot my dusty car. Something zings in my brain—hope, maybe. A bright, hot rush of it. *I was* right. And so was Mom.

She needs me. She needs me to pull sense from the muck of her mumbling.

And I will. *Six days*. Six days to make this right.

I remember going along to West Palm sometimes as a kid, with Dad, to see some of the houses he was working on. On the way, we'd always stop at a convenience store for Sno Balls—Twinkie-type snacks filled with cream and covered in coconut icing.

He'd tell me the houses he was working on were ours until someone bought them up, or moved in—let me choose what color to make the door, or the shingles. I'd almost always choose purple, so every one would be a little bit like Oh Susannah. For a long time, every time I passed a house with even the littlest bit of purple, I considered it part-mine.

Dad was forced out of his career as a builder because of the failing market. He agreed to become part of a giant commercial real estate venture because Ted Oakley was behind it—because he didn't see any other way to keep his hands in a thing he loved. Maybe he thinks Ghost Town will help resurrect Miami's bombed-out housing market. Just like he probably thought by marrying Mom he could make her better.

I used to think this heroic: my sturdy, stable dad, capable of anything. But now I realize that he's just drawn to dying, helpless things. The unsaveables.

Like Mom.

Maybe, like me.

I plug Greg Foster's address into my GPS: the place is seventy-five miles away, and it's almost rush hour. But I don't care. I play a dumb top-forty pop station on the radio and sing along, loudly, to every song on the long drive there to distract myself from my nerves. *What will he say?* I wonder. *What will he know?*

Raina and I used to speculate, during a couple three-hour long phone sessions my last semester in art school, why Greg Foster left Mom's case halfway through. Raina thought maybe he was in love with my mom, and it drove him so mad he could no longer focus on the case and was forced to quit to save his own sanity. I thought maybe he was a drunk. Then Rain thought maybe he was both a drunk *and* desperately in love with Mom, and, in his drunkenness, made a pass, which caused her to fire him.

I wonder how different all of this would feel with Stern beside me, alive, in the passenger seat, if the kid who had died that night almost a year ago had been someone else entirely, someone neither of us knew. He'd want to be here—to confront Greg Foster with me, hold my hand as we walked toward him, faces set in hard, serious lines that mean *don't fuck with us; we mean business.* And I ache, as much as I have since the day Stern and I kissed, for a person beside me who understands exactly what I need without my ever having to say it.

Even if the world stays gray forever, I just don't think it would be so bad if I knew I could have Stern, permanent, solid, for real.

Traffic clears up after Boca, and the rest of the drive on 95 and onto Route 1 is smooth. The sky is already beginning to darken as I turn off the highway. My car hums along the narrowing roads of West Palm, as I move beyond the more populated business district full of high-rises and condos and little shops to a winding, hilly residential neighborhood marked by a giant sign, arced between two palms, that reads: *Palm Grove*. So, the address I have is his *home*.

Now I *really* wish Stern were here. But he's not.

I'm fine. I'll be fine. I tell myself this as I turn onto Greg's street—Formosa Lane—past big, lush, wide-windowed homes with bucket-tiled roofs and three-car garages. Some instinct tells me to turn my music down, and I do, as though I might hear his voice flitting to me through the heavy palms.

*Your destination is ahead, on the right.* My navigation system seems to scream in the new silence of my car. My heartbeat quickens, whole body flushing, as I inch up to Greg's house, parking a whole house away—just in case.

*Just in case what?* I'm not even sure what I'm afraid of.

West Palm feels cooler, somehow, than Miami. The sky is layered like a gray neopolitan. Bet it's beautiful in color—a vivid melt of tangerine and periwinkle and vermillion. I imagine all those colors stretched along the spotless sidewalk, creating a separate sky beneath my feet—a downward heaven. I take a deep breath, keep walking.

Greg Foster's home is just as impressive and large as the rest of them—dotted with palms and sweet acacia, a heavy, grassy, sweet smell lifted from the earth. No part of his house is purple.

I lift the heavy brass knocker in my hand and strike it, twice, firmly against the door.

No answer. I press my ear closer to the door, try to

listen for sounds or movement within, but I hear nothing. If there is anything to hear, it's too quiet, lost in the buzz of a neighbor's lawnmower, the distant gossip of birds. I try again, knocking even harder this time. *Come on. Be home. Be home, dammit.* I fight an urge to scream it through the slim crack beneath the door—to the whole neighborhood, even. *Show yourself, Greg Foster.*

I let my head rest against the door for a second. I strike one final time against the door before giving up. He's not home.

On my way down the driveway, the neighbor—a pretty older lady, in her sixties, maybe—a baseball cap over her pixie-cut hair, exercise pants, a short-sleeved shirt with *Breast Cancer Survivor* in dark, bold letters across the front—clicks her lawnmower off and starts walking toward me across her wide, newly tended lawn, waving broadly. "Hello!" she calls to me, coming closer. "Can I help you with something?"

"Maybe." I step toward her, to the places where Greg's poorly tended lawn meets her fine-trimmed one. "I'm looking for Greg Foster."

A worried, close-lipped smile crosses her face. "I'm Debra Kilmurray," she says, reaching out with both hands to shake mine. Her skin is dark gray—she must spend a lot of time in the sun—and beginning to liver-spot, brown circles dotted between her knuckles.

"Olivia Tithe," I say, shaking back. "So, um, do you know Mr. Foster?"

She removes her baseball cap, holds it at her side. "Oh, honey. Yes—I did." She blushes a little. "Were you a friend of his?" she asks.

I spit out the first lie that comes to me. "He's my uncle." She raises her eyebrows. "Estranged uncle, I mean . . . I haven't seen him in a really long time . . . big falling out with my mom, all that." I stare at the ground. Mud always looks like cement this time of day, when the sun dips into evening.

"So Greg had a niece and never even told me about it." She clicks her tongue, shakes her head. "Go figure. I thought he didn't have any family . . . the way he left all of his money to some charity. A forest preserve, I think. He was a big nature lover. Always watching birds, planting things in his garden. All that." She clicks her tongue again, speaking softly. "A very sweet man."

"Wait—*left* all of his money? What are you—?"

"Oh, sweetheart." She puts her free hand to her chest, gasps a little. "You really don't know? I can't believe no one would have—"

"Know what?" I ask, bewildered.

"Oh, no. I'm sorry, sweetheart, that I have to tell you this, but Greg"—she pauses momentarily—"Greg passed away. Terrible story . . ."

"What happened to him?" I manage to stammer. "And when?"

The woman tilts her head and looks at me with concern.

"Six months ago," she says. "The house has been on the

market ever since, but, as soon as people find out what happened, they get scared away, I suppose." Then she lowers her voice, her eyes moving away from mine to stare steadily at the dirt beneath us. "It was the cleaning lady who found him, you know. Hanging right in the middle of his bedroom—neck broken and everything."

# thirteen

"I'll call you if I think of anything else," Debra Kilmurray tells me before I walk, dazed, back to my car. I scribbled my number down for her as soon as I regained control of my speech, insisted she take it—just in case. Night has settled full-dark, and I feel like I'm swimming in it.

The wheels of my Capri spill me forward, shifting through the smooth-paved streets like a submarine. The trees float above like soft kelp, like coral reef hiding all sorts of secret, watchful things.

I drive with a constant chord of questions, wrapping itself tighter and tighter around me: what does it mean that Greg Foster is dead? *Does* it mean anything? How come no one *told* me about it?

Greg Foster lawyered the first half of Mom's case. He seemed to be making so much progress, too—he passed on *very optimistic* updates to Dad; he told me not to worry. He told me he was going to get her out of Broadwaithe, that it wouldn't be long, that we had a very strong case. And then he ditched her. Ditched her amidst his steady stream of put-on optimism and, according to Debra Kilmurray, hung himself in his bedroom. Carol Kohl took up the reigns and suddenly everything became *hopeless* and *plea bargain* and *insanity as silver lining*. Everything became There's No Way Out Of This So Just Give Up Now.

All I want to do when I get home is rush into Dad's arms, bury my head in his white T-shirt, smelling of sand and salt and acacia from the thick of plants in the back garden of our old house, and tell him every single thing I'm feeling. And he'll say: *You just lay your head down and shut your eyes and I'll stay here the whole time and make sure no nightmares try to climb in.*

But I can't. Heather's Prius is in the driveway. Which means she's home. Which means going inside and seeing her and Dad together—nuzzling or watching a movie in the living room or setting up some cheesy game night for all of us to play together. I'd rather be knocked off the side of the road than have to walk inside and feign excitement about Scrabble or Boggle. So, I sit in the driveway, eyeing the flickering light of the TV screen. I dig my phone out of my bag to see what Raina's doing, but before I can dial, it starts ringing: a number I don't recognize. I let it ring three times before answering: "Hello?"

"Olivia Tithe."

The voice takes me a second to place. "Austin," I say, trying to suppress the weird nervousness I feel vining up my throat at the sound of his voice. An image of our almost-kiss pops into my head. And then the much paler image of Stern's face that, at the last second, replaced his own. "Did I . . . give you my phone number?"

"Nope. It's listed on your Facebook page. What are you doing right now?"

"Well, I was maybe going to go to this party thing in Lauderdale with Raina," I lie. "But I don't know . . . why?" I check out my hair in the rearview mirror, shake it loose from my ponytail holder.

"Sounds like you're free. Meet me at the marina. I've got a surprise for you."

"A surprise?"

"I'll give you a hint: It's not as good as half-naked night swimming, but, it also won't get us arrested. Well—it *probably* won't." I can hear the smile in his voice.

It's hard to believe that Austin Morse actually went out of his way to find my phone number. And call it. *Weird.* I can't imagine there aren't a million and a half private school girls who wear the right clothes and drive glittering-new sweet-sixteen BMWs throwing themselves at him.

But maybe he's tired of those girls. Maybe he really has secretly been into weirdos like me all along.

"Fine," I say. It's just the distraction I need. "When?"

"Now, Olivia Tithe. I'll be there in ten." *Click.*

I text Dad from the driveway: *going to a movie with Raina. Be back later. Love, Liv.*

He responds, seconds later: *Not 2 late!! Have fun. I love u.*

I rest my cell phone in my lap and check my hair once more in the rearview, little buzzy plucks of nerves working their way through my belly.

I put my hair into a loose braid, smear cherry-scented gloss across my lips, spray some of the jasmine body spritz Raina left a while ago in my glove compartment all over myself, and hit the gas.

*Austin Morse.* Dad always told me never to underestimate just how much a person can surprise you. It sure happened to him, to all of us, after all: a big old giant smack-in-the-face of a surprise.

Austin's "surprise" that *probably* won't get us arrested turns out to be a sailboat.

The first thing I think of when I see it is that it looks like a giant white banana with benches for sitting, ropes for pulling, a mast that seems too tall for its smallish body, a giant, billowing mainsail with three stripes down its center, a smaller, plainer sail he calls the *jib*.

"Don't fall." Austin catches me at the waist as the sailboat rises suddenly in the crest of a wave. Now that we're out of the marina, the wind picks up and the waves are choppier. The mainsail puffs out and sucks back in, collecting the air, absorbing the wind. The stripes wave in and out, back and forth like they're dancing.

"I wasn't going to," I say. I don't pull away immediately. "I've been on sailboats before, Austin Morse. They aren't *only* for the overprivileged." The tips of his fingers linger on my waist. Warmth radiates up through my stomach.

"Oh, you didn't hear? The mayor made some new laws while you were gone. You have to show your Dad's pay stubs before you can sail out of this marina now."

It's not even that funny, but the way he says it—so deadpan—makes me laugh. And relax—finally. It feels good, being around him, being paid attention to in a way that's not about Mom and Stern, that's not about pain. I thought that all my mourning and pining for Stern meant there was no room for another person.

But maybe the heart is an organ on constant-ready, always waiting to try again, always open to the next best thing.

Both sails make a sound like muffled clapping, the mainsail bubbling out like someone's putting his big mouth up to it and blowing right in, the *jib* simmering beneath it. I rock back on the smooth wooden bench as Austin pulls the main sail taut so the boat immediately tilts to the side for a moment before righting itself. His face is tight with concentration. He tugs the creases out of both sails so they spread smooth like cellophane over a serving dish.

"You really get to learn this stuff at Finnegan?"

"Yeah," he says. "But I'd been wanting to learn for a while. This was my dad's boat. He left it to me." I can't help staring at his lips, at the shadows made in the crease of his arm muscles.

"Do you remember much about him?" I inhale deeply—

brine, kelp, the way-down-deep, full cold—think of Mom, and her stories about mermaids that return to me now in dreams.

"Not really. I think I remember him feeding me a hot dog at a Marlins game. But it could have been a dream. I was only three when he died. He got cancer right after I was born, so Mom says he was in the hospital most of the time anyway, but I don't remember any of that." He pulls a lighter out of the pocket of his plaid shorts, sparks it a few times, and drops it back in his pocket.

"I do remember you, though, when you were little." He smiles. His teeth are very white, supernova white or some astral shit like that. "I remember some party your parents had when we were four or five, and that you were naked and refused to put any clothes on—"

"What? I *don't* remember that."

"But I do. My mom wouldn't let me play with you even though I wanted to; I think she was threatened by what a sexy four-year-old you were. I think she thought you would corrupt me."

"Gross," I say, hugging my arms across my chest. "I can't believe you just used the words 'sexy' and 'four-year-old' in the same sentence."

"Well, I wouldn't use them for just anyone, you know." He raises his eyebrows, and I can't help but smile.

"You're weirder than I thought you were, Austin."

"I'm just a man on his dead father's boat, looking for answers to all of life's toughest questions. Right?"

I'm not sure how to respond—all I can think is, *maybe his dad's in the Gray Space, along with Stern.*

"It's nice out here," I say finally.

Austin shoots me a look I can't decipher. "It's better than hanging around the house, where my mom is constantly on some new self-improvement kick and Ted is out all hours at the condo. Or *wherever* he goes."

"What do you mean 'wherever he goes'?"

Austin doesn't answer right away. He just stares up at the black sheet of the sky. I stare up with him at that same blackness, the bigness of it spinning all sorts of strange philosophies through my head. All the usual, corny stuff about how small we all are and how far the ocean goes and how getting swallowed up in the unendingness of it all is both the loneliest sensation in the world and also the most comforting.

The boat slides between waves. The sails *whapp* in the wind.

"He's just so busy all the time," he says abruptly. "My mom argues a lot with him, whenever he comes home in the middle of the night." He leans closer to me, one hand still at the helm, guiding us steady through the water. "I think he might be screwing around, behind her back or something. Or maybe she knows. And I know my mom can be a bitch sometimes, but, I really think it would kill her. He's my dad, you know? He raised me, and he makes my mom happy—or he *used* to. But he's also sort of taught me not to trust anyone." He shakes his head. He looks almost startled, like he'd never expected any of that to come out. "Sorry, Tithe. Didn't mean to get all serious on you. I've never really told that to anyone before."

I don't quite know what to say, sort of walloped by the fact that Austin Morse even has thoughts that run this deep.

I wonder if his suspicions about Ted are accurate. Is Ted that kind of person? Even though he's been around in the background for so many years, it hits me that I don't really know much about him.

And then, I wonder if it even matters—the real thing is that Austin feels betrayed. Like the rules somehow changed while he wasn't looking.

"I get it," I answer softly. "I mean, I get parents turning out to not be who you thought they were. Being a disappointment. Believe me, I get it. And it sucks."

"Yeah," he says, focusing on the water. "So what about you, Tithe? Tell me something good." He bites his lip. I can smell the cologne he's wearing—citrus and fig and some other dark layer. Tar. Mulch. I have to fight an urge to tackle his mouth with my own and tug him, hard, into me. It's the same feeling of excitement I used to get when painting—smearing oils wildly across a fresh canvas, open wide to take me in, all those base, earthy smells of paint and linseed oil and charcoal and linen.

It almost—*almost*—makes the ghost of Stern feel like a distant breeze, a confusing dream.

I can feel the heat coming off of Austin's body and at

the same time, the coldness spreading inside my chest every time I think of Stern. "I used to paint a lot of nudes, at school," I blurt out, trying to clear out the coldness. Maybe if I keep talking, it'll all go away. Everything except this moment, everything except Austin. "Old women, fat dudes. They'd get up in front of us and pull off their robes and sit there under the lights for probably like three hours, but it always went by so quick. I loved it. I loved drawing big naked fat people. They're so much more fun than skinnies. Full of wrinkles and shadows."

"So, you're saying, for example, Matthew Pauls would be a lot more fun to paint than me because he weighs like three-hundo?"

I laugh, feeling the ice in my chest break apart just a little more. "Exactly."

"If you had the choice, you'd be on a boat with him tonight instead of me, wouldn't you?"

"You got it." I grin.

Austin laughs, flicks me playfully below the knee. "So why did you stop painting if you loved it so much?" He turns the boat to the left, wind catching in the sails that sends us rocking slightly backward. The stripes of the mainsail dance some more, rippling in and out of focus.

I pause for a moment, preparing my answer. "I wasn't very good at it," I finally say. I can't tell him that for me the world has dissolved into gray; then he'd think I was nuts. And I want him to like me, weirdly enough. I think I need him to like me.

"Really?" He's so close, still emitting that strong, strange, boy scent. "That surprises me. You see things in such a unique way." *He has no idea.* "Did your mom paint, too? Or just play piano?"

My face stars to burn. "Just played," I reply, feeling my fingers begin to tingle—they do this sometimes when I start to feel sick, or nervous, or anxious. I run them through my hair, try to focus on the perfectly cut angles of his face, the constellation of freckles across his nose.

He inches the fingers of his free hand closer to me, to the between-space of my knees. I can feel the heat and tension of them, pulsing toward me. *Oh my god.* "Where'd they send her again?"

My whole body's so hot at this point I'm just waiting to spontaneously combust. I mumble: "Broadwaithe. For now."

"Man . . . that's got to be tough." He looks at me, his fingers still lingering between my knees. "Aren't certain kinds of insanity genetic?"

I stare at him, hot-faced, hot-mouthed. "I don't . . . why would you say that?" I hug my knees together and pull them into my chest. "You—you think I'm crazy?" *Can he see it? Can everyone see it?*

"No, no. Of course not. Sorry—bad joke." He puts a hand over my sandaled foot. I move my foot away, burning up to hell inside.

"Because I'm *not* crazy. Jesus, Austin. Why would you even say that?"

He reasserts his warm palm on top of my foot. "That

was a really stupid joke to make and I'm sorry. I'm really sorry. The truth is, I think . . . you're just crazy *hot*. And really fun. And probably the sanest person I know. And the smartest." The sea slaps the sides of the boat. He tugs the mainsail taut again, stares at me with those big, moonglow eyes. "I like you, Olivia."

My stomach surges, a hot pulse of saliva filling my mouth like it does just before you puke. I swallow it down, steady my hands beside me on the boat bench. The waves keep slapping the sides and I feel like they're somehow *inside* me, sloshing around, trying to rush out my mouth in a thick, briny fist.

"I need to go back to shore," I say, scooting closer to the smooth painted edge of the boat; the tips of waves peak like foamy fingers, try to pull me down into the deep dark. I lean back, stare up into the star-freckled sky. "I think I'm gonna be sick."

And then I am: on the floor of Austin's dead dad's boat, and into the deep dark sea, with its fine, finger-spray of foam.

# fourteen

A lamp is still burning in the living room, casting a glow on the driveway. It's almost twelve. Heather and Dad must still be up. They might even be waiting for me, sitting jittery on the sofa, sipping coffee and praying I'm not bleeding in a ditch somewhere.

I twist my key carefully in the front door lock, still queasy from the boat ride, from wondering the whole way home if, despite his claims otherwise, Austin saw something—*sees* something—a hint or glint, twitch or tick, that indicates to the world in no uncertain terms how quickly I'm unraveling.

When I step inside, there's no rush of worried greeting: Dad and Heather are passed out on the couch in the living room, surrounded by messy stacks of RSVP cards. He's got one arm around her. Her thin face is mostly obscured in the nook of his shoulder, her pin-straight blonde hair messy for once, a halo of untended frizz, one arm slung around his waist. Johnny Cash is skipping in the old CD system Dad brought with him from Oh Susannah and I creep quietly to the console beside the spanking new big screen TV to turn it off, the sounds of their sleeping breath audible now, even sweet.

She snores a little in her sleep—a ragged puttering sound from her perfect little doll nose. Dad's breath moves like a little steamroller through his tall, thin body and out his lips in a little *puh*. I leave the lamp on so they don't wake up in the dark and tiptoe back over the soft carpeting, before padding upstairs to my room. My cell phone buzzes from my purse. Probably Raina. I ignore it; don't feel much like talking.

I switch on the cracked old clown lamp that takes up most of my nightstand and start to undress, my whole body heavy with exhaustion. I stare at the gray curves and dark-shadow dips of my body in the mirror, remembering the two months in seventh grade I did this for hours on end, at night, before bed. I'd tried to starve myself: allowed myself one slice of salted bread with lettuce and an apple per day. I was so self-conscious, so unsure. But I had everything then. Everything. And I didn't even realize it.

I turn away from the mirror, and tug on my big, old nightshirt, a shirt Dad used to wear in college. I start to climb into my unmade bed but stop when I notice something crumpled up in the comforter and sheets—a body—something warm. Breathing slowly, carefully, I tug them back.

"Wynn!" I sigh. "Jesus . . ." She blinks sleepily at the sound of my voice, rubbing her eyes with one hand.

"Livieeeee!" Wynn squeals, leaping up in bed to clutch me around the neck. "You're home!" She's dressed in her Little Mermaid pajamas. I notice several sheets of paper scattered in bed beside her—old drawings, I'm guessing, by the shadow of lines peaking through their undersides.

I exhale loudly. "Wynn," I say in my best Serious Adult tone, lifting her arms from around my neck, moving to crouch beside the bed. She looks at me with puppy-dog eyes, blonde curls haloed around her face. "Why aren't you sleeping in your own bed, and"—I motion my head toward the drawings—"where did you find those?" "

Her eyes go even wider, pleading with mine. "I woke up and I wasn't sleepy anymore, Livie," she starts, dancing her fingers over the comforter toward mine. "And I came in here to find you and I found your drawings first and I really really liked them and"—she pauses, tactically, dancing her fingers over my hand, biting her teeth over her bottom lip—"will you draw me? Because you're a good drawer and I wanna show Kimmy and Lisa. Livie. Please? Pleeease?"

I lift the drawings from the bed and quickly shuffle through them—old sketches from middle school and the beginning of high school: our old house; a sketch of our sweet, old mutt, Cody, I'd made as practice for a painting I made Mom for Mother's Day one year; a picture of Raina on the beach, with seaweed for hair. "It's not nice to go through someone's things, Wynn. That's my private stuff. And you don't go through someone's private stuff."

"But," she starts to whine, "I wasn't tired and-and-and I found them by accident." She looks up at me, eyes still thoroughly puppy-dogged, hugging my comforter into her chest. "I said I'm sorry so will you draw me now? I'll never do it again, cross my heart hope to die stick a needle in my eye. Kimmy taught me that yesterday even though Mommy thinks it's not nice," she says, proudly, twisting one of her curls around her pointer finger.

"I—I'm really tired, Wynny," I say, rolling the pieces of paper together and shoving them, this time, into the way-back of my closet.

"Please?" Her voice crests into a desperate whine. Dr. Levine's request, so strangely urgent, returns to me: *keep sketching, just stick to black and white for now.*

I turn back to Wynn.

"All right, Panda." I scoop her up, giggling, and fling her over my shoulder. "I'll draw you, but you have to get in *your* bed first."

I stoop to lift the sketchpad and a charcoal pencil from my book bag, carry her to her pink-carpeted, ballet-slippered room, click the ladybug nightlight on. When it's dark, everything looks to me like it's covered in fog—the outlines and edges and architecture of a room the only things I can truly decipher without having, first, to be shuffled through a whole mess of memory and logic. She leaps into bed, snuggling beneath her covers, burrowing beneath her piles of stuffed animals. I flip my sketchbook open to the next blank page.

"Are you ready, Wynn? Because you can't move once I start."

She hugs the stuffed panda I gave her to her chest, gives it a little kiss on the beak. "You're gonna be okay, Panda," she tells it, very seriously. "You're gonna have real sweet dreams and I'll be right here the whole time." It's what Heather says to her before bed sometimes, too, when Wynn's too scared to sleep. I wonder if she learned that in the support group where she met Dad. I wonder if they say it to each other before sleep. Maybe there's a whole group of people out there who've lived with "emotionally unstable" people and need someone to reassure them that they'll *be here the whole time* every night before sleep. Wynn looks up at me, then, radiant, smiling so the gaps of her three missing baby teeth show. "Ready."

I start moving charcoal across page, struggling at first, not trusting my hand, my eye, second-guessing the sweep of my lines across a page. But then, when I draw in the strawberry-roundness of her face, start to fill in her wide, light-lashed eyes, button nose, kewpie mouth—that *thing* begins to happen. That time-lapse thing when past and present and future just melt into one long, patient, quiet moment where nothing matters but this.

I stop noticing the almost apple-juice scent that Wynn's room carries, the photographs of Wynn and Heather holding mittened hands in front of a giant pyramid of pumpkins somewhere up North, the lone photograph of Wynn's father's smiling gray face stuffed behind a sheet of glass and held tight in a smooth wood frame, small balloons painted in two of the four corners.

I stop noticing anything at all but the mass of line and shadow that bring Wynn—finally asleep, snoring softly—alive on the page before me. I finish the drawing, plant a very soft kiss at the top of her forehead.

Back in my room, I lean against the wood frame of my bed and let my hand hover over a new blank page in my sketchbook. I'm trying to remember the details of Mom's face—every inch of her skin, the shadow of her cheekbones, exact curve of her jaw, the little c-curve of her earlobes, the tip of her nose she always thought was too bulbous, the sea-surge of hair down her back. But it's hard. The images keep getting spliced with Broadwaithe Mom—*Gray Space* Mom—choppy slats of hair poking out at odd angles behind her ears, down her neck. I make several drawings, shade bags under her eyes huge and scary and wrong. Try again. And again. But they all come out wrong. Her face isn't solid to me anymore. It's lost to that other realm. Silent. A place where art cannot exist.

*Except,* I remind myself, *The Gray Space doesn't exist. It can't be real.*

I look down, disgusted at my attempts: they're awful. Total shit. I tear them from the book, crumple them into hard little balls in my fist, and hurl them into the wastebasket beside my desk. In a surge of frustration, I rip the comforter off my bed, biting hard into it to stop from screaming. I can't stop; I rip the silk sheets off my bed, too.

Mom always thought silk sheets were a silly, unnecessary luxury and now she's sleeping on steel wool with a toilet five inches from her head and I've got *silk* and big billowing window treatments, all bought with money from Ghost Town. So that we can look like everyone else, so that Dad can prove that he's above it all. That what happened can't hold him back. That she can't hold him back. He's got bigger, better, more expensive things now.

My cell phone buzzes on my nightstand. *1 new text message*. From Raina. *Why are you ignoring me? Meet me and Tif at Beast Beach!! Champagne of beers. Bonfire. Maybe some fly honeys. Come onnnn, yo . . .*

I ignore it.

The sheets lie in a pile next to the trash can and I toss the sketchbook on top, away from me. How stupid I am to have thought there was salvation in this—in making time slow down with a pencil in my hands, in creating, in thinking I could escape myself.

You can never escape.

I click off my lamp, climb on top my bare mattress. Cold and uncomfortable, I press my knees against my chest beneath my sleep shirt and wriggle around awhile until I'm too tired to wriggle anymore and everything goes full black.

My dream feels more real to me than reality has felt lately. I'm in my bed, and Stern's beside me, and he's warm. We're both pretending to be asleep, but I can't sleep because his hands are on my body. Every one of my cells seems drawn, magnetized, straight into the spot where his hands meet my skin. So warm. He's so warm, and he smells like he's always smelled—like the detergent his mom uses to wash his clothes with a little sweet-bitter tug of the Marlboro cigarettes his dad smokes and then the just-him smell. And his face is too beautiful to look away from. Just too freaking beautiful. His lips—parted just slightly. And his body is too close to allow for sleep. And every single part of me is buzzing.

I can hear him breathe. I can feel his heartbeat in the inches of sheet and bedcover between us. There's a little bit of light peaking out through the semitranslucence of my window shades. Our knees are touching. I could scream with happiness.

*Don't close your eyes,* I keep telling myself. *Stay here forever. If you stay awake, you can stay here forever.* There's a little smile on his face, like he's dreaming of something very, very nice. He starts humming the tune to "Oh! Susannah" under his breath, like he's trying to lullaby me further into sleep though I don't want it. But, at the soothing sound of his hum, I'm suddenly too tired to keep my lids up. *Don't you cry for me, I come from Alabama with a*—too tired. So tired. *Hold on—*

*Hold on—just another minute—with a banjo on my knee—just one more second—*

* * *

"Liver! Liv. Yo! Wake up."

I groan, hug my knees tighter into my chest. It's suddenly so cold. It feels too early to be morning. But there's sunlight ripping through my big curtain-drawn window.

Morning. Sunday. *Five days left.*

Someone blows directly into my right ear and I shoot up in bed, startled wide-awake now. Two top buttons of Stern's Christmas flannel are unbuttoned.

"Stern!" I look away, cheeks flushing, because I'm worried that he actually *can* see straight into my thoughts and knows that I spent all night dreaming of him beside me in bed, trying to make it last forever. "What are you doing here? What *time* is it?" I catch him looking at me in my big nightshirt and nothing else and scramble for my comforter on the floor, wrap it around me, suddenly self-conscious.

"Dunno, Liver." He looks around, noting the light, the clock on my nightstand. "Eleven-something. Seventeen. Eleven-seventeen."

I'd be way late for work—if I'd even planned on going in the first place.

"Isn't there, like, some ghost version of knocking?" I cross my arms, pretending to be annoyed, but his presence is comforting to me, somehow. Maybe this is how Mom feels about her own delusions—they're all like close friends you start to miss when they don't show up for a little while.

Stern laughs at my sudden modesty. "Nervous about something?" he asks.

I shrug, embarrassed by the fact that I'm embarrassed—by a *ghost*. "Guess it's not like you haven't seen all this before anyway." Truth is—you can't really make it through a childhood without seeing your best friends naked for one reason or another.

He glances at me, a glint of interest in his eye—and of alarmingly genuine surprise. "Have I?"

I just nod, wondering just how selective his post-death memory is. If he doesn't remember any of the events surrounding his death, and he doesn't remember the countless occasions of childhood-bath-taking or truth-or-dare-strip-downs or late-night-skinny-dippings, is there any way in hell he remembers our kiss?

"You know, I was wondering when you'd show again," I say. "It's starting to weird me out when you don't haunt me."

He smiles shyly. "You know what? That might be the nicest thing you've ever said to me. Unless I just can't remember anything nicer. Which is highly probable. Anyway . . . I'm just here for the scantily clad women."

My heart skips a beat as he sits beside me on my bed, leans close, wide-eyed. I inhale deeply, wanting him to smell like himself, but he smells like air. Like nothing.

"Liver, I had a memory. A *memory*," he says, excited.

"Oh, yeah?" I ask, weirdly nervous. *Is he going to bring up the kiss? Right now?* My heart thumps. I wait for him to continue.

He scratches at his scalp. "And then next thing I *knew*,

I was *here*. I watched you while you slept. I never knew you were a snorer. . . ."

I stand from my bed, horrified, somewhat confused—*is he gonna bring it up or what?*—and lift a wrinkled halter dress from the floor. I pull off my nightshirt and wriggle the dress over my head. "That's really creepy, Stern."

He laughs. "I'm kidding. I just got here. *You* brought me here. You have a big something to do with it, you know, so don't act like I'm the only creepy one here." *He knows. He knows about the dream. The kiss. Everything.* "Anyway." He unfolds his long legs from beneath him, turning over to rest his stomach on the edge of my bed, knees on the floor, elbows beneath his chin. His eyes are childlike, excited. "I heard music, Liv. I haven't felt *happy* like that in . . . well, in forever, it feels like. It was like being lifted out of a swamp. And then you were there. Or, here, I mean. I was here. With you."

"Oh." My heartbeat returns to normal. *Oh* is all I can say right now. I guess, through all of it, part of me hoped he'd come to me *this* time because he was ready to confess to everything he remembered and everything he needed to say involving his undying love for me, and all related topics. *Stupid.* I'm so stupid. He had a *memory*, something that actually might help us. That's what's important here. Not some impossible, transcendent love connection I've concocted in my many hours of misery and missing him.

He closes his eyes, starts playing an invisible piano on

the bed. His whole body seems to grow brighter, like it's being lit from the inside. It's hard not to see Mom's old excitement in him—the way she looked when she'd play. Sometimes, she wouldn't let me in the studio because she needed to focus, and so I'd watch her secretly through a crack in the door. "I remember . . . a big recital. A competition, maybe," he goes on. "I was nervous, really nervous about it."

"Juilliard. That's what you must be thinking of. It's the last concert you played." I stare at him, waiting for something new to come. "Ring any other bells?"

He shakes his head. "That's all I really remember. Just that it happened. This big thing. My stomach hurting before." He gulps. "Everything's getting blurrier, the longer I'm here. Or, at least, almost everything." He looks at me. "You're still clear, who you were. *Are*," he corrects himself. "Who you *are*."

Ignoring the flood in my heart for more important matters, I grab my laptop, and plop back onto the bed, dragging up articles from the *Herald* about his burgeoning musical career, his shocking death—articles I used to look through obsessively, right after he'd died, making myself sick. *Lucas Stern was a child prodigy; pure genius. Had his young life not been cut tragically short, he would have been at the top of his class, the top of his field, the top of the world.*

And then more, the same ones I'd spent hours analyzing for clues. Stern just shrugs, none of it seeming to trigger anything at all but little mutters of surprise, grief, and, sometimes, glee.

I notice the picture of a girl named Tanya Leavin at the bottom of one of the articles. It mentions her death in relation to his—her body, still missing, never found—of both of their deaths representing a general sense of failure within the Miami PD in the prevention of violent crimes. Something about her face—her eyes, maybe—reminds me so much of Raina it makes my stomach churn.

My eyes move to her neck—there's something funny about it, like it's twisted in a weird way, but looking closer, I realize she's wearing a scarf just a few shades lighter than her actual skin tone. Pink, probably. She looks like the kind of girl who'd wear a pink scarf.

I close the article and look back to Stern. Something has just occurred to me. I'm almost afraid to ask. He's playing invisible keys again. His whole body leans into it, following the music in his head.

"Hey, Stern?" I swallow down the lump in my throat. He turns to look at me, still playing the air. "Do you think—do you think your parents know anything?"

He stops playing, moves his arms back by his sides. "My parents?"

"I mean, about my mom. Do you think they might know something about who really did it?"

"No way." He frowns. "If they did, they never would have let your mom get put away."

"Have you—have you see them?"

A troubled look crosses his face. "It doesn't work like that," he says, shaking his curly head, slow. "I wish I could, but, I can't."

I almost think of asking him if he'd visit Raina, too, if he had the choice, but I'm too ashamed. I'm actually turning possessive of a ghost.

His hands have picked up again at the air piano.

"Liver," he says, eyes flashing, "I have to play it. The song I was working on for the competition. Elvira Madigan. If I play it, it might help me remember." He moves quickly toward the door of my bedroom.

"We don't have a piano."

"Your mom was my piano *teacher,*" he says, fingers still skating across an invisible surface. "There has to be a piano around here somewhere."

"Maybe I brought the wrong one," I mutter to Stern as I try to turn the key I found in Dad's desk in the locked door of Mom's storage unit. Number 108B: a door among many doors in a cold, windowless, warehouse space with tall-ceilinged hallways, a flickering overhead light, the smell of raw paint. Dad's been storing Mom's piano for her since she's been locked up, way the hell out here in Liberty City—a crumbling, poverty-struck part of town—claiming there'd be no room for himself, Heather, Wynn, me, *and* a baby grand no one would even play. But I don't buy it. I think the truth is it'd just make him too sad to see it every day. Because, secretly, I think he misses her, bad. Regrets Heather, the overhasty replacement. Realizes he's the real reason all of our lives are fucked.

I smack the door with the side of my clenched fist. "This stupid lock!"

"Relax. Ease it in," Stern says. Always the moderator, always the person to calm me down. I look to him—all that height, a strange, slender column, stark and beautiful. He steps right beside me, the icy tingle of his skin sending rivers of cold up my arms. "You're just nervous."

"I'm not nervous," I lie. Pins and needles in my hand, on the doorknob. We're almost touching, and it sends a different chill through me, and a familiar buzzy warmth, too.

The key finally turns in the lock and the door swings open on its rusty hinge. We step into the small, dark room. I flip on the light, which flickers over the dusty space. Over the piano.

Her piano. Stuffed there into the cobwebbed corner, closed up.

I move slowly toward mom's vintage Steinway baby grand, hover there for a few long moments, breathing the piano in, watching it, as though it might suddenly grow feet and run the hell out of here. I run my hand slowly across the bench before I sit. It's cold.

Stern follows. I'm grateful for his nearness, his bone-chill, as I lift the heavy lid, breathe in the scent of the ivory keys beneath like they might keep something of Mom inside of them, spill her out.

Stern sits down beside me. He seems to vibrate there, holding his hands over the keys, shaking a little. "Damn," he says, softly, trying to make the keys move. But they won't.

His eyes bore into them. He finally gives up and sits with his hands in his lap. "I can't even touch the keys." His voice is suddenly bitter, defeated.

I stare at the shiny stretch of black and white, take a deep breath, and burst out: "I—I went colorblind. Out of nowhere. Right before you died."

He looks at me funny, cocking his head. "Seriously? You can't see any colors at all?"

"Just black and white and shades of gray. Everything looks like it's covered in dust," I tell him, pressing lightly against a key. A dull note sounds out. "Food, people, clothes, traffic lights. My world is one giant Pompeii."

"And nothing happened? There was no . . . trigger?" he asks. I bite my lip, watching him, assessing the flickering of his own eyes. Once again, my curiosity refuses to abate: *does he know? Does he remember what happened between us?*

I shake my head, push away the stampede of anxieties, of negatives in my brain, to make way for this thought: *tell him. You have to tell him.* "It happened the last time I saw you." I feel a hot pulse rising in my chest. I have no other choice—the moment is bursting inside of me, demanding release.

But if he remembers our kiss, he doesn't say anything about it.

"Liv." He slides just a little bit closer to me. "We have to help each other out," he says softly.

It's not what I expected him to say after my big confession. "Help each other out?" I repeat.

"Yeah," he says, his voice smooth, sure. "You're a colorblind painter. I'm a dead pianist. Right?"

"So? How does that help anything?" The light flickers bright for several seconds and then settles darker around us. I shift on the bench.

"Like this." He stands and moves behind me, and then I feel him, wrapped around me, all around me. His legs straddle my legs, his arms wrap around my arms, his fingers press against my fingers, onto the keys. My whole body trembles, hot and freezing at the same time; his body is a storm, hovering around me. I press back into him, shivering, burning up, scared, sad, amazed, unsure what he wants me to do, how he wants me to sit, how long we'll stay like this. His fingers begin to move mine along the keys, clumsily at first—learning my hands, the shape of my fingers, how deep he needs to press to make this work. I can hardly breathe. I can hardly think.

So I give in. I release into him. His fingers press against mine—slowly at first, picking up speed—moving, sweeping, storming across the keys.

The music pours from me, from us, electric and whole-bodied, passionate. It shivers through me. My legs quiver, fresh blood rushes through my fingers. The notes curl and ache and it's almost like I can *taste* them, like I can see each one separately, shining, vibrantly formed.

The song he played, over and over again—it's like I'm inside of it now. Transported back to those last, hot, lazy days when everything was safe. Mom was safe. Stern was safe.

And for the briefest flicker of a moment, I swear I can see color again. The cream of his skin, the red of my dress, the blue tips of his sneakers. I stare at Stern's hands wrapped around my own but still separate, not there, not whole . . . and I ache more than ever for him to be solid, to be able to pull him into me for real and kiss his warm, solid, living mouth one more time, two more times, a million more times.

"Wake up," I whisper to him, feeling suddenly like it really might be possible. "Wake up and be alive."

"I think this is as close as I can get." He whispers it softly into my ear, as the sonata crescendos and our bodies connect at some other point, some point higher-up in the body, higher than the human form, higher than life or death or skin or blood.

The sonata finishes. I didn't want for it to finish, because it means that I'm not there anymore—faraway, in the safe past-place of those notes. Stern stays wrapped around me for a few moments, still shaking, shaking in the way he does right before he disappears. I press a little closer into him, worrying that he will, needing him to stay. And I can *feel* it: the place he goes when he's not with me—the endless dark, the bone-ache of it.

Even when he pulls away, the impression of him lingers on my skin. His face is twisted, and he grips the sides of the bench again like he's got a terrible stomachache.

"What's wrong? Are you okay?" I move closer to him, but he edges away, putting one hand up to stop me.

"It was . . . it was painful to be so close to you."

"I'm sorry," I say quietly.

"But it's painful either way, Liver. You know that, don't you?" He sits at the other end of the bench and we stare at each other. He bites his own bottom lip, moves a tuft of thick hair behind his ear. I press a foot on and off the pedals at the bottom of Mom's piano.

We sit in silence for a while—but somehow, it's a comfortable silence.

"So," I finally ask, "Did it help? Do you remember anything else?"

He sighs. "I don't know. I don't think so," he admits. "It felt really good, though." He looks at me for a second and then looks back at his hands.

We sit on my mother's cold piano bench for what feels like an hour, not speaking, not needing to speak. Just feeling the vibration of each other's bodies—my warmth and his ice—letting the frigid room hold us in for a little while longer like two small lost children. Which we are.

"Let's get out of here," I say, finally, standing up and shutting the lid to the piano, left open for all these months without Mom to monitor its proper upkeep. As soon as I do, though, a rush of papers hidden, stuffed, behind the lid come spilling out onto the floor. I stoop to collect them back up, tenderly. They must have been things Mom was working on just before shit hit the fan. She wasn't necessarily the most neat or organized of people, but this was part of her charm. At least, I always thought so.

"What's all that?" Stern asks, peering over my shoulder.

"Compositions, I guess," I mutter distractedly, blowing the dust from each new sheet. "Some recommendation letters . . . one addressed to the Juilliard admissions board," I say, skimming the paper in my hands. "It's about you, Stern." I move back beside him on the bench and continue skimming, reporting back the interesting bits. "Mom wrote this right before the competition, right before . . . everything. About someone named Marietta Jones who—who did something to you?" I read further. "Misconduct," I quote, slowly, from Mom's scribble. My eyes meet Stern's in the flickering darkness. He sucks with some intensity on his bottom lip, struggling to reclaim everything death has erased from his brain.

"What else does it say? Just read it to me."

"Okay—it's sort of hard to make out some parts 'cause it's messy and kind of scratched-up, but," I continue, squinting at the page, "I'll do my best." I clear my throat dramatically and begin to read: "To whom it may concern . . . I must inform you of an incident of misconduct involving two current scholarship competitors—Marietta Jones, and a student of mine, Lucas Stern. Learning that Lucas was to play the same piece that she had planned to play, Marietta directly confronted my student in the parking lot after a pre-recital practice on July 15, and told him that she would 'do anything she could to make sure he didn't play.' It is my belief that her threat was a serious one, indicating an intent to inflict physical harm. In light of this information, I feel that Marietta Jones must be eliminated from the competition, based on rule 12A listed in the competition handbook indicating an absolute zero tolerance policy for threats of, or actuated violence between competitors. Please feel free to contact me with any further questions. Miriam Tithe."

Stern and I meet eyes again, both of us momentarily stunned. My hands start trembling so hard I think I might rip this magical piece of paper in two. "Marietta Jones?"

Stern shrugs, still struggling, always struggling, now. "Marietta Jones . . ." he repeats, uncertainly. "Marietta Jones. Marietta Jones. Marietta Jones."

And then, suddenly, it clicks. *"Tuna Face!"* I cry.

"Tuna Face?" He gives me a funny look.

"The girl who was stirring up all sorts of shit before the competition! I can't believe I didn't think of it before! You told me about her, like, a bunch of times. I just—I didn't know her real name. Because you always *only* ever referred to her as Tuna Face."

He laughs briefly, looks down at his hands. "Tuna Face. That's pretty funny. What did she do to me?"

"She actually expected you to change your piece last minute because she was a senior or some crap. And you wouldn't, and that's when she threatened you, and why Mom must have written that letter. Man . . . I'd forgotten all about that girl. "

He looks back up at me, his eyes suddenly mournful. "Juilliard—I wanted it, pretty badly, didn't I?"

"Since you were five. It was, like, all you'd talk about."

"Wow." He wraps his arms around himself, shivering. "That must have been pretty annoying. . . . Maybe that's why Marietta did it. She just wanted to shut me up."

"Maybe. That, and she was totally nuts. The really crazy thing is—you weren't even really *in* the running for the scholarship that year, because you were just a junior."

"Then why did I—"

"You told me you just wanted to play the best thing so they'd notice you, for next year, when you applied. Because you *would* have gone there," I add, fervently. "That's why she was afraid. Because everyone knew that you were brilliant and that even though you were a junior, you would have beat all of them, because you deserved it. I mean, you practiced like a freaking maniac. I was there. Every day, right upstairs, listening." My voice breaks at the end and I feel stomach-sick as I look at him there on the bench, all balled into himself. I want, desperately, for him to remember or, at least, to stop forgetting. "If the letter's still here, though," he asks, "does that mean that your Mom never sent it?"

"I don't know. This is obviously just a draft, and since she wrote it right before shit went down, she might not have gotten the chance to type it up, or send it at all. . . ." My breath catches in my throat and my chest suddenly feels all lit up. "Or, maybe she meant to, but then Marietta found out . . . and she couldn't."

I sit back on the bench and hug myself. My fingers are thick with cold. "Marietta must have found out somehow that Mom was planning to do this—I mean, knowing Mom, she would have called Marietta, or at least her parents or something first and tried to straighten things out. It would make sense . . . for Marietta to make sure Mom was blamed. She was posing a direct threat to her whole career, or at least that's how Marietta must have seen it."

"So wait . . . you think this girl really might have killed me and framed your mom just so she would win some competition that I couldn't have even *won* that year?" He shakes his head, a single inky curl coming loose on his forehead. "That's—that's insane."

"Yeah—the competition *and* her reputation. And Stern—some of these kids *are* insane. You told me all sorts of crazy shit about what people'd do when they were stressed out and overly ambitious. Art kids are the same way—some of them at least. When there're awards involved. *Prestige* and all that. The competitions make them crazy. She obviously hated you, and *threatened* you," I remind him, waving the letter in the air. "You wouldn't have told my mom about it if it wasn't something serious, right? It would never have come to this."

"Yeah, Liv . . . I guess not." His voice is husky and soft. A voice I could listen to anywhere and feel instantly at home. "So . . . what do we do?" he asks—and when he looks up at me just then, I see him for a moment as he was when we were five years old, and everything was easy, and we had so much time.

Thick-throated, I fold the paper carefully in my hand. "We find her," I say, jaw clenched, head throbbing, heart thump-thump-thumping. "Today. Now."

And then, staring at my best friend's face—the flickering image of him inside of this ancient-smelling room, full of Mom's old life, all of our old lives—I stop time for a moment. I twist it backward, way backward. I twist it so far back that his heart's beating again, and his skin is warm, and no one has found any reason to bash his head in and toss him into the water to die.

Because who could think anything—anything at all—was more important than life?

And it's this thought that makes me turn to him, unthinkingly, and lean forward and push through the strange slow-motion field of time and life and death, and start to bring my face toward his.

"Liv. No," he cries out, like he's trying to stop me, like he's in great pain. I pull back and our eyes meet for an *inch* of a second, and before I can even murmur *Stern* or *oh god I've loved you all this time you dead dum-dum:* poof. There he goes. Like he was never there in the first place.

And I guess it was my fault.

But for one second, time rewound itself, and he came back to me. I had him.

I lean against the still-open piano, pulsing fresh with anger, and the same gut-punch ache I feel every time I lose him—and pulsing, too, with some terrible little flame of joy, burning somewhere deep inside of me.

# fifteen

I kiss Mom's piano goodbye, finish closing it up with the gentleness of someone laying a baby down to sleep, and hurry through the flicker-lit halls of E-Z-Store and out to my car.

I'm still processing: Stern's legs wrapped around me, his arms, his fingers over mine—feeling all the bewildering intensity of him in those moments we played, our fingers sliding together over Mom's keys like it was some intimate party trick we'd been practicing for years.

Storm clouds gather in the distance. I signal my left turn out of the parking lot, try to turn the wheel to the left when I realize: I can't. Something's very wrong—my whole car, too, feels lower to the ground—like it's scraping against the road. I pull, best I can, to the curb at the end of the street, shift my sad clunker-junker into park, and step outside as the first fat drops of rain start to fall.

My tire—no, *all* of my tires—are flat. I stoop closer, searching for punctures, bits of lodged glass, nails. I notice there's a flat, inch-long slit through the side of the driver's side front wheel.

Curious, I step around and examine the three remaining tires: all of them have the same inch-long slit. No glass. No small, sharp-toothed animals. The same exact slit. I step back, feeling suddenly dizzy, realizing: someone did this on purpose.

There's a thick knot in my throat. I climb back into my ruined ride, feeling suddenly exposed. Who would do something like that? And why?

A prank—a stupid prank. Probably nothing more than that.

Raina would know what to do right now. Raina always has the answers, and even when she doesn't, she knows how to make me feel better.

Her Rihanna ringback tone cycles three times before she picks up. "Liv! Where the eff have you been all my life, girl?"

"Rain." My voice catches in my throat as I say her name. I miss her. I miss feeling normal. I try not to cry but obviously she can tell something's off.

"Liv—what's wrong? Are you okay?"

"Can you come get me, Rain?" I gasp. The rain pounds the roof.

"What? What happened? Where are you?"

"Liberty City."

"Pork and Beans? Geez—what are you doing there alone? Aren't you supposed to be at work?"

"I played hooky again," I tell her, pausing. "I had to follow a lead."

"A *lead*?"

"Just come get me. I'm calling a tow-truck as soon as I get off the phone with you. It's the E-Z-Store on northwest 62nd."

I sketch while I wait for her to come. I sketch the rain-stooped trees; sketch the boxy clots of housing projects on the other side of the highway. I sketch the power lines that swoop between lampposts and soggy laundry, drooping on clotheslines. It speeds time forward, so I hardly notice how long I sit alone in my car, waiting to be collected.

Raina folds me into her arms as soon as I get inside her mom's Toyota station wagon. Her soft T-shirt smells of cigarettes. Something about that dull, nicotine scent mingled with her own particular Raina smell—sage and peach and sandalwood—makes the re-formed knot in my throat threaten to crack open again. "I missed you," I say.

"Missed you too, little lady." She sighs as we pull onto the highway. "The tow truck's going to pull your poor baby somewhere nice?"

"Yeah. Autobody shop near home." I shuffle through her iPod, avoiding her eyes.

She peers at me sideways as she drives. "You're too skinny—I can see your ribs poking out."

"I'm fine. Just haven't been too hungry recently."

"Are you going anorexic on me? Because I swear to god—"

"No, I'm not going *anorexic* on you," I interrupt. "I—I've just had a lot on my mind, I guess. It's just—it's really hard to explain."

"Well, why don't you *try*, Liv? I'm your best friend. If you don't tell me what's going on with you, how am I supposed to help?"

"You *can't* help, Raina." I turn and stare out the window. This is why I've been avoiding her; I knew this would happen.

"How do you know? You're not the only person in the world who's ever dealt with anything bad, okay?" She's driving ramrod straight, both hands on the wheel—very un-Rain. She's angry, I realize. "You're shutting me out."

"Okay, fine!" I burst out. "My mom's sentencing is next week and my dad won't talk about it and nobody can tell me how to help her." I'm starting to break inside, to flood. "She's not supposed to *be* in a place like that. She's dying in there, Raina. She's going to die if I don't fix this. And—" I bite my tongue and watch the highway disappear behind us, a long black tongue.

"And . . . ?" she pries.

"Stern." *Okay. Roll it out slow, Olivia. Roll it out slow.*

"Stern?"

I take a deep breath, keep fiddling with the iPod, and the window, and the stain on Raina's car seat. Another deep breath. *Tell her,* my brain urges my lips. *You have to tell her.*

"This sounds insane, Raina, okay, I know that, but . . . I've seen him."

A pause. "What do you mean, you've *seen* him?"

"I've seen him a few times. His ghost."

"*What?*" She's driving more slowly now, like she's forgetting she needs to press the gas to make the car move.

"I did *not* believe it at first—I thought I was hallucinating—but now . . . he showed me some box Mom had that I never knew about. Full of caramels. He says Mom didn't kill him, and—and so we were playing the piano to help jog his memory about what really happened that night. That's why I was in Pork and Beans today—it's where Dad's been storing Mom's piano—and then some shithead slashed my tires. And I don't know what I'm supposed to do from here, or how I'm supposed to help. They both need my help. But—but I don't know if I can, Rain."

"Liv," she says, very gently. Familiar streets wind around us now. The sky's beginning to calm, rain sucked back into the upper atmosphere. Her hands are pale angles against the dark round of the steering wheel. The trees cut the sky into segments, disordered lines and shapes. "You're driving yourself crazy. Okay? *You* are not crazy, but you're grieving, hard, and—and that can make you . . . see things. I remember after my grandma died—and, you know, she lived with us for like ten years, so we were really, really close—I thought I used to see her sometimes, standing in my doorway, or hiding in my closet." She laughs a little. "I was so sure she was just hiding in my closet."

"Well, maybe she *was*—"

"No, just listen, Liv. She wasn't. But I wanted so badly for her to be there that I *invented* her. It's not that unusual. I saw this grief counselor, you know, my mom sent us all to this lady, and at the time of course I fought against it, but, girl, it helped."

I fix my eyes on the blur of passing trees. On the cut-up sky. "I don't need to see a grief counselor, Raina. I need to help my mom, and I need to help Stern."

"It's not up to you—what happens to your mom—it's not something you can change. As much as you want to, you can't. And Stern is *dead*," she says, like I'm stupid, like I just really *don't get it*. "He's not coming back. I know it's not what you want to hear, but I think, maybe you need to just . . . let it go."

"Let it go? How am I supposed to let it go? My mom wouldn't let it go if *I* was in there. She'd fight until she fixed it."

Raina has pulled the car over onto the side of the road at some point, but I've only just realized that we're not moving. "But you can't fix it, Liv. That's what I'm saying. You can't *solve* all of this shit for everyone. It's not your job."

I shake my head, anger surging in my chest. "See? I didn't say anything because I knew you wouldn't get it."

"I *do* get it, Liv. I *know* Miriam, and there's no way in hell she'd be okay with what you're going through right now. If she knew you were suffering this much for her sake, *that's* what would kill her. And you know I'm right."

There's no more use in trying to convince her of something she's not ready to believe—I'd probably have the same reaction if she told me what I told her. Ghosts. *Right.* I *did* have the same reaction. I release a weird, choked, sob-laugh. "I know. She'd hate it. She'd be so sad." I stare at my hands. "I don't know what else to do. No one teaches you this."

"Let it go, Liv. Let it go. Your mom's a really strong lady, like you said. She's going to be okay, whatever happens. She'll pull through. She'll fight."

We're silent for the next few minutes as we drive through a Miami whose grayness feels unbearably heavy right now, to Coconut Grove, to Dad's too-smooth concrete driveway. I still can't see this house as *my* home. My home includes Mom and is full of African masks and ceramic dishes and sheet music and instruments and poetry and mismatched glass jars full of handpicked flowers. And I would do anything to have that back again. Anything.

Raina unbuckles her seat belt and turns to me, her eyes watery and warm, some distant part of my brain still vaguely registering their cinnamon color, or the absence of their cinnamon color, at least. She leans over and wraps her arms around me in a tight hug. "I miss you, Liv. And I want everything to be okay. I want *you* to be okay. God, I really do."

I hug her back.

"You should come over tonight," she says, wiping her

eyes with the back of a hand. "We can watch old *True Blood* episodes! And make appletinis!"

I try and gulp down my doubt, the permanent choke that's been lodged in my throat since I came back to Miami. Maybe she's right. Maybe I should go to her house and watch TV and drink some sweet liquory thing and forget about everything else. It's the kind of thing other girls do, girls with regular mothers and regular families and regular brains.

"That sounds good." But then Stern's face flickers through my mind, and I know that I can't. I shake my head. "But I'm sorry, Rain. I have work to do."

"Work?" she asks, incredulous. "What kind of *work* do you have to do? Why can't you just *hang out* with me, instead of driving yourself—"

"Crazy! I get it!" I burst out, chest burning hot, heart beating madly. "You think I'm crazy. You know what? You're right. I'm *not* normal. I can't just do *normal* things like sit around drinking apple-fucking-tinis and watching *True Blood* while my mother rots in a cell. And if that's what you need from a friend"—I grip the handle of the car door—"then maybe you should just call somebody else. Like *Tif*. Or *Hilary*."

"Are you seriously going to give me shit for making new—"

It's too late. I leap out of the car, slam the door shut. A wave of anger takes over my body and I ride it, not thinking, not caring.

Raina puts the window down, calls out to me: "Liv—stop. Talk to me. Liv!" Her voice sounds stung, split-apart and separated into strands of bewilderment. "I never said I thought you were *crazy*."

I keep marching toward the front door. Don't turn around. Don't give in.

"You can't ignore me forever!" Raina calls out. "I'm not going to let you. I just hope you know that."

I shut the front door behind me and press my back against it. I hear Raina's car pull away, tires squealing down the street. I feel my heart shrink up even smaller. I try to steady my breath. Dad and Heather and Wynn aren't home. Stern's in his thick black hole of nothingness.

And I'm alone.

# sixteen

*Please enjoy this Verizon ringback tone while your party is reached.* A Lupe Fiasco song; only half a verse plays until he answers. "Well, well, well." Austin pauses briefly—a muffled cough, the sound of a door being shut. "It's you."

"It's me," I say, clutching my phone tightly, suddenly a little nervous.

"I thought maybe you'd died of seasickness last night and no one'd bothered to tell me. Listen, I'm sorry I didn't get to take you out on a date that didn't end in you vomiting."

"I take it that's not how your date's usually end up?"

"Not exactly." He clears his throat. "Are you okay though, for real?"

I pause, sucking in a deep breath. "Austin—I—" and then it breaks open, spills out. "No. Not really."

"What's wrong?" He sounds surprised, and genuinely concerned. "Do I hear crying over there, Tithe?"

"I'm not crying," I say quickly, swiping a hand across

my nose. Then I tell him about the slashed tires and he listens patiently, in silence.

"Holy shit. That's messed up. Why would someone do that? You don't seem like the type to get into a lot of catfights."

"I don't. Maybe it was a prank, but . . ." I squeeze my cell phone extra hard. "It could have been something personal, too."

"I'm not really following you."

"It's this piano thing—has to do with Mom, and this competition—I—I can't really get into it right now."

*Can't get into the ghost-Stern of it. The Gray Space of it. The crazy.*

"Wanna come here?" he asks. I hear someone calling for him from another room. "Hold on a second." His palm muffles the receiver, but I make out my name, and Ted's voice, though the rest is indecipherable. "Ted just asked if you wanted to come for dinner. It must be some kind of occasion, if he's eating at home."

My breath catches in my throat. "Oh. Um. I don't—I don't know if I can." I pause, inhale a thick gulp of air-conditioned air. "Can you—do you think you can just come over here?"

A brief pause. "I was supposed to hang with the boys in a few, but I can hang with them any time. And you're a slippery little sucker." I can hear the little smile spreading across his face. The stupidly adorable, smug little smile.

"Good," I say. The resolve tightens inside of me. I've

started this and I won't stop. I won't let it go, no matter what Raina says. "I have a favor to ask you."

Marietta Jones's address is listed in her info section on Facebook. Over a thousand articles pop up when I google her name: *Marietta Jones earns Golden Ticket to Juilliard; Jones Beats out Best-of-the-best for Admission Into Top-Tier Music School; Pianist Perseveres Despite Lifelong Battle with Anxiety and Depression*—all from *The Sun Sentinel* and the *Palm Beach Post* in West Palm Beach, where her family lives.

Thankfully, Austin doesn't ask too many questions, other than to say, "I didn't know you were into threesomes, Liv," when I pass him her address.

We plug Marietta Jones' address into Austin's navigation system and start to drive. He lets me fiddle with his iPod and I wrestle Bon Iver out of a whole host of rap and R&B and top-forty.

"I knew you would pick this," he says, sounding almost triumphant as he pushes the sunglasses from the top of his head to cover his eyes from the sun's midafternoon glare.

"What's *that* supposed to mean?"

"Nothing." He shakes his head, but I can tell he's holding something back. He cracks a smile. "Okay. I'll admit something—I just downloaded this guy's music onto my 'pod because I thought you might like it."

"You just . . . guessed?" I sit up straighter in my soft leather seat and examine the calm perfection of his profile—little slope of his strong-bridged nose, clear-water eyes, long-lashed, bow of his lips. "Women's intuition?"

"Not exactly. I saw that you liked him on your Facebook page. There it is. Feel free to laugh."

"No. I think—I think you're sweet, Austin."

He smiles his big, lit-up grin. Blindingly white teeth. Amazing how easily a couple of minutes in the presence of Austin Morse—his citrus-and-spice scent, the heat off his skin, the flush of his cheeks, the little freckles dotted across his nose—can suddenly mute my brain to Stern and the events of this morning.

I don't know how that happens—how you can love one person and want another so damn bad at the exact same time.

My phone buzzes so many times with repeated texts from Raina (*Liv stop. You're being immature; Liv. This is ridic; SERIOUSLY LIV STOP IGNORING ME)* that I eventually turn it off entirely. By this point, we're stuck in the weird knot of three o'clock traffic, and "For Emma, Forever Ago" has ended.

Austin switches us over to the radio. "Don't worry, Tithe," he tells me as he fiddles with the smooth black dial, stopping when *'60s on 6* flashes across the little strip of screen. "I know what you want."

I roll my eyes at him. I pull my sketchbook out of my purse and lay into it—into the blurs of passing cars with wide sweeping lines, the wispy humps of stratocumulus clouds, the assaulting bright of the sun. I don't notice that we've pulled off the highway and into a neighborhood—into *her* neighborhood—until Austin turns the radio off and announces: "Snap to it, Red. We're here."

I shut my sketchbook and sit straight up, suddenly terrified.

I plead with him silently not to turn off the car. Maybe he'll just put it right into reverse, or try to talk me out of confronting Marietta.

"Look, I really haven't thought this through," I admit, my breath coming fast. "Like, at all."

"Well, it's a little too late for that." He gets out of the car and opens my door for me; I watch his muscles flex beneath his soft white T-shirt. "Buck up, Tithe. We've got this. We've got this chick on lockdown." Macho Austin Morse, at it again. Weirdly, it makes me feel better. I step out of the car with shaking legs.

We walk from the long driveway to the Jones' large three-story, wide-windowed home, all still and silent. My heart flutters in my chest. Austin grabs my hand, suddenly, as we reach the front door. Surprised, I let him hold it.

"I've got your back, Olivia," he says, kissing my knuckles with soft lips. "Seriously. You just let me know."

I take a deep breath, ring the bell, hear the knob twist almost instantly from the inside like someone's been planted by the door, waiting for some action. Expecting it. The door opens; a slight, dark-skinned girl with eyes that seem to take up most of her face stands in the frame in a tutu, unscuffed toe shoes—pink I'm sure, if I could properly see—a gray that's calmer than yellow, darker than white, creamy, somehow. "Jones residence," she says, with such well-trained poise it comes across unnatural, slightly robotic. I hesitate, look briefly down at her—she stands in fourth position, right foot crossed and pointed out at an impossible-looking angle in front of her left foot, pointed just as uncomfortably in the other direction. Definitely a robot.

Austin speaks up first. "We're looking for Marietta," he says, calm, cool, smooth—the very attractive boy who *has my back*.

The girl raises her eyebrows, raises up onto the hard point of her shoes arching her whole spine back in a slight, graceful arc. "Why?" she asks, returning center, pointing her right toe left right, left right in front of her.

"We're friends of hers," he says without skipping a beat.

"Ummm . . ." The girl smirks. "I seriously doubt that."

"And why's that?" Austin asks.

"Because Marietta doesn't have any friends."

A brief, awkward silence.

"Look," I say. My impatience is mounting. I watch her perfect little body move through an intentionally distracting warm-up routine. "We're music acquaintances, okay?" I step closer to the doorway and peer inside—long, clean, glassy hallways—a big mirror in the foyer, no family photos in sight, the edge of a shiny Steinway grand in the living room visible from where I stand snooping. "And I need her advice about a piece I'm going to play soon . . . it's an audition piece . . . for Juilliard." I bite my lips, hoping she won't read the lie on my face.

Just then, there's a noise from inside. A girl's fingers appear, curled around the upstairs banister. The fingers—clean, well-manicured—are all I can see clearly. Everything else is in shadow.

"I don't know who you are and I'm not interested in talking." Marietta's steely voice echoes through the big, open house. "Shut the door, Annabelle. I'm taking a nap." The fingers disappear from the banister. A door shuts.

Annabelle moves to shut the front door. Austin and I both put our hands out to stop her. "You're her sister?" I ask.

"Yes." She twists the toe of her left foot into the ground, spins around twice, landing perfectly.

"You're a really good dancer," I say, smiling at her, trying a new tack. A soft floral smell reaches me from inside, mingled with something metallic, robustly sanitized. "Do you want to go to Juilliard, too?"

"Mayyybe," she says, cocking her head now to look at me, raising her arms overhead, fingers arched. "But if you were coming here to ask Etta about Juilliard, she *definitely* won't talk to you."

"Why not?" I ask.

"Yeah," Austin chimes in beside me. "Does going to Juilliard make her too good to talk to 'regular' people now?"

Annabelle laughs openly at us, as though to demonstrate

how completely pathetic she finds us. "You guys are bad liars." She spins around once more, lifting her right foot about six inches off the ground and arching it behind her weirdly muscular back. "If you were *really* friends with her, you'd know that Juilliard *revoked* her acceptance." She narrows her eyes, smirking. "She broke a girl's fingers at her high school. Another pianist—right before their senior year."

Austin and I share a look of surprise. Sabotage.

"And she stole this guy's inhaler. He wasn't even a pianist. He played violin. She just didn't like him. He almost died." Annabelle crosses her arms and smirks. "And you know what? The inhaler was in her piano the *whole time*. Stupid."

"Wow," Austin says. "Sounds pretty *psycho*."

"You don't understand," Annabelle says, "and you couldn't." She again starts to shut the door in our faces. Austin puts his hand out, as before, to stop her. She tries to push back but he's far stronger.

"Come on, just talk to us. What don't we understand?" Austin asks her.

"Ugh." She gives up trying to close the door. She looks around quickly, and then steps outside with us, closing the door behind her. She blinks in the sunlight, shields her eyes with the flat of her little hand—even this pedestrian move looks graceful. Out here, in the light, she looks even younger. "We don't have a choice, okay? You don't know what it's like with our parents. . . ." She shoots another worried glance over her shoulder. "We have to be the best," she continues, dropping her voice. "Or else."

"Annabelle!" A man's voice sounds, loud, angry, muffled from within the house. Annabelle leaps where she stands. "That's my dad. I gotta go." My heart sinks a little as she turns to the door, starts to open it.

"Hold on, Annabelle. One more question." Austin's voice is smokey, a voice that would make any girl stop dead in her tracks and turn—which Annabelle does, blushing. "Was your sister in Miami this morning?"

"Miami?" She shakes her head. "She hasn't left the house in weeks. She's been depressed ever since . . . You Know What."

"ANNABELLE!"

Annabelle jumps again, twists the door open a crack and leaps inside, mouthing *bye* to us before shutting it in our faces.

We stand there on the front step, staring at the closed front door, the smell of sweet acacia lining the front lawn growing suddenly rank, awful.

Five days and nothing solved. Five days and not a single step closer to helping Stern—or my mom. Austin moves his hand to my back and ushers me toward the car. I let him guide me; I don't have the will, or the energy, to move myself.

We sit in his car, at the end of Marietta Jones's driveway. It's nearly six now. Late afternoon light pours its last balmy dregs through the windows.

"So, I guess she's not the one who slashed your tires, then," Austin says.

I close my eyes, lean my head against my window. "Guess not." Between the door and Austin's car I grew exhausted somehow.

"So maybe it was just . . . someone random?"

"No. I don't think it was random." I draw my knees into my chest. Austin doesn't yell at me for putting my feet on the seat.

"Why? What's the deal here, Tithe? Spill it."

I sigh, deep, and wrestle the words out. "It has to do with my mom."

"Yeah, you said that earlier."

"All of this shit started happening when"—I stop myself from mentioning Stern—"when I started to think maybe . . . maybe she didn't do it after all. Ever since I've started looking into her case, I feel weird—like someone's watching me or something." I stare at him, anxiety flashing: *Including you. You were an asshole . . . now you want to date me all of the sudden.* "And everyone's telling me to stop looking, to let it go. It's like . . . it's like there's something else going on. Something bigger."

"Wait, wait . . . let me get this straight. You think there's a chance Marietta Jones killed that kid instead of your mom?" He runs his hand along the gearshift. "And everyone is, like, covering for her?"

*That kid.* It occurs to me: Austin hardly even knew who Stern *was*.

"Did you hear what her sister said? That they had to be the best, *or else*? I mean . . . who knows what she could have been driven to do? She already almost killed some violin player! Maybe she hired someone. Maybe the same people she got to knock Stern off are the same people who slashed my tires." Increasingly, as I talk, it seems possible. No. More than possible—it seems right. "Maybe she's not really depressed. Maybe she's faking it, because she's worried I'm getting closer. She's hiding out, you know?"

"Hiding out?" Austin shakes his head. He winces, like he's just swallowed a mouthful of lemon juice. And I know what's coming next. "I don't know, Olivia. From an outside perspective, it seems pretty whack." I start to protest, but he hushes me. "Just hear me out." He reaches for my hand again. I don't mean to relent, but somehow I've got to—under his spell, his touch, the warm, citrus-spice tangle of his scent. "My dad put the best lawyer in town on her case," he continues, softly, in that smoky *let me undress you* voice of his. "If there was any *chance* she was innocent—even if she did it, and there was some weird legal loophole that would have gotten her off—she'd be free right now. And if the best lawyer in Miami couldn't do anything, there's nothing you can do."

"See what I mean? Why is everyone discouraging me?" I snap. I feel dark, helpless.

"Because we're on the outside of it, and you're not." He turns the key in the ignition and, finally, we start to pull away. "Everyone else can see what you can't: that you just need to let it go. And trust that when *everyone* you know is saying it, they might know something you don't."

*Everyone besides Stern.* My breath sticks in my throat, shallow, tight. The palm trees sway like grass skirts above us.

I study his face in profile: his insanely perfect, Greek-god face. If Austin ever knew suffering the way some kids learn it, early, when it sits there for life like a malignant, steady-growing tumor, most of it's lost to him now. His dad died when he was too young to miss him. Lucky boy, to have the kind of suffering that ends up benign, removable by time, or drastically reduced. I didn't learn it early. But I've sure learned it by now.

*Everyone gets theirs in the end*; it was something I remember my mom telling me one day after I'd come home crying from school because Bobby Roache thought my hair looked too much like tomato sauce and threw a rock at my forehead on the school bus. *He'll get his in the end, Livie. Everyone gets theirs in the end.*

Austin's right. I do want to let go. At this point, I just want to let go of everything. "You're right," I say in a small voice.

"I know." He tries to get me to smile, but I'm too tired to fake it right now. A few moments later, he starts Bon Iver back up on his iPod. He drives with one hand only on the steering wheel, the other teasing the gearshift. "Look. My mom's been texting me since I left to pick you up. Dinner's at six and she made some linguini and crab shit and if you don't come she'll pretty much stab me in the eye."

Exhausted as I am, this time I manage to smile. "Eye-stabbing? That's pretty serious. Sounds like I'm not the only one with a crazy mom." I fiddle with my hands in my lap. "But I don't think I can, Austin. I'm really—"

"Hungry? Me, too. And, look, Clare and Ted seriously won't get off my back until you do. You *have* to come. It's Sunday Dinner. It's like, a thing. Also, I won't be able to drive you around anymore if I've only got one working eye."

"You'd adjust. Eventually."

"You're a tough one, Red. You know that?"

"I don't know anything, Austin."

"So that's a yes then? Cause I kind of want to know right now if I'm going to be able to play lacrosse this year or not."

"I guess I'll let you keep both eyes," I say, pressing my knees into my chest, staring out at the wide-bright of the streetlamps, which click on to greet the rising dark. "But only because I'm in no position to forfeit a chauffeur."

# seventeen

We're so glad you could join us, Olivia," Ted says, winking as he pours wine into each of our glasses. I love Ted Oakley for not thinking twice before pouring two sixteen-year-old kids giant glasses of wine. Austin and I both set to drinking ours. I wonder if this "double date" with his parents weirds him out as much as it weirds me out.

Austin is sitting close to me at the dark-wood table. His knee just touches my knee, but heat radiates between us. I push the crab around on my plate. Clare smiles encouragingly at me.

"Good?" she asks, leaning slightly forward to better hear my answer.

I nod enthusiastically, smile back, chew, swallow, smile some more. "It's great, thank you. Really, really great." Their kitchen is bigger than Oh Susannah: shiny-tiled, tall-ceilinged, an island with a giant, gleaming stovetop for cooking, two separate convection ovens, giant fridge, six-foot-tall expressionistic paintings Clare probably bought for a million bucks a pop.

Austin stifles a laugh by shoving a forkful of pasta into his mouth, which makes *me* laugh. I haven't really had much to eat today. Four or five sips into my wine, I'm already feeling tipsy.

"Ausy—where's your napkin?" Clare asks, like he's a little kid. "Why isn't it on your lap?" He reaches for it, gruffly, off the table and settles it across his lap.

"There, Mom. Happy now?"

"Austin. Enough with the lip," Ted says. "We have a guest."

I feel Austin's fingers at the inside of my knee, tickling slowly up my thigh. I swat it away, noticing Clare's eyes on us from across the table. She and Ted exchange a glance. I clear my throat and take another gulp of wine.

"So, how is everything at home, Olivia?" Ted asks. "You're glad to be back? Job at the park okay?"

"Yeah, it's. . . okay." I pack my mouth full of pasta so he won't try to ask me too much else. I notice how dark the skin is beneath his eyes, like he hasn't slept—not proper, at least—for a while.

"Just okay?" He is obviously not deterred.

"No, I mean, everything's fine. I've just been tired, I guess. It's hard to sit on a bench most of the day and wait for something to happen."

"Tired? Have you been sick, honey?" Clare asks, peering at me with concern.

"I mean, you know . . ." I meet Austin's eyes and quickly look away. "The hearing. Mom stuff." *Don't act like your life is perfect, either,* I think, remembering what Austin told me on the boat—about Ted and Clare, his late nights, the lies he may or may not be telling. If nothing else, they're both masters of illusion. I'm starting to think that most people are, in one way or another.

Ted frowns and nods. "Any news on that front?"

"I've just been . . . looking into things," I say, taking another sip.

"What sorts of things?" Clare asks.

"I've been talking to some people," I elaborate vaguely. I wonder what they would do if I confessed that one of the "people" I've been talking to is a ghost.

"Are you having any success?" Ted asks, standing up from the table to more easily top off everyone's glasses with fresh wine.

The wine has made me feel open, friendly, eager to talk. I sit back in my chair. "Not yet," I tell them honestly. "But I feel like I'm getting closer to understanding what really happened. And I know everyone keeps trying to tell me to give it up, but I'm still not convinced. At all." I shrug, look to Ted, standing beside Clare's chair now, appealing to him with my eyes. "I'm not going to give up. I know she didn't do it. I *know* it."

"Shit!" Ted exclaims, jumping back—he's accidentally knocked Clare's glass over, and wine is spilling everywhere, including all over his crisp white dress shirt, narrowly missing Clare. "Damn it!" The wine blooms down his shirt like ink into snow.

"Calm down, Teddy," Clare says, standing from the table to wet a napkin at the sink and bring it to him. "I'll take it to the dry cleaner's tomorrow." She lays another napkin on top of the wet table and I watch it sop up the liquid like a thirsty plant.

"This is brand new," he huffs, rubbing frantically at the stain with the wet linen napkin. "Jesus, Clare. Can't you *do* something? Don't you have any stain remover?"

Austin looks over at me, rolling his eyes as his mother stands up from the table, sighing, and disappears from the kitchen, into a room I can only assume is packed with cleaning products she typically pays someone else to use. Ted sighs heavily, glances briefly over at Austin and then at me. No one says anything for a few moments—we listen to Clare rustle.

"So, Ted," Austin says, finally cutting through the silence. "Are you going to finish your pasta, or . . . ?"

Still obviously disgruntled, Ted stares at the table, at the stain on his shirt. "You take it, Aus," he says, pushing the plate toward Austin. He inhales, and all at once returns to the cool-collected-in-control version of Ted Oakley I've always known. The Ted Oakley who gets things done. The Ted Oakley who knows just who to call in a pinch. His phone rings then, tinny, from his pocket; he pulls it out and examines the screen, sighing as he rubs his head. "I'd better take this," he says, smiling apologetically. "I hope you'll forgive my rudeness, Olivia. Clients. They've got no manners. Total barbarians, calling in the middle of dinner." He stands up before Clare has the chance to return with the stain remover, puts a hand on my shoulder. "So glad you could come by. It's always so nice to see you around. Come back any time, you got that? I promise, next time—no wine spills or embarrassing outbursts." He makes his way toward his office. I hear his door click shut.

"Sorry," Austin says, shrugging. "He doesn't usually freak out like that, at least not in front of other people."

I sit without saying anything for a minute, fiddling with my napkin. Then I burst out: "So, why did he?"

Austin snaps his head around to face me. "What?"

"Ted. Why do you think he freaked? I mean . . . I started talking about the hearing, and then . . ."

"I told you. He's been super stressed out the past couple of weeks—you know, lots of money riding on Elysian Fields, I guess. Stuff with Mom."

"Oh." There's a twisted-up feeling in my belly I can't shake. "That sucks."

"He'll get over it," Austin says. I can feel his breath, close, close to my skin. And even that smells good—sweet with wine, slightly peppery. His citrus-spice weaves around my head, softening me to a sudden sleepiness. I turn to check the time on the wall clock over the stove: almost eight o'clock. Late. Dad's probably a wreck—I turned my phone off earlier to shield myself from Raina's barrage of texts. He probably assumes I'm dead by now.

I grab my bag up from beneath the table and check my cell phone. Just as expected, my inbox is bombed by messages from Raina and from Dad. But mainly from Dad. I don't read them.

"You okay, Red?" Austin asks, grabbing a noodle from Ted's plate and chomping on it. Red. That word barely means anything to me now. It could be anything. It could be nothing.

"My dad," I tell him. "He's sent me like fifty text messages in the past four hours."

"You didn't tell him you were coming here for dinner?"

I shake my head weakly, feeling wobbly in the eyes, double-sleepy now.

"You're such a rebel, Olivia," he says, putting his hand over my bare knee and squeezing it, hard. "Such a devil."

My brain is soft-edged from the wine. For a second, I'm just a regular sixteen-year-old again, flirting with a boy, wanting to touch him, to be touched, to run out into the surf, shedding my clothes to the wet sand. I move my hand to his thigh for just a second, move it up, and up, before releasing it. "Think I can bum a ride back to hell?"

# eighteen

"Olivia Jane." *Busted.* Dad's voice, angry, rings out from the kitchen.

I step gingerly into the line of fire. He's drinking whiskey in a rocks glass at the kitchen table. "Dad—I'm sorry I didn't text—I was out with—"

"I don't want to hear it, Olivia," He shakes his head, taps lightly against the table with the edge of the glass. There are circles dark as Ted Oakley's under his eyes. Maybe Ghost Town is sucking them both dry. "The bridesmaid fitting has been on the calendar for over a *month*, Liv. Do you know how disappointed Heather was? I texted you about twenty times and heard nothing."

Shit. "My phone died. I totally forgot." I shuffle my feet along the tile floor. I can't tell him I actually *did* have better things to do than try on some stupid Ann Taylor dress built for middle-aged back-in-the-saddle types trying to hook a husband. "It wasn't on purpose, okay?"

"You say that, Liv, but I don't think you mean it." He runs a hand through his thinning hair. "You've never been good at hiding what you're thinking. And it kills me that you're so unsupportive. It really does."

"You really expect me to be *supportive*?" I stare at him, stare at the face of my Dad, and wonder why it looks so different to me now. Why it suddenly looks alien—like this house, his kitchen, his fiancé, his whole life after Mom.

"I expect you to consider the feelings of others. Sometimes you don't think through your decisions, and you end up doing hurtful things as a result."

I practically jump out of my chair at this, but the *don't you go anywhere young lady* expression on his face keeps me put. "I *told* you I didn't mean to miss the bridesmaid fitting. It was a *mistake*. You make mistakes. Big ones. Blond ones." I don't mean to say it; it just pops out. He sits back in his chair and starts shaking his head. "But I'm not allowed to do the same thing? Are you even *listening* to yourself?"

"I'm not the one who needs to listen." He rubs his eyes. Suddenly, he looks tired. "Look, Olivia. I think it's time you give talking to someone another try."

"What, like a *shrink*?" I sink back in my chair for a moment, feeling my whole body go sharp with a fiery heat. The words of my first-and-only shrink to date remain burned into my memory: *there's really nothing psychiatry can do to ward off schizophrenia, Olivia. Unfortunately, all we can do is wait, and medicate.* He'd smiled at that last part—his funny little rhyme.

I fix Dad with a sharp stare. "Are you serious?"

"Yes, Liv. I know the first time we tried was a whole mess," he says, softly, "but that was a hell of a long time ago, and that guy was a real quack. We'll find you a better one this time—someone who can help. We'll do our research this time." He reaches across the table for my shaking hand, but I pull it away. "You've gone through stuff you're too young to understand—and by too young I *don't* mean not smart enough, so don't leap down my throat. Just too damn young."

My breath comes quick and sharp. "So now you think I'm crazy. You think I'm like her." I pull my knees into my chest and stare at the tile floor. It gleams beneath the overhead light like it's just been washed. It's too clean in here. Sterile.

"Liv, now you're just being immature. You know I don't think that." He sighs, pulls at his chin. A scruffy beard used to grow there. Mom loved it. His five o'clock shadow. She'd say his chin gave the best back-scratches of all time, when it was just a little bit prickly. "There's a lot of change in your life right now . . ."

"Oh? You mean changes like Heather?" I make a face.

"Don't you talk to me that way, Olivia Jane. Don't you even dare," he warns. "I know this is hard for you, but I love her, and you're going to have to give her a chance. You haven't even let yourself get to know her—just decided point-blank you weren't going to like her, day one. You have got to stop giving her such a hard time."

"Why should I?" I spit, watching water bead up around

the edge of Dad's glass. "I mean, what do you even *see* in her, Dad? She's got nothing in her head!" I tap my palm dramatically against my temple like it's a block of wood. "She's an idiot. She's—"

"You watch your mouth, Olivia," Dad cuts in sharply. "Heather's an incredible woman, and very strong. She understands more than you know about"—he imitates my head-tapping gesture—"this whole thing."

"What whole thing, Dad?" I challenge. "Is she crazy, too, and just really good at hiding it?"

"Her first husband killed himself," Dad responds matter-of-factly, which shuts me up right away. "When Wynn was just about a year old, Liv. Put a gun to his own head, right in their bedroom. She walked in, found him like that."

All the air goes out of me, and for a second, all I can think about is baby Wynn, never getting a chance to meet her own father.

Like Austin.

I'm quiet, shaking a little, not sure what to do with all of this information. It's too much. It's all too much. "I'm sorry, Dad. I'm sorry about that. I didn't know."

My dad stares into his drink. His mouth is set in a firm line. "He was a manic-depressive, on a bad spell. His meds stopped working for him. He didn't see another way out, I guess. As you can imagine, this pretty much gutted Heather. She's done a lot of work to move on, but it's a process. Just like it is for all of us, when the unthinkable happens. She's not so different from us, Liv." He lifts his chin slightly, scratches at his neck with his long fingers before returning them to the coolness of his glass. "So don't go on assuming you know anything about what a person's gone through." His eyes are dark and steady and serious. "Heather understands what we went through with Mom. What we're *going* through."

I clear my throat. "Then how come you guys act like Mom never existed? *She's* not dead, Dad. And you used to love her. You did. You used to love her. How did you just stop?" I swallow the tears, rolling into my mouth, angry that I've cracked, that I've spilled, that I'm spilling. "You got sick of her and went to some dumb support group to help deal with her and instead of helping, you just replaced her. And you replaced Oh Susannah, and your old life, and your old job. Everything." I stare at him, hard. "You *replaced* her, Dad."

"Replaced her?" He sits back in his chair and looks at me, openmouthed, stunned. For a moment, we sit in silence. Then he stands, using the table to help heave him to his feet, looking suddenly like an old man. He passes into the darkened hallway without another word. I sit, swallowing the taste of saline, fighting the heave in my chest, thinking he has gone upstairs. I watch the time blink on the microwave clock. *8:17. 8:18.* It blurs around the edges as I stare at it.

But then he's back. He's holding a twine-bound stack of letters. He plunks them softly on the table. He rests his hand on top the letters, tenderly, as though they were the head of a small child he wants to comfort. "I've written a letter to your mother every week for the whole ten months she's been in that place." His voice cracks. "When she's lucid, she answers. I stuck with her best I could; I don't know what else to say about that. I know you think things could have gone different, but they didn't. They went like this. And the thing about your mom is, Liv, she wants us to be happy." He sits back down, scoots his chair around the table to sit beside me. "It's in all of her letters. She wants us to be happy. Because she loves us."

"No." I shake my head, willing it away, willing it all back. Time. History. Every bad thing that's ever happened. "No. Not like this."

"Livie Livie Livie!"

Wynn rushes into the kitchen, wearing her pj's, before I can continue. Her feet squeak across the floor. She hops straight into my lap, wraps her arms around my neck, and gives me little bumblebee kisses on my face.

"Hi, Wynn," I say. I realize I'm shaking.

Wynn puts one little finger against the wet beneath my eye. "Why are you sad, Livie?"

I hug her to me and she blocks Dad from my sight. "I'm okay, Wynny," I whisper to her, though my chest aches with anger, with a deep, gnawing sadness. "It's fine."

I hear the front door open and close. I swivel around and see Heather kicking off her suede flats in the hall, carrying a Walmart bag.

"Mommy!" Wynn yelps, wiggling out of our hug. Heather comes into the kitchen, placing the bag on the counter by the sink, and leans over to kiss Wynn. All four of us now. The happy little family.

Dad stands from his chair, crosses to her, kisses her lightly on the mouth. The little stack of letters still sits there on the table, the length of twine a wavy shape beside it. I try to shut my ears from their "sweet" little greetings—*honey*s and *love*s and *I missed you*s. Wynn's still in my lap, making my hair into little corkscrews with her fingers.

"Olivia," Dad says curtly. "I believe there's something you'd like to say to Heather."

I sit there, silent for a moment, Dad and Heather looming over me, Wynn twirling and making funny little cat noises in my ear. After all that, he still has the nerve to put me through this. An apology from *me*, when he's the one who should be apologizing. Unfair. I'm sorry her husband offed himself, but, it's not my problem. I shouldn't have to apologize for all the damned crimes of the world, for every bad thing people do to each other.

But I have no other option. I take a deep breath. "I'm sorry," I mumble. It's the best I can do. I focus on Wynn's white-blonde curl-haloed head so I don't have to look at Heather, or at Dad. I don't want to see Heather's face and imagine that day, baby Wynn in her arms, she found her husband's brains spattered on the rug. I don't want to see her as human.

"Thank you, Olivia. I appreciate that. But, know what?" Heather leaves Dad's side to come to mine. Wynn reaches her arms up in my lap and Heather reaches back, pulling her up from my lap and into her arms. "It all turned out okay. I peeked at some of the dresses in your closet, and ordered something for you that should fit." She puts a hand on my shoulder. "If it doesn't, we can always make tweaks when it comes in."

I shift in my chair, force a smile.

"Okay."

"I hope you know how much it means to me to have you by my side on my big day." Her smile is painfully, annoyingly genuine. Her *big day*. But the cold, hard, undeniable truth is: Dad *does* look beaming-happy, lit-up, when he's with her. And she with him. And I guess that makes me the asshole who wants to take that away, for the sake of honor and broken promises and broken family bonds and broken mothers.

"Thank you, Heather," I say, forcing the small part of me that really means it to inflate. "And I really am sorry I forgot about the fitting today. I feel awful." Once I say it, I realize I really do.

"Oh, honey, it's really not a big deal. I know you've got a lot on your mind. I'd have probably forgotten it, too, if I wasn't the one getting married." She looks between me and Dad. Her eyes bug out a little bit. I try and guess the color of her button-up—much darker than her skin, lighter than the night sky; a shade slightly richer than a stop sign. Burgundy, maybe, or dark red. "Have you two eaten yet? I fed Wynn earlier, but I'm starving."

Dad shakes his head. "I was waiting for you."

"I ate a couple of hours ago," I say quickly, still focusing my eyes on Wynn so I'm not forced to make eye contact with either of them. "Maybe I can take Wynn out for a walk while you two get some food?"

Dad and Heather exchange a glance. "That would be great, Olivia," Heather says, hand to her chest. "It'd be really nice to have some alone time. It's been a little while."

"Yessssss!" Wynn says, bouncing in my arms. "Yes yes yes!"

"Cool. We won't be gone too long. By the way, Heather," I say, deciding to test my powers. "I like that color on you. It's great with your skin."

She stretches an arm out, tugs at the sleeve. "Yeah? I wasn't sure about this dark red with my hair." She winks. "But if a painter says so, then it must be true!"

A shiver runs through me—*I was right*. Momentarily, I feel elated, like I've bridged some gap, transcended the Gray Space, for just a moment.

"No problem." I continue to avoid Dad's eyes. "We'll see you later, okay?"

"Home by nine for bedtime," Heather calls after us. "That's just for tonight, Wynn! So don't get used to it!" As Wynn and I slip into the hallway, I nuzzle my nose into the top of her head.

"Where should we go, Wynn?" I ask her, before putting her down so she can slip on her shoes. "The beach?"

"The beach! Nine! Wowowowowow."

"Oh, and Dad?" I shout from the hall. "Long story, but I have to borrow your car, okay? I lent mine to Raina!" I haven't explained the slashed tires, or the tow.

And I figure what's one more lie, on top of all the others?

Wynn sticks half her body out the window of the car the whole short drive to the beach, like she's a caged animal, released just today to the outside world. I point to Elysian Fields as we pass it; "Look Wynn, Ghost Town," I say, and she repeats it, with awe, amazement, like they're the first words she's ever spoke: "Ghost Town." Outside: the smell of milkweed, crinum lily—sweet and grassy, just slightly acrid at the end of it. Wynn sniffs deep, wriggling around in her seat. "Does that mean ghosts live there?"

"I don't know, Wynn, maybe. That's not what it's really called. Raina and I made it up." I inch Dad's Chevy into the beach lot, just two streets away from the winding entrance to Ghost Town. I can't bear to park in front of the actual place—some fear of leaving any part of myself there alone at night pricking at me when I consider it.

"I'm scared of ghosts. I hope if they live there they stay in there. Even Pop-pop Wooshie."

"Don't worry, Wynny. You're safe."

"Promise?"

I cross my fingers so she can see them. "Promise."

There's just the tiniest lip of sunlight left by the time we reach the actual beach, sandwiched between the different darks of sky and ocean, so the horizon looks like one huge, horizontal Oreo cookie. Ghost Town looms, practically within spitting distance. Wynn clutches my hand tight and we run through the sand—my old house is up ahead and we start walking toward it. "Shhhhh shhhhhhhushhhhh . . ." Wynn imitates the wave sounds, jumps around on little peaks in the sand, makes them flush with her sandals. "Shhhh shhhhhhushhhhhh." I point to it ahead—the sturdy, boxy, two-story house I know better than any place in the world. "That's where I grew up."

"The *purple* one?" Wynn asks, so excited about this that her voice squeaks.

"The purple one." It only looks a sick ashy shade to me now.

"Wowowowowow." She pauses, grips around my leg now. "It's like a *princess* house."

My heart hammers in my chest—haven't been inside the place since last summer, right before I left for art school, when, aside from the divorce, everything was still pretty much normal and Mom wasn't a murderer and Lucas Stern was a living breathing human being. But, suddenly, I need to be closer. "Do you want to see it, Wynny?" I kneel on the sand, meet her at eye-level.

"Yes I do want to see it, Livie. Can we really go? Can we go now?" Her big round eyes are glittering.

I stand up, take her hand again in mine. So tiny, so warm.

"Wowowowowow."

"Wynn—stop doing that." She zips her lips. Tosses away the key.

We climb the dune separating the backyard from the beach, pulling off our sandals to better trek through the gritty sand, and the clusters of big, ferny pawpaw poking out between the tall grasses. I search for evidence of Mom along the way—a ring she might have lost, a thin silk scarf flown off her neck long ago, wrapped between the weeds—but there's no trace of her. "My mom and I used to do this every day. She'd carry me when I was really little. Do you want me to carry you?"

"Nope. I like the sand in my toes a whole lot."

"Well, aren't you an independent lady?"

"That's what Mommy says. She lets me pick out what I want for lunch, too. She lets me pick out cookies."

"Oh yeah? What'd you pick out today, then?"

"Ummmm. Chocolate chip ones," Wynn announces. "And she lets me pick out what shape I want my sandwich in and I wanted a heart. And she let me put the cookie cutter on the bread and I got to cut it myself." Wynn swishes the bottom of her pj's as she walks, extra slow, so she can dig her toes in.

It occurs to me that Heather is a really good mother. She raised Wynn by herself, after everything that happened, but has never once complained. She's strong. And so I guess a small, stubborn part of me understands why Dad is drawn to her. Why he needs her. Why she's good for him.

"My Mommy used to let me pick out my lunch, too, but I don't know if I ever got to cut *my* sandwiches into a heart, so you must be a *really* lucky lady." I point to the space beneath the stilt-raised house, about three feet high, the cover of rocky dirt beneath it. "My best friends and I used to sneak away and play games under there." We stop and Wynn puts her hands on the side of the house and swings herself underneath.

"Raina?"

"And Stern." I swing myself underneath the house, too, then, and we sit there in the dirt, side by side.

"Do you still play with them?" Wynn asks, grabbing a fistful of soft, milky dirt and releasing it back to the ground.

"Well, sort of. But, it's different when you get older, Wynn."

"How come?" She wrinkles her nose.

"It's harder. And your friends change . . . and you change." I leave out: *And you fall in love, and they kiss you and say it was just a mistake, and they die, and your eyes stop working right.*

"Oh." Wynn reaches for my hand, her eyes big and scared. "Can we go now?"

We skirt past the side of the funny beautiful purple house I grew up in, the moon big behind us. Mosquitoes hover in tight swarms. Wynn tries to shoo them away with her whole body—bouncing and wriggling around when they come at her. I feel cloaked in some mist of childhood here—small and sort of scared, but filled, too, with a sense of wholeness and protection.

The area of grass and palm tree and dirt where Mom's vegetable and herb garden used to be is littered, heavily, with trash and pieces of glass. Several windows are broken, spidery cracks all through the glass, spray paint bright on the front door: *Child killer. Devil. 666 I HOPE YOU ROT.*

I have the instinct to shield Wynn's eyes, but I don't. I freeze. Because there's someone coming toward us, from the other side of the house—someone small and hunched. There's a shopping cart behind her, loaded with trash, and she's mumbling something, seemingly at us. Wynn hugs around my leg. "What's that, Livie?"

I put my hand on her head. "Don't worry. Don't worry. Here—" I urge her off my leg, take her hand, and we start to walk back around the other side of the house, away. *Creak-a-creak-a-creak-a*: her shopping cart follows us. Cans jangle within it.

"*Chica.*" The ragged, accented voice is familiar—the stoop of her back, the wild frizz of her hair, the haloed quality of it in the moonlight. Of course—this is the beach she always stalks, late at night, digging for "treasure." I turn to her. To Medusa.

"I don't have anything to give you, Medusa. I'm sorry."

I keep a tight grip on Wynn's hand. Wynn is staring at her, even bigger-eyed, sucking her thumb. I pull her along. *Creak-a-creak-a-creak-a.*

"I see you, *chica*. I see." She pauses, her footsteps still close behind. "*Ten cuidado*. Be careful."

Something icy scales the length of my back. Wynn stares up at me. "Why does she talk funny?" she asks.

"She just does," I whisper, picking her up, drawing her close to me. She wraps her arms around my neck. Curious, and a little desperate, I stare hard at Medusa, at the shadows made in the deep, weathered creases of her skin.

"What are you talking about?"

She mumbles under her breath, scratching at herself. "The shadow man," she says then, suddenly sharp, eyes focused and direct. *"El hombre del sombra vendrá para ti también."*

"The shadow man?" I come closer to her—she reeks of soggy garbage; I breathe through my mouth. Wynn whines a little in my arms. "What are you talking about? Who's the shadow man?" I narrow my eyes at her, waiting. "Jesus! Say something!"

Wynn grips more tightly around my neck and I put a hand on top her head, murmur a reassurance to her.

Medusa goes blank, shuts down. Her eyes seem to swim in their sockets, tick around like a clock. She's mumbling now, starts biting at her hands.

I turn and walk briskly away from my now-ramshackle old home, back down the dune, across the beach, up to my car. I can still hear the sounds of her babbling halfway to the parking lot.

I place Wynn into the front seat and buckle her in. She's awake but oddly, stoically quiet. Medusa's warning continues to echo inside of my head the whole ride home: *Ten cuidado. Be careful. The shadow man. El hombre del sombra.*

*She's a crazy person,* I remind myself. *A babbling, confused homeless woman.*

So why am I shaking so hard?

# nineteen

Four days.

"Olivia?" Hound-dog-faced George, Boss of the Carousel, stands over me.

"George. Hey." I straighten up on the bench where I've been dozing for the past half-hour in lieu of the hawk-eyed carousel-watching I'm paid minimum wage to do. "Sorry—I just shut my eyes for a second."

My sleep last night was filled with that jittery monsters-hiding-in-the-closet fear that used to grip me nights as a little kid. Back then, I'd just run into Mom and Dad's room, wedge myself between them in their bed, and *bam*—out like a light.

I'm already in hot water with George. He called Ted Oakley, who knows George well and got me the job. Ted passed on George's disappointment, along with confirmation via Austin that I had, in fact, called out of work all weekend, to Dad this morning, like a big, crappy game of telephone. And Dad called me before I could sleep through my alarm to tell me if I didn't get my butt out of bed and haul on over to work there'd be major hell to pay.

So, here I am.

"The carousel's looking *pre-tty* dirty. Did you wash it last week?" George crosses his arms over his belly, stares down at me. Milky gray sweat beads up on his rat-gray skin. It looks like there's dark dirt, settled into the folds of his face. "You know, Olivia, it's part of your work here to hose that carousel off. Every single week. While there's no one on it right now, I'd say it's a great time to—"

"—wash it down. Yes, sir. Yep. On top of it, George," I interrupt. I try I stand up from my bench, put on a cheery smile, avoid answering his last question because, no, I did not wash the stupid carousel last week. I skip off toward the supply shed on the other side of the park before he can get on my case about anything else I'm failing to do to stupid Park and Rec standards.

"I'll be back later to check in," he calls after me.

I track the hose from the shed back to carousel. Aiming first at the base and platform and then at each pole-suspended pony, I douse the whole structure in a wide, lazy circle. Grainy gray dirt drips down the ponies, scalp to nuzzle; it snakes down their manes and long white noses, settling there in new little dirt clumps so that they're just as dirty-looking as before, but in a new way. *Great.*

Cleaning the carousel is always a two-part process: a wide sweep followed by tedious detail work, wiping the rearranged dirt from each pony's head and mane. I have no idea how the carousel gets so damn dirty, since it probably has a grand total of forty paying customers a week. Maybe dirt gnomes come at night, just to screw with me.

I turn the hose off and wind it back onto its giant plastic spool in the shed. Digging out a dusty bucket, I squeeze in some liquid soap, turn on the spider-web-covered faucet protruding from one wall. As the water slowly fills the bucket, I can't help but think of Raina. If she were here, we could make fun of hound-dog George together, of the ridiculous tasks we're both forced to do, for crap money, at work.

I sigh, jostle the bucket around with my foot a bit to redistribute the bubbles. I shouldn't have freaked out like that at her in the car. She did a nice thing for me, and I repaid her by being a total bitch. So she thinks I need some help. Who wouldn't?

Once the bucket is full, I drag it across the grass by its tendon-thin metal handle and set it beside the carousel. I dip a sponge in, soaking my arm up to the elbow.

The work is slow and painfully boring. I move down the line, doing a sloppy job, struggling to wash the dirt from each painted plaster face and mane with maximum efficiency and minimum effort.

It's then that I notice a folded piece of paper scotch-taped to the dark gray ear of the carousel's only unicorn.

Sponge still clenched in my fist, water sliding down my arm, I look around to see if anyone's watching before I pull it off the unicorn's ear and unfold it.

*Like mother like daughter*

I blink at it, like I might be able to burn it up with my eyes.

*No punctuation*—stupidly, it's the first thing that occurs to me.

The sound of kids approaching shoots me out of my trance and into action. I rip the note from the unicorn's ear and crumple it in my hand, drop the sponge back into the bucket, walk to the nearest trash can, and rip the horrible little piece of paper into confetti-small pieces. I look around—feeling those eyes on me again. Those invisible eyes that never connect to anything but air, space, ether. Nothing.

It's still three hours from the end of my shift, and George said he would come back to check on me. But I don't care. I lock the gate over the carousel, retrieve my bike from the grass, and ride to Rotisserie Chicken Outpost No. 5, the sweaty little hut in the middle of Wynnwood strip mall # 3 where Raina cashiers on Tuesdays, Wednesdays, and Thursdays until seven-thirty.

*Four days*. Not enough time. Not nearly enough time.

The cold hard truth is: I can't do this without her. I need to sink into her shoulder and bawl my eyes out. I need her to let me. I need to let myself.

But when I arrive, some rail-thin blond chick is flipping the pages of an *Us Weekly* behind the counter. Not Raina. I struggle not to break down in front of a girl I don't even know—Rain's absence alone makes everything I need to cry about right now well up fresh. I wheel my bike to the entranceway and peek my head inside.

"Hey," the girl quickly shuts the mag, gives me a once-over, then re-slops her spine back into the lazy c-curve of *I-don't-give-a-shit*.

"You need somethin'?"

The chicken smell is overpowering. "Do you know where Raina is?"

"Oh. Um . . ." I watch her chew her thin lower lip in thought. "She's at some—revealing?"

I shake my head, confused. "Revealing?"

She opens her mouth and runs her tongue back and forth behind her upper teeth. "Yeah. Some thing for a friend who bit it."

I feel my whole body go cold. *The unveiling*. It's today.

I check the time on my cell phone, murmur a quick "Thanks." I hop on my bike again, pushing off, pedaling fast. They were supposed to be at the cemetery at ten-thirty, but it's almost one o'clock now. I wasn't even planning to go, so why am I so angry with myself for missing it?

Maybe it's because I've missed the best, and most obvious, opportunity to finally see Stern's parents—practically my second family—after so long.

Or maybe it's that she's there and not me. That she knew, and I didn't.

I ride to Stern's house very slowly. A big part of me is hoping that I'll arrive too late—or even too early, so I won't have to see his relatives, and Raina, gathered in their living room along the yellow U-shaped couch Stern and I used to love to play on.

Seeing his parents again for the first time since his funeral will only cement the fact that he is gone—the solid part of him, at least. If I stretch out the space between here and there, maybe I can withhold, even for a few more minutes, that part of my brain that has not yet accommodated the loss of not only Stern, but also of his family, and of his rancher-style house in the thick of the woods, and of all the trees we used to climb, and all the mud pies we'd challenge each other to eat before we chickened out at the last moment and threw them in each other's faces instead, wet mud caking our skin, dripping from our eyelashes.

Stern: the first boy to whom I showed signs of my slow-growing boobs in a game of truth or dare. Stern: the boy who taught me how to eat a whole hunk of sea-foam green wasabi without choking to death; who taught me that the femoral artery was one of the best places to stab a person to death, if it ever came down to it; who spat on a horse once, between the eyes, after it bucked me to the dirt for no good reason and I broke my wrist in three places.

And then, somehow, weaving between the stacks of my memories, I find that I have arrived in front of Stern's brick-front house with the yellow U-shaped couch and towering army of trees and rusty basketball hoop bent just slightly to the left in the driveway.

Also in the driveway: Raina's muddy-bottomed Toyota. Deep green. I know its color from memory, but it's more than that. I can't see it, but I can sense it. I'm getting better at this game.

I lock my bike to a skinny tree in the neighbor's lawn and walk to the front door—already feeling myself go to goo in my center, light-headed. My palms are sweating and my forehead is sweating and I am definitely going to cry, any minute now.

The front door is already cracked open, and I slip in very quietly, putting my finger at the spine of the door so it won't make a noise when I re-shut the screen. I hear muffled conversation coming from a part of the living room that's out of view. I stand in the foyer for a moment and take it all in: the same family-photo-glutted walls, the quaint little kitchen with its hand-painted tiles and spoons and cast-irons hanging on hooks from the walls. A table at the entrance full of tiny, sparkle-eyed ceramic border collies. The bathroom in the foyer—door flung open—the overstuffed magazine rack and gleaming full-length mirror over the back of the door and framed Far Side cartoons. I always loved that bathroom.

Stern's mom's voice rings softly from a few feet away, and it soothes me. It calms me. This is right. I should be here. These are my people. These are my family. I take a step forward, and catch the tail end of a hushed sentence: ". . . said that to you? And you really think Olivia believes it?"

My whole body goes cold. Blood thrums between my ears.

"I can't tell if she does, honestly, Mrs. Stern." Raina's voice.

*Impossible. She couldn't possibly be telling them . . .*

"And she really said she *saw* him?" Stern's dad.

My heart stops. She is. My private confession: my grief.

"I wasn't sure if I should bring it up or not, especially right now," Raina says, voice full of faux-grief that I'm sure she's using to just *melt* their hearts right now, to poison them to me even further. "I really think she needs help, and I honestly didn't know who else to tell. Her dad's stressed out enough as it is, with the sentencing, and his wedding . . ."

Stern's mom starts crying softly—little back of the throat sobs I can tell she's trying to stave off. "She must miss him so much. She must just . . ." She trails off.

"I guess so," Raina says. "I really think she needs help. But she gets so angry if I even suggest it, you know? She won't listen."

"They really did love each other, those two," Mark says, voice low and creaky. "All three of you. Such an amazing friendship you had."

"We did. And now, I just . . . I feel like I'm losing her, too, you know?" Raina says, choked up. I adjust my footing slightly just then and a floorboard creeks. *Shit. Shit. Shit.* Raina stops mid-sentence. They all go silent. "Hello?" Beth calls out. "Is someone there?"

I stand stock-still. I've been caught.

The three of them move into the foyer, and come into sight.

They see me standing there, frozen, horrified.

Beth's hands flutter to her chest, her face going pale like *I'm* a ghost. Her tiny frame is even tinier than I remember it—deeper bags under her eyes. Dark, dark gray. Mark, too, looks gaunt and sad, so many shadows dug into his skin. And Raina just looks stunned. Or maybe I'm just seeing myself again, reflected in all of their faces.

"Olivia! Oh, honey—" Beth puts her hand to her mouth and starts to cry. Mark takes her shoulders. Raina takes her hand.

"I shouldn't have come," I choke out. "I'm sorry. For everything." And just before everything bursts right out of me—all my anger, all my grief, all my missing—I rush back out the door and onto my bike.

I'm struggling to unlock it when Raina bursts through the Stern's door and runs, panting, to stop me. "Liv. I didn't know you were coming. I . . . I didn't know you were there."

"That's why you don't talk about someone behind her back," I growl. "You never know when she might show up."

She tries to push the little bike-lock key out of my hands and take it but I push away from her, keep working the key in the lock. Her lip quivers as she watches me struggle, folding her arms around her chest.

"I only want to help you," she sobs. "That's all anyone wants. We love you."

"If you *loved* me," I shout, "you wouldn't go behind my back, to Stern's parents' house, and tell them you think I'm *crazy*. And you wouldn't repeat something I told you in confidence. But you just can't *stand* not being the center of attention, can you? You know what, Rain? If you really want to help me, then you'll just back the fuck off, okay?"

She shakes her head, tears running down her cheeks. But she doesn't try and defend herself. She turns on a heel—that long, stupid braid clapping against her back as she runs back inside. I notice Stern's parents have been standing there the whole time. Watching us. Judging me.

Heaving, belly twisted in a tight, terrible knot, I finally get the lock from the tree and hightail it out of there. I speed like crazy—everything a blur.

Mom's sentencing is in four days, and, I realize, the only person still on my side, still willing to help, is the person, two months ago, whose guts I hated. Austin Morse. The only friend I've got left.

# twenty

I call Austin as soon as I get home and realize it's the last place I want to be: alone, in my bed, thinking of Stern. Not wanting him to come, and desperate for him at the same time. Instead, I get up and walk to the end of the block, out of sight of my house; text Dad before he gets hysterical: *phone about to die. hanging out w/ Raina until late.*

Then I turn off my phone. I've been doing that a lot lately.

I leap up from the concrete soon as Austin arrives. I fling open the car door, fall into the soft leather seat. I suck that sob that has been lodged in my chest way down deep.

"So, Red, where do you want to go?"

"Just drive," I answer, looking away, drawing my knees into my chest and resting my cheek against the cold of the window. "I don't care where." *I needed him, and he came.* My body registers this in some grateful, hungry, exhausted way.

Streetlights blur past in wide streaks and I trace them with the tip of my finger along the glass. Austin moves his right hand from the gearshift to my thigh. He holds it tight, like he's worried I might float away—and his fingers there, warm, tracing along the inseam of my cut-offs, makes me tingle all over.

It's exactly the distraction I need. With Austin next to me, I don't have to think about Stern. Raina. My dad. Heather.

I don't have to think of my mom, and how there's hardly any time left at all.

He moves his hand back to the wheel to turn a hard right. I notice the thick clump of landmarks—cluster of copper palm trees in the middle of Arthur Square, the dug-out construction plots, waiting to be laid with concrete and limestone and shale and built up into other big-time high-rises, how close we are to the beach, to Oh Susannah.

"What are we doing at Ghost Town?" I ask him.

He turns just slightly to flash me a slow smile. "I have keys to an empty condo," he says. "And I thought we could check out the facilities. Make sure they're up to par before the residents move in. I mean, don't get any ideas, Tithe," he says, grinning, showing off his dimples, "I just want to talk."

We hang another right into the long, winding driveway that leads to the manicured front of the complex. I go stiff and knotty all over, the way I always do when I'm near

Ghost Town, until he runs the fingers of his right hand back through the palm of my left, and small parts of me begin, slowly, to soften.

He parks the car in the cul-de-sac in front of the visitor parking lot and we get out. My shorts cling to my thighs. It's hot, as always. The crickets are already singing out of tune in the tall grass, but everything else is dead quiet. I feel like I'm floating outside of my own body, like I'm watching from above as we walk to the front entrance. Austin turns the key gently into the big, curtain-darkened glass doors and we step inside, to the AC blasted lobby that leads, straight ahead, to elevators, stairs, the baby grand I try to ignore for the instant lump it brings to my throat, the Oceanus Ballroom; left to mail and laundry, garage and side entrances; right to the admin offices.

I'm not used to the lobby's huge glass windows being curtained-off, but they are—they were the only thing that made this whole place inviting in the least, even though they face the parking lot. It's dead-dark inside, and the elevators aren't running yet, so we use the light of his cell phone to find our way to the stairs. Our hands brush together as we climb. "Hey," he whispers, playfully. "No funny business, Tithe."

"Well, if they didn't make this staircase so *narrow*," I answer, pressing into the side of his body like we've got no choice but to squeeze together, "maybe I wouldn't have to."

"Yeah, it's really too bad about how little space we've

got to walk," Austin says, pressing back into me. "I'm definitely going to have to bring this to Ted's attention."

Something in me is beginning to loosen. Images of Stern's ghost on the beach, and in my room, and at the piano in my mom's studio float through my mind as we make our way through the darkness. I try to banish each one.

We climb, pressed together, for what feels like a long time. Our hands brush again and he interlaces his fingers with mine. My skin goes hot. His palm feels clammy. The staircase smells like the inside of an old wine cellar, maybe—vaguely sweet and raw and very cold. When we reach the door that says *Floor 6*, he pulls his hand from mine to open it.

We stop outside a door marked *#608* and we kick our sandals off and organize them beside the door. The hallway carpet is plush, very soft. His cell phone, our only source of light in the windowless hallway, makes our toes look like bright little aliens against a floor of material dark as mulch, soft as fresh dirt.

"Well, here we are." He almost sounds nervous as he jiggles the keys into the door and pulls it open for us.

"Whoa. Here we are, indeed." I'm temporarily amazed as we step inside the palatial condo, its marble floors flooded with slowly waning sunlight from the floor-to-ceiling windows looking right onto the ocean. I feel the heat off Austin's body centimeters behind me, feel it at my back, against my skin as I walk to the big glass door leading to the porch and slide it open so sweet salty ocean air floods in to us, sends my hair wild for a moment around my face.

My whole body is buzzing—wondering what Austin's hands will feel like on my skin. Wondering how he'll touch me, if we'll work, wrapped in each other, what his mouth will feel like on my mouth. Wondering if being with him will quiet all the anxious, spinning wheels of my brain.

I come back in and we sit down on the cold marble floor beside each other. I feel him looking at me, searching for something, and then something comes—a quiet sob I try to suppress but can't. Despite my attempts to blot them out, the events of this afternoon are still beating through me. Stern is still beating through me. I push him away, with every cell of my being, to focus on Austin.

Austin is life, new life—beautiful, funny, unexpectedly kind Austin—big hands and freckles and muscles and reassuring confidence.

"Olivia," he says, urging me to look at him. I do, finally. "Remember what we talked about? You need to let it go. Let all this shit go with your mom. Please, promise me."

I shake my head. He thinks this is about Mom—and I know that, in part at least, he's right, and this tugs at me even more. "All this *shit*?" I repeat.

"I didn't mean it like that. You know I didn't. Come here, Red." He grabs my shoulders, and I try to shed his hands but he won't let me, his grip strong, insistent. "Just relax."

"It's hard to relax when someone's telling you to relax."

"I'm not telling you. I'm making you." His fingers knead along my shoulders, up my neck, down my spine, down, down. I shiver beneath his touch. "Does that feel good?"

"I don't know," I answer.

"You don't know?" He sounds hurt, like no one's ever told him before that he can actually do something less-than-perfectly.

"Harder," I answer.

"Really?"

"I'm not going to break, Austin."

A pause. His hands find my ribcage, move slowly upward, fingers very close now to the bottom of my breasts. I shiver some more, waiting, wanting him. He moves his mouth right up to my ear. "You sure about that?"

"Yeah," I murmur. "I'm sure."

"Well, then . . ." And then he flips me around—strong hands, strong arms—to face him and his mouth is touching my mouth, slow and electric, and he's kissing me. Sentence left unfinished, hanging there forever between the cliff and the long, steep, rocky fall. His big hands move up and down my arms, my waist, my legs, grip me hard, like he's never wanted to touch someone so badly before. Like he can't get enough.

Austin's lips, Austin Morse's lips, are soft. Our tongues move together, test the ridges of each other's teeth and lips. He wraps his arm around my waist and pushes my back against the sliding glass door, running his hands over my chest, soft, then moving them downward as I feel my legs go to jelly, my brain go to jelly, everything in me rushing, buzzing, humming.

"Olivia." He runs his fingers, slowly, to the button of my shorts. He works quickly. I help him. I want them off. Our fingers work together at the button until it comes loose, and he pulls at the zipper, slides it down, slides the shorts down over my legs, over my feet, to the other side of the room. His hands return to my legs, to my thighs, to the soft triangle of my underwear.

I move my hands up and down the ridges of his chest, slide his shirt up over his head. He pulls my tank top over my head. I've never hooked up with a boy like Austin before—a boy so flawlessly sure of himself, he doesn't even need to ask me what I want.

"You're beautiful. God—you're so beautiful," he whispers into my ear, his breath tickly and warm. "I've wanted to do this for a long time." He kisses my mouth, and the little divot in my neck.

"Wait—" I freeze beneath him—I hear something. *Someone.*

He kisses my neck, my ear. "What's the matter?" He tries to pull me closer to him but I inch away.

"No—stop for a sec." I crane my ear toward the wall to my left. "Do you hear that? Someone's crying. . . ." I sit up. "Do you really *not* hear that?"

He sits up, too, hair mussed, his bee-stung lips moving

toward my ear. He nibbles at it. "You're probably just hearing the gulls outside."

"No. It's—it's not coming from outside." I meet his eye. He bites his bottom lip. "Has anyone moved in here yet?"

"Nope. We're all alone. Trust me. Okay?" He moves one finger to my chest, traces a line between my breasts, down my belly button. And the rush in my skull just then mutes every other sound.

"Okay," I say. And we're at it again. He lifts me so I'm on top of him, my legs wrapped around his hips. He lowers me back to the ground, kissing my stomach, kissing lower, and lower, and lower. Even though the marble floor is cold and hard against my spine, I don't notice it. I don't notice anything else. But his lips. His tongue. His breath on my skin.

*Buzzzzzzzz.* His cell phone. We pause, breathing hard. "Ignore it," he says. *Buzzzzzzzz.*

I smile, playfully, reach my hand out toward the pocket of his discarded shorts. "You supposed to be fooling around with some other chick tonight, Morse?"

"Hey—stop. Just put it down—" he tries to bat it out of my hands.

"Don't worry," I say, opening the screen. "I won't tell her I'm—"

But then, I freeze, eyes locked on the text on the screen.

*Are you keeping an eye on her?*

"Who is it?" Austin asks. But I barely register the words he's saying.

I just keep staring at the message, trying to make sense of it: *Are you keeping an eye on her?*

"*Who* is it, Tithe?"

*Are you keeping an eye on her?*

I push him off of me, grab my shirt from the floor, start to re-dress. "Ted," I answer, staring at him hard. "He wants to know if you're *keeping an eye on me*."

He grabs his phone from the floor, stares at the screen, looks back at me, horrified. "Olivia—I can explain."

"What does he mean, *are you keeping an eye on me*?" I'm suddenly so cold, I can barely stop my teeth from chattering. "Answer me, Austin. Have you been, like, *babysitting* me or something? Is that what this is?"

He reaches for my hand but I scoot away, searching for my tossed-off clothing. "No. Please, Olivia. Not at all." He shakes his head, rubs the back of his neck. I grab my crumpled-up shorts and underwear and wriggle them over my legs.

"You're lying," I spit out. "And you suck at it."

He sighs, grabbing up his own clothes, holding them up to his chest instead of actually putting them on. "Okay," he says. "Ted asked me to take you on a date, as a favor. But that was only at the beginning—"

"A favor?" My voice comes out like a screech, like the sound of the distant gulls. I close my eyes, open them again. The room is spinning. "So, I'm some *charity* case?"

"Listen—it was just at *first*."

"And what were you supposed to get, huh? What was your big prize for doing him that favor?"

Austin looks away. "A new car," he mumbles.

"A new *car*?" The room is spinning. I have to get out of here. "Oh, *awesome*, that's *fucking awesome*. You know what? Fuck you, Austin. I never should have fucking *believed* you were honestly this *changed*—"

"Olivia, *listen* to me. I'm trying to be honest with you. I like you! I really do! I wouldn't have done anything with you if—"

"Yeah, well I wouldn't have done anything with *you*, either!" I'm fighting to get into my jean shorts. My fingers are shaking so hard I can barely get them buttoned. "You think that every single girl in the world is just *dying* to hook up with you."

"Come on, Olivia. Please. Don't be like that. I'm trying to be honest."

"It's a little too late for that, Austin. I know what I am to you. I know what I am to Ted. Totally bat-shit insane. Just like my mother."

"You're wrong. What do I have to do to convince you?" he moves toward me, tries to grab me at the waist. I scoot away, put my hands over my chest.

"Some crazy who needs to be watched all the time. You never actually cared."

"That's not true."

I grab my purse from the floor, run to the door, and let

myself out—Austin still only in boxers, clothes hugged into his chest, calling to me as I make my stumbling escape through the dark: "Come on. Quit it with the bullshit, Olivia. Come back here."

Finally, I reach the lobby, run across the marble floor, breath ragged. I hear the sobbing again, the distant wail of a girl, and it is not until I'm outside that I realize I'm the one crying.

# twenty-one

I think of Mom as I half-jog-half-walk home, down the boardwalk, from Ghost Town.

I think of how it started for her—when her brain started twisting things up and spitting them out her mouth all wrong.

All these people—the well-meaning people trying to keep me safe—I know, logically, that's all they want to do. So why do I feel so much resentment? Why does every new truth feel like a knife in the gut? And why does it feel like *I'm* the only person in the whole world on the outside of what's going on *inside* of me?

*Damn.* Austin. I was just supposed to be using *him.* As a distraction. As a not-Stern . . . as an anything-but-Stern. It wasn't supposed to get this far. I wasn't supposed to maybe on some level kind of *like* Austin.

But I do. I did. I really liked being around him. I thought he'd grown up a little, that he was different, that we had something there. . . . *God.* To think I really believed that Austin-fucking-Morse actually, truly cared for me, of his own volition. To think I *bought* into his bullshit act. Austin Morse dated me for a new car. *A car.* Jesus.

I'm so stupid. So, so stupid. So blind. To think I've wasted even a spare minute of time with him, when I've got so little of it to spare.

Four days. It's all I've got.

Stern, Stern, why did you have to die? Why didn't you stay?

I turn my cell phone back on. One new text from Dad: *Be safe, darlin'. Not too late. Luv, Dad.* The only times he's calm like this are when he's immersed in Heather. And I'm actually grateful for it. If not for her, he'd be his own one-father-crazy-show by now—forty thousand texts per every hour he doesn't hear from me. He probably wouldn't even let me out of the house anymore, not at this point.

The seagulls shriek from the sand, shaking their bills, flurrying their wings. Their cries sound nothing like the cries I heard in Ghost Town.

I can't imagine what Austin's doing right now and I don't care. Maybe he's still standing gape-mouthed in the doorway, expecting me to return, to strip naked right before I fall, desperate, into his chest, to confess to all my pathetic weaknesses and ask him to save me from myself.

Then that warm feeling floods my legs, just for an instant—his hands on my waist, my chest, his lips on my neck. *Ugh.* I almost let him take off my underwear.

I stuff my hands into the pockets of my shorts and kick some crumpled-up trash out of my path as I walk. The sky is dark now. I wonder if Austin really thinks I'm beautiful, sexy, amazing . . . or if Ted bribed him to say all that, too. Maybe it was Ted who told him all the moves to make: *Get her loosed-up with a massage. Compliment her. And then undress her, son. Compliment her some more. Pretend not to care if she's wearing granny-panties.*

*But Da-ad . . .*

*Don't 'but dad' me, Austin. Olivia really needs our support right now. If you don't tell her how much you like her boobs, she might just go kill herself.*

I'm halfway home when my phone buzzes inside my purse. Probably Austin, calling with more excuses. I lift it out, blink at the number on the screen.

Unknown.

I skirt a clot of preteens clogging up about half a block of the boardwalk, find a quiet bench ahead before I answer. "Hello?" My voice comes out all wobbly.

"Olivia?" A woman's voice. An older woman.

"Yes . . . ?" I wait.

The woman sighs. "Oh, good. I was worried I'd written the number wrong." She laughs a little, then clears her throat. "It's Deb Kilmurray—Greg Foster's neighbor. We met on Saturday?"

My belly releases some of its knots. "Oh, yeah. Of course." I try to keep the confusion from my voice. I can't imagine why she would be calling. I expected Dad, or Austin, or Raina. Not her.

"How are you, honey?"

“I’m fine,” I say cautiously. “How are you?”

“Fine, fine. You said to call if I had any more information about your uncle,” she says, clearing her throat.

“My . . . ?” For a second I forget that I told her Greg Foster was my estranged relative. I catch myself just in time. “Oh, right. Of course.” I press the soles of my sandals against the edge of the bench, fiddle with a loose splinter on the arm. I wait for her to continue.

“Well, really, it’s not new information. That is, I mean, I was just wrong. I’m not even sure whether it matters. . . .” I hear the sound of rustling behind her—she’s sorting through papers? “Oh, dear. I’m bungling this, aren’t I? I just thought you might want to know. I was wrong about where—where Greg—excuse me, Mr. Foster—left his money. I think I told you he left it to a nature preserve, but—”

“You did. You said he was a big bird watcher or whatever.” Something tightens in my stomach. I have a breathless feeling.

“He was, and that’s why I think I made the mistake—because of the Cullen Nature Preserve. But, it wasn’t the nature preserve. It was the hospital that he left his money to. Shepherd-Cullen Hospital—they specialize in schizophrenia research, apparently.”

“What did you just say?” I say slowly into the phone: now suddenly an alien piece of plastic in my fist.

“Oh. Is the connection bad?” A muffled sound of tapping against the receiver: “I said that Greg Foster left all of his money to a psychiatric hospital called Shepherd-Cullen. Over four million dollars. To their schizophrenia research department. And you know what?" she continues, her voice slightly higher-pitched. "He didn't even leave it in his own name."

"Whose name did he leave it in?"

"What was it? Oh, yes, I have it written down right here—Miriam Tithe. That was her name."

My heart near stops.

*Mom.*

"Hello? Are you there?"

"I—yes. I'm here," I hear myself say. Everything is spinning around me. The ocean, the boardwalk, the clot of preteens sharing a single bottle of beer in a paper bag. *Mom.*

"I just find it very strange," Mrs. Kilmurray babbles on. "He was so friendly—we used to chat quite frequently. . . . But he never once mentioned . . ."

*He abandoned her case, killed himself, and left all of his money in Mom's name. Why?*

"I'm—I'm sorry, Ms. Kilmurray. I have to go," I stammer.

"Oh! Of course, dear. Let me know if I can—"

*Click.*

It's almost ten by the time I get home; I hear the TV on in Dad and Heather's room. *CSI: Miami.* Wynn must be asleep by now. But someone left the small light over the kitchen sink on for me, a chocolate-dipped fortune cookie tied with ribbon on the kitchen table. The cellophane wrapper says *David and Heather*, is dotted with tiny white hearts—a sample of what they'll have at the wedding, I bet.

I wonder what he and Mom had at their wedding.

I take the cookie and pad upstairs to my room, press my back against the frame of my bed, and try to make sense of the senseless. *Four days.* Greg Foster. *Four days.* What an absurd number. I can't help but feel the universe is trickling out new bits of the puzzle, so slow, just to mess with me. Stern.

I gather my laptop onto my knees on the floor, drag up every article I can find from last year, when Stern was killed. Almost sixty separate tabs. Each one containing the possibility of something I've overlooked, of a pattern hidden between the endless stream of words, like in one of those Magic Eye puzzles.

I focus on my favorite picture: a wide-angle shot of Stern, dressed up nice in a suit and skinny tie, leaned against Mom's piano. His eyes in the photograph are dark and serious, and I imagine they contain a tiny mirror reflecting the rest of the Mom's studio: her Turkish rugs and stacks of books and sheet music, the vintage ceramic lamp on top of the piano, a small framed drawing I'd made for her in a distant corner of the shot.

I wonder, as I stare into his eyes in the photograph, if he can see me right back, if everything, somewhere, is still exactly as it used to be.

But what I really want is to go back and make things different. I wish I never once dismissed my mother on the phone when she annoyed me. I wish I'd never passed up a single chance to hug her, fiercely, to walk with her through the thick broke-bark trees behind our house, along the surf, to set up a picnic blanket with her in the middle of the night when the waves were always terrifying and huge and cold.

Every single time I missed helping her prepare dinner so I could wait around the mall for Jose Ruiz or Rece Zayden or Mark "the loon" Looner to maybe show up and mostly ignore me, every time I did not tell her exactly how much I loved her—with every cell, with every breath, with every streak of paint, every sway of my fingers down a page—I want it back.

*Four days.* I stare at more articles, more pictures, because I can't stop. And when I reach the pictures of Tanya Leavin, the girl who disappeared the exact same time Stern did, who looks so much like Raina, I can't ignore the cramped, unsettled feeling that comes into my belly. I've made a real mess of things, with everyone who's bothered to care.

I set the computer down. But I'm still itching to do something, itching for a distraction. In the closet, I drag out the box of my old art supplies from school—a box I haven't bothered to open since I left, months ago. I rip the packing tape off the cardboard slowly, letting my hands hover over the flaps of the box before I air out its innards.

The smell of it gets me first—the mineral smell of all the hard tubes of my oil paints, scattered within a lidless shoebox on top of my charcoals and sketchbooks, my linseed oil and gouache and watercolor, dirtied-up chamois, a hardened tangle of paint rags, and a long, slender wood box full of sable-hair wood-handled paintbrushes and reed pens, their tips black with old India ink.

I'm transported by this smell—to dark-curtained rooms full of easels and brushes and the paint-spattered floor, to stretcher boards and the grain of loose linen and the way my fingers would ache after stretching too many canvases in a row, to everything my life used to be, when my parents' separation was the worst thing that could possibly happen, and was (I thought) only temporary, at worst. When I still had Stern to show snow to on Skype.

My fingers fumble through the shoebox, lifting all my paints, one by one, onto the floor in a sunburst arc. I can't tell which color is which anymore without great, inexact effort, or by the names stated explicitly on their labels. There is still some oily wetness around the neck of one of the tubes. It gets on my fingers as I lift it out—red, I'd guess. Only slightly darker than a stop sign, and definitely red. Red oils take forever to dry, longer than any other color.

Near the bottom of the shoebox, my fingers grip something distinctly un-paint-like. They inch the foreign object out and onto my palm. A CD.

I flip it over. Marked with dark pen across its center:

*L.STERN, PIANO GOD*, and subtitled: *Lucas Stern vs. Juilliard: Practice sessions of our nation's foremost musical savant.*

My heart thwunks around in my chest, stunned that I'd forgotten about this for so, so long. The CD he gave me *to remember him by*. That's what he'd said that day—the day we kissed, dust and heat rising around us like a fog. The day my eyes changed. The last day I ever saw him, alive. I never listened to it.

I just stare at it for a long time before pulling another relic out of my closet—a CD player from early middle school—and plugging it into the socket near my bed. My hands are shaking a little bit, my throat all lumpy. I slip the CD inside and press play.

At first: a few seconds of thick silence that make me think he forgot to even press *record* before he started playing, but then, it's him. It's him. His voice. My whole body starts shaking. His living voice.

*Hi, Liver. It's me, Lucas Stern, piano god. (See front of CD for confirmation of this title.) I made you this CD to preserve, in memory, a time in my life prior to my being internationally adored, and accepted early to Juilliard, of course. Duh. So . . .* he whistles, long, soft; *here goes, baby. Here goes. Oh—and one more thing—thanks for, uh, thanks for listening. And, ya know . . . for being my best friend. Okay. Enough with the corny sentimental shit.*

I drag myself onto my bed and shut my eyes and listen because I can do nothing else. Every note he plays swallows me new, reincarnates me, swallows me up again. I can't stop seeing his face as he'd play—so serious, his eyes so supernaturally clear, almost—like he understood something big in those moments, bigger than the shit we know in the trap of our skulls. Big like life, and death, and love. Big like things ancient and overwhelming and universal but still somehow ungraspable to most.

Then an off note in the recording startles me from my reverie—a note just a little bit flatter than I remember it being, every time I'd hear him play in Mom's studio. *Weird. Stern was* never *off.* The song repeats itself, or, more accurately—Stern repeats the song, over and over again. And each time the note comes around, it's flat. Definitely flat. I let the tape continue to play, all knotted up by nostalgia, suddenly moved to pull out one of my old sketchbooks from my art supply box and give it a flip-through.

I flip through sheaths of crappy old sketches and stop at an old sketch of Stern's face. He was in my room that day—I see him still—sitting with his spine against the wood frame of my bed. He wanted me to draw him like a tintype, flat-mouthed. I started. *No smiling*, I kept telling him, but then he keep cracking up, because he wasn't allowed to. *Stern, I can't draw you if you keep moving. You're just going to look like a freak—all of your features out of place.* He was laughing so hard, hyena-ish, he even stopped worrying about covering up the little gap between his front teeth. And so I caught it, exaggerated the gap so that in the drawing he looks like he's missing a whole tooth up there.

*You look like a proper hick, now, Sternum,* I'd told him. And he donkeyed-out his teeth, and with an invisible banjo, began to sing, *Oh! Susannah, don't you cry for me, I come from Alabama with a banj-y on mah kneeeee.* Over the notes of his recording, I start to sing our old song, quietly, to myself as I stare at my haywire charcoal scrawl of his face, tears coming again, fast and loose: "I come from Alabama, a banjo on my knee, I'm goin' to Louisiana, my true love—"

"—for to see, it rained all night the day I left, the weather it was dry, the sun so hot I froze to death, Liver. Don't you cry."

He's here. Real, or mirage. I don't even care. He's *here*.

"Stern!" I cry out.

He has big circles under his eyes, and a face that is not quite fixed in the solid way of the living, and, behind his lips: a glimpse into that dark valley of the whole of existence.

"Liv." He looks at me—those dark, serious eyes. "It's getting harder for me to come. Much harder. But I did it."

He pauses for a moment. I see his chest rising, kind of wavering in and out, as though he's short of breath. I watch his body shiver within his Christmas flannel, the pale, grainy gray of his skin. I miss him. Even when he's here, next to me. A logical part of me knows it's not true, it's not real. And I miss him, the certainty of him. His eyes go wide. "Hey—why does this sound so familiar?"

"It's your recital song," I remind him, practically pleading, as though that will bring it all back: his memory, his life. "The one we just played, in Mom's studio." We listen together for a few more moments, silent.

"You were recording it?"

I shake my head slowly. "You made me a CD. I just found it."

"When did I do that? When is this from?"

"It's from the last time I saw you. Right before I went back to school." I gulp down a new lump in my stupid lumpy throat. I try and smile. "But you must have been off your game."

"Off my game?" He smiles, pale, perfect. "Impossible."

"Listen."

I skip it back and we listen for a bit. The flat note comes around and I watch his face tilt slightly to the left, wincing. "*See?* That note!"

"It *is* off. But it's not me. The whole scale is fucked up. . . ." He closes his eyes, bites his lip, starts playing air scales along with the music. "It's the piano."

"It can't be Mom's," I say. "Hers was *always* tuned, like, religiously. What piano did you record this on?"

And as soon as I ask it, the answer falls out of my mouth. "Ghost Town."

We stare at each other for a second. "But, wait—Ghost Town wasn't even *done* before . . ." At the last second, I can't say it. Stupid.

"Before I died," he finishes for me. His whole body is

shaking, the light half-wavery quality of skin almost glowing behind the gray of it.

"But the lobby was done," I say slowly. A strange prickly feeling is working its way up my back. "It was furnished and everything, so they could show it off to perspective dickwad clients. Anyway, they have that baby grand in the lobby. You must have gone there, Stern. You must have played there sometimes."

Stern closes his eyes. For a long time, he is quiet. Then he says: "I must have found some way to sneak in—so I could practice at night." His face almost glows as rare memories flow through him in tiny waves. "I remember walking up dunes . . . all that saw grass. It smelled muddy."

My chest is hammering, hot, wild. I try to work it out in my head—what might have happened. *If he wasn't at Mom's that night—and he remembers sneaking into Ghost Town to practice*—"you must have been there the night it happened!" I say, my words all hot and rushing together.

He shrugs. "I don't know. It's a blank."

"Okay, just close your eyes for a second," I tell him, "and listen to the recording. Assuming you were there, it's what you would have been playing, so, maybe . . . maybe something will come back." I search his face as he listens, as though I can pry my way into his brain and dislodge the clogs of his memory with my eyeballs. "Anything? Even something fuzzy?"

Stern's eyes move over the drawing, his pointer finger hovering right over all the vectors separating black from white, shape from nothing. "I remember light reflecting through the windows—sudden light." His face is carved in thought, trying to remember. "But that's it. Everything else is shadow."

"Those windows face the parking lot," I say slowly. "Sudden light could mean headlights. Did someone show up while you were playing? Do you remember hearing anything?"

He bites his lip, his face contorted, as though he's in pain. "Yelling," he finally says.

"Yelling?" I prompt, urging him on.

He opens his eyes. "Voices. An argument."

"What kind of voices? Do you remember what they were saying?"

Stern's face shows signs of pain, of struggle. He's trying to stay here, just to remain with me, as Nowhere tries to pull him back, back to the darkness. He wraps his arms around himself, keeps shaking.

"What's happening? Are you okay?" I'm terrified he'll disappear before anything can be solved, again. "Please. Please try and stay."

"I'm trying, Liv. It's hard. . . ." His breath is coming short. "Everything's so foggy. I'm—I'm having trouble even remembering why I'm here—what I'm doing."

I bite my lip, thinking. We sit in silence for a minute, suspended; consumed. "Ghost Town," I announce, leaping to my feet. The fire in my belly is rising, rising. "Maybe there's some kind of record somewhere of that night—documents that prove people would have been there—workers? Or, what if there was a break-in? Something you got caught up in, by accident? Though . . ." I stop to consider, pushing the hair from my eyes, "there'd be police reports, if there was, and I feel like it's something I would have already known about. Something Dad would have told me. . . ." Despite the frigid air-conditioning of the condo, my forehead's beaded with sweat. "Ghost Town," I repeat, sure—truly—of nothing else in the world. "We have to go there. Now."

Stern manages to nod.

I just hope he can stay long enough for me to get him there. I race around my room, searching for the key to Ghost Town that Dad gave me last week. I rummage through every paint-smattered pair of shorts, every windbreaker, every inch of carpeting. Finally, I turn to Stern, who's pacing diagonally across the room, seeming almost to float above the ground. "*Shit.*"

"What?" He stops pacing, a single dark curl falling over his eye. "What's wrong?"

"The key's missing. It's gone."

"Are you sure?" He tugs at the ends of his sleeves. "There's got to be another one somewhere."

"Yeah—there should be; my dad has, like, four of everything. But he keeps them hidden. He's a weirdo. He probably came in here when I was gone and took back the key he'd given me. He's probably worried I would abuse my privileges."

"Which you would have," Stern points out, smiling weakly. He looks patchy, less solid than usual. He's pacing, bouncing up and down on his toes, flexing and unflexing his fingers. "Can't you call him?"

When that fire starts burning inside of him, Stern can't be stopped. It probably explains why he's able to keep coming back to me, why he never gave up on me, on getting where he needs to go. It explains why he was Mom's favorite student, too. He had more passion than anyone she'd ever met, ever taught, ever witnessed.

I shake my head. "He'd ask too many questions. Ever since I flunked out of school, he thinks all of my intentions are delinquent. If I asked him for a set of keys, he'd stand there watching every move I made."

Stern keeps up his furious pacing. "Is there anyone else you *can* call?"

I think for a moment. My stomach feels leaden now.

Austin.

# twenty-two

I pick up my cell phone. Austin's already called me four times, texted once more. *Olivia, we really need to talk. Please call me. –A.*

*A,* I text. *Still not ready to talk. Soon. But can you do me a favor?*

*Ok.* He texts back, right away. *Anything.*

I turn away from Stern, not wanting him to see what I write next. *Leave the lobby door to Ghost Town open for me? Think I might have dropped my bra somewhere on the floor on my way out.*

I watch the cell phone in my hands, still turned away. Austin responds, again, almost instantly: *Sure, no problem.*

Nerves vein through my belly. I turn back around. Stern stares at me. "Well?" he asks.

"We're in."

"Who did you text?"

"Austin Morse," I say. He shoots me a look and I turn away again, suddenly feeling dirty, self-conscious, exposed. I step into my huge closet and quickly change from my cutoffs and T-shirt into a soft black cotton dress that I pull off my floor and soft-soled flats.

"You think that's a good idea?"

I turn back to him. "Unless you can slip through walls at will, we don't have any other options." I throw my cell phone into my purse, take in a thick gulp of air. "We're going to get to the bottom of this, Lucas."

He smiles sadly at me. I haven't called him by his real name in years. No one has, other than his parents. But, somehow, it returns us for a moment to who we are, in our cells, who we will always be—something he hasn't yet forgotten. Olivia and Lucas. My Lucas. For a moment, we stand there, facing each other, held in the stillness.

Then my cell phone buzzes, and the moment shatters. I read Austin's text: *Unlocked.* So curt.

I move to Stern, swift, and put my mouth to his cold cheek. The gesture doesn't quite work—something ripples, like the air between us refuses to breach the space that separates the living from the dead. And so I cannot touch him—not really, not like I'd like to.

So he follows me outside, both of us quieter than death as we close the front door.

I hop on my bike and Stern climbs on behind me.

He shivers against my back as we ride. I know our closeness must hurt him. But for me, it's a miracle just to have him a little bit longer. If Stern is stuck, if Mom is stuck, I, too, am stuck.

*Four days.* Wish Mom could be outside right now—wide open view, so much space, all the thick trees wiggling their roots into the soil. Plumeria—a passing breeze, armed with that heavy, soapy smell.

Soon things will be different. She gave me life and I will save hers. I will make it better.

Stern hangs on, somehow. Neither of us speak. I pedal harder, sweat pouring down my face, salt on my lips, on my tongue. It's the ache in my belly, the second heart that pounds for her, that propels me faster than usual. Palms blur past, the gray shine of their skin and leaves, the wide mother arms of the banyan, the waving wrists of wild sage.

Soon, Ghost Town looms to my right as I pull my bike up the driveway and Stern and I hop off. The eerie quiet sets me on edge. I walk slowly through the lawn to the entrance, twist the knob: unlocked, just as Austin said it'd be.

Stern and I meet eyes. My stomach is a system of hard knots as we walk quietly through the wide, dark, marbled lobby. I'm glad he's here with me. I think it's the only reason I'm able to go through with this at all. He's the only reason I was ever able to go through most everything, after all.

The parlor room with the baby grand is off to our right, and we immediately go in and start wandering the room in the darkness, looking for some sign, or hint, some glimmer of hope.

I stare around at the cheesy Monet on the far wall with its gilt frame, the lush potted ferns in either corner by the windows. If someone had broken in—what would they have possibly wanted with some parlor furniture and an otherwise virtually empty condo building? But maybe they were after something inside the office . . . ? Computer equipment, telephones?

"I'm going to look over here," I whisper to Stern, and turn down a dark corridor to the office. The door is part-open. I reach along the wall for the light switch but decide not to: I can't shake the niggling feeling that Austin might still be here, in the building, desperate to talk. And what if he is? What if he comes in and finds me like this, snooping around? Will he tell Ted? What excuse will I give him?

Heart beating quick, I start at the bottom drawer and pull out a file full of loose papers—searching in the darkness for anything that might lead me back to what happened that night, to who might have been here, arguing.

Nothing. No clues. I'm starting to feel hopeless. A knot is building in my throat, threatening to choke me. I don't know what I expected to find—a note written in blood? A signed testimonial from a murderer?

*Think, Olivia, think.* Stern broke in so he could play on the piano. If it *was* a break-in, why would anyone have any real interest in actually forcing their way into this place?

Maybe for the same reason Austin brought me earlier . . . for all the empty space, the dark corners, the places to take off clothing. I spot a spare set of keys, just sitting out in plain sight on the desk.

And another thought occurs to me.

Maybe it wasn't a break-in.

Maybe the person who showed up that night had a key.

Except no one had keys to the unfinished building at that point other than my father . . .

And Ted.

"Olivia," a low male voice says from behind me.

I freeze, letting several papers fall from my hands. Everything goes still; for all I know, time itself has momentarily stopped. And then I turn around, and face him.

# twenty-three

*Click*. Ted Oakley turns and carefully locks the door behind him. My heart speeds up. Ted. Ted could have been here that night. Ted could have been here with one of his girls—Austin said there might have been a bunch of them.

I will Stern to come back to me. Could he still be in the parlor room? *Lucas. Lucas. My Lucas.* "What—what are you doing here? Where's Austin?" I say, all the tone sucked out of my voice. No fear, no passion. A flatliner of a voice.

He doesn't answer my question. "Olivia," he says my name again slowly, in his same concerned-father tone. "Austin is sleeping. As you should be. Do you know what time it is?"

I stare at him, look around. "Yes." I start shaking. I don't want to be shaking, I don't want him to know that I'm terrified. That I'm suddenly terrified of *him*. "I know what time it is," I say, trying to keep my voice steady. "Austin was supposed to meet me here," I lie. "He texted me. We were going to meet."

Ted stares at me, like I'm the craziest bat he's ever seen. "I don't know what you're talking about, honey. Austin went to sleep hours ago. He's got practice in the morning." His voice is slow and obnoxiously calm. He steps closer to me, puts a hand out toward my head like he means to take my temperature. "Are you feeling all right? Should we call up your father and have him come get you?"

I back away from him, straight into his desk, sick of being treated like a child, like an idiot, like a crazy person. "That's not true. I got a text back from him. I . . . *someone* sent me a text."

Ted smiles and shakes his head.

I go on. "You—you had him keep an *eye* on me. It wasn't because you were worried about me, was it? No . . ." it's all dawning on me now, so fast and heavy my brain can barely keep up with the racing of my heart. "No, you asked him to spy on me because I was looking into Mom's case, because I realized she didn't do it. There's no way she did it." *You did it*, I think, but I don't say it. Something stops me—something about the definiteness of that statement that I think might push him over whatever edge he's teetering on.

Might push *me* over the edge. And still, still, I don't want it to be true.

Ted stands there, looking at me like I'm on drugs, like I've just told him if he drinks my Kool-Aid, he'll be transported to a magical otherworldly place where everything is free and nobody ages. "Oh—honey—you're *not* okay, are you?" He approaches me, lays his big-lug hand on my shoulder, rubbing it gently before I shuck it off. The bump in his nose leaves a crooked shadow on his face.

"I've been worried about you," Ted says gently. "We all have. This is how it started for your mother, you know, when she was about your age, wasn't it? Have you been . . . imagining things?"

"What? No. I'm not *imagining* things. Why does *everyone* think—?"

"You know, Olivia," he interrupts, "it *is* genetic. I'm sorry to say, most schizophrenics experience their first episode as teenagers." There's a worried little smile on his now clean-shaven face; his hands smooth at his suit jacket. He's wearing a suit. At midnight. Ink black. "I'm just worried about you—understand? I don't know what you're looking for." He motions to the open files, the scattered papers. "But you're not going to find anything here. Do you understand me? There's nothing to find. You think that everything is working against you, that something is *wrong*, that everyone's trying to *harm* you." He shakes his head, stooping to collect the paper on the floor and place it neatly back into the bottom drawer of the desk. "That's paranoid, sweetie."

"Why are you here?" I blurt out, watching him shut the drawer, and straighten up. "If I'm just imagining things, what are you doing here?"

"Well, some of us have to *work* quite late, little miss. I know you don't understand that. Your parents never did too much working in their lives, after all—not to pass judgment, mind you. But, well—we all get where we are for a reason." Something's happening to his voice—it's getting higher, faster.

"Someone took Austin's phone tonight. Someone texted me. Was it you? You knew I would be here, didn't you?" He's still looking at me with a furrowed brow, like everything I'm saying is entirely ridiculous.

And some part of me thinks he's right. How could Stern's murderer possibly be Ted? I must be insane to even think it. He's been such a saint to us. He brought Dad in on Ghost Town as his business partner when he needed work, and he got Mom a new lawyer right after Greg Foster quit . . . Greg Foster, who killed himself just after leaving the case. Greg Foster, who left an enormous amount of money in Mom's name.

The pieces are starting to slot together in my skull. There's a rushing between my ears.

Greg Foster was going to get Mom acquitted. He told us so. But then he suddenly split and Carol took over, thanks again to Ted, and that was that.

Ted *wanted* Mom to get locked up.

"You framed her," I say suddenly, certainty settling through my bones. My whole body goes hot, then cold, then hot again—like someone's standing inside of it, flipping a switch.

"Honey, I really don't know what you're—"

"My question is *why*," I say, cutting him off, trying to keep my voice from shaking.

His facial muscles start to twitch just slightly. "No one knows why mental illness strikes, Olivia. It's one of the many tragedies—"

"No! Why him? Why Stern? What happened that night?"

Ted has pulled his phone out of his pocket and begins dialing a number. I knock the phone from his hands, then back away quickly, my back against the wall. He looks at me in utter shock.

"Tell me what happened that night. I want to know about your girlfriend, the one you brought over here. Were you just here to screw around?"

A flash of something that almost looks like sadness passes across Ted's face and wrinkles his brow. But his voice is unemotional. "Who told you about Tanya?"

I suck in a deep breath. "Tanya . . . " I say slowly, drawing it out, remembering. Ever so slowly. The girl who looks like Raina. *Tanya Leavin.*

The girl who disappeared around the time of Stern's death. The one who was wearing a pink scarf in the newspaper photo.

Disappeared. She disappeared. "What did you do to her?" My mind is spinning and I feel sick. *I need to call my dad. I need Stern. I need to scream.*

"You don't know what you're saying, Olivia. You're *sick*. Okay?" He comes back over to me, takes my wrists hard in his hands. I try to tug away, but he's gripping too hard. "Sit down. Okay? Just *sit down*, Olivia. Just. Sit." He forces me down, into Dad's swivel-back leather office chair, his hands moving to my shoulders, pushing them back.

"Stop. Get off of me." I try to swipe at him, to push him out of the way, but he moves the chair back to the wall, holds me there, stands guard, staring down at me. "Get *off* of me."

"Listen," he says, little circles of spit collecting at the corners of his mouth. "You don't know what you're talking about. You're imagining things." He leans his face toward mine—his breath smells of liquor. His whole body smells of it—whiskey. "Do you understand me?" His voice breaks when he says it.

I rocket out of the chair, toward the door. But he blocks my path, grabs me again at the shoulders. The man who pretended to care, for so long, so long. I cry out, struggling to break free of his grip.

"Olivia, I don't want to hurt you, that's not what I want," he says, his jaw clenching tightly. His clothes aren't clean, I realize—there's a long ovular stain (coffee?) down the front of his button-up though the rest of him is, as usual, impeccable. I can't take my eyes off the stain. Ted Oakley never has stains.

"You've already hurt me," I say. My voice comes out small and breathy. The room starts to wobble. "You killed my best friend. You sent my mom to jail in your place. You pretend to be so freaking great and kind and caring but you're—you're a liar." Impossible to hold it back anymore, I let it fly. "You're a killer. And I'm going to tell everyone, so they know, so everybody knows." And then I spit. I spit in his eyes—that's where I aim, at least—and, momentarily stunned, his grip softens on my shoulders and I reach for the door handle, jiggling it open. I'm two leaps out the door when he forces me back in, his hold firmer than ever around my arms. He's almost hugging me.

"I never wanted to hurt anyone. I had no choice. If I could make a different choice, Olivia," he says, his voice shaking, soft, "I would."

"You *had* to?" I'm so scared and so angry, I feel like I'm going to explode as I struggle to get out of his grasp.

"It wasn't easy." He's shaking his head. I think he might be crying. "No. It wasn't easy. I didn't want to—to hurt any of them." He's starting to break down, to shake. My body shakes, too, as his arms tremble around me. "I'm not a killer."

A hot surge of anger goes clean through me. "You're a *coward*. You ruined my mother's life." I try to push him away from me but he's too strong—grabs onto my arms tighter and wrestles them tightly behind my back, presses me face-first against the wall behind the desk.

"I didn't want to kill Tanya. I didn't want to kill her." He's breathing hard, practically sobbing.

"Oh my god." The final piece clicks into place. Stern saw Ted with Tanya. He saw him *kill* her. "She was a *kid*, and so was he," I manage to get out, and then he knocks my head back against the wall, and I let out a whimper.

"You were screwing her. You were cheating on Clare." My chest is fire. My lungs are fire. "Why did you do it?"

"You watch your *mouth*. You know nothing."

"I know you're a coward," I retort, and he knocks my head into the wall again, hard. I bite my tongue, and blood fills my throat. Metallic and thick.

"I love my wife. I love Austin. And I didn't want that all to go away. I had to do what was best for my family."

"What's *best*?"

But he's hardly listening to me now, just holding me too tightly for me to move. "I'm not—I'm not an immoral man," he says. My wrists throb within his grip. "I have a *family*, Olivia. You don't understand because you're just a kid. Tanya didn't understand, either. She wasn't married, she didn't have *children*. But I did. I *do*. The stakes were higher for me. I did it for them. For my family, Olivia." His grip loosens and I try to push him away, but he tightens instantly, presses his hand to the back of my head. "It would have been the end of my life. And Clare's life. And Austin's life."

"What about *Tanya's* life? What about Lucas Stern? And the people who cared about him? You don't even know—how many people's lives you destroyed. He didn't do anything wrong. You killed him just for being at the wrong place at the wrong time." I try to turn myself around, to face him, to claw his eyes out. But he leans an elbow into me, flattens me against the smooth cold office wall.

"I tried to talk to him. I *tried*. He wouldn't listen to me."

I can feel his whole body trembling behind me. His hands tighten again over my wrists. "I offered him money—so much money and he wouldn't even hear it. Stupid kid. I didn't have a choice—I didn't have any choice. I didn't—" He chokes on a sob—a weird old man sob so pitiful and sickening I could die right there.

"You're disgusting. You're a goddamn—" *Thwack.*

Blinding pain in my head. I sink to the ground. Everything is spinning, I try to sit up but I can't. I feel him moving away from me. Time passes—I don't know how much. I can't move. I can't see.

And then I see Ted, through the haze settled over my eyes—climbing on a chair, dismantling something above the doorway—an alarm. Wires hanging limp against the wall. Then he's opened the door to the hallway and returns with something in his hand, a large bottle, glass: a spilling sound—liquid hitting solid, spattering the desk and the carpet. A familiar, biting smell—whiskey. A loud crash, the sound of something shattering. Everything happens so quick, I can't get my bearings, I can't get it straight.

His voice reaches me, hollowed out, from far away.

"I'm sorry, Olivia," he says. His voice comes out wobbly, strangled—he's crying. "I'm so sorry. I'd hoped we could talk, that you'd be reasonable. I care about you, Olivia, like a daughter. You have to know that. Olivia, honey, I didn't plan this, not for a second. You have to understand"—the sound of a struck match, sudden skin of heat, tickling my arms, my legs—"it'll look like an accident this way." The door slams shut, the lock twists. I can hardly open my eyes because there's smoke beginning to rise from the carpet, to weave itself around me.

The office is on fire.

# twenty-four

The office is full of fog and black air. My lungs are beginning to fill—so quickly it happens, so quietly thick and painful. I try to pull myself up on something—move toward the door, away from the fire snaking toward me, licking up the carpet, wild, the legs of the desk—but it seems I'm somehow stranded on a blank island, nothing in my path but the heat.

My brain clicks in and out of seeing, of hearing. Blink. Open-mouthed. No sound. Too hot. So hot.

I start to crawl—crawl through the places not burning—but my head still throbs, and my wrists hurt. The space I've got is shrinking. I claw at the carpeting, pulling myself, pulling, pulling. I try to scream, but my voice won't come. *Please. Help me. Someone help me.* And then I think of him—if this is what it felt like as he died, if choking on smoke and choking on water feel like the same thing when they both just equal death. *Stern.*

I see his face—like it's right in front of me as I pull myself forward. Every cell in my body stretching too wide, pain searing through every single inch. I have to reach that face. I have to reach that door. I can hear the flames, the mouth of them, devouring in snaps and roars.

The wires hanging from the wall belonged to the smoke detector. That's why there's no scream from above, no call for help.

I try to call out again, to cry, but I'm coughing so hard there's no space for words.

The carpeting is wet beneath my hands, sodden with liquor. I try to suck in clean air, but there is no clean air. The smell is like a big whopping smack in the face—my lungs will explode—I will explode. *Stern*. I reach for him—for the door—reach up and up, to the handle. My hand brushes the door handle, tries to jiggle it. Locked.

My head goes blank, and then: a gap in the air, in the fabric of the room, in the weave of time; a well-deep hole through which I slip. Light in my head—an image, a memory. Dad holding my hands, spinning me around and around through the sprinkler on the grass. The water cutting little rainbows through the sunlight. Mom watching from the porch, waving. Her hand disappearing every time I spin, giggling, through the water.

Sprinklers. Pipes. Water.

*The blueprints*. The CAD. An image roars back to me for a second—the paper from dad's files The snakes. I drew to cover them, drew flowers and leaves over the little rectangles that showed where the pipes connect.

Then it's fog again. And the sprinkler—one more time—

Dad's face illuminated by the shards of sunlight through the trees. The water spiraling out from the swing-circles our wet hair made through the air.

Blank again. I fight to stay awake. Stern's voice skates around me, and I can almost feel the individual notes of his voice floating like snowflakes through ash and flame. I don't know if he's here or not.

My hands reach through the thickening smoke and touch the legs of the chair—wet, too, with whiskey, but not yet huge with fire. I struggle to lift myself up from the ground, to pull myself up to my feet. To reach the fire alarm beside the doorway, the wires I watched him disconnect. In the haze of my head I think I'll be able to reconnect them. That this will be the easiest way to end the thickness clotting every breathing living part of me. The smoke is like a fortress. I steady myself against the wall with the flat of my palms, trying to keep my knees from buckling, trying to keep every bone in my body from giving up right there. I reach through the thick air, feel my way to a little square box protruding from the wall: *Fire alarm.*

I paw desperately for the wires, coughing. My chest is full-up. Can't breathe. Can't breathe. I reconnect them by touch, not sure if I'm doing it right, everything slipping away.

Nothing happens. My fingers find the fire alarm again, one more time—and then they find it—a small switch—click it on.

And then the room fills with screaming. Everything is wet, pouring from the sprinkler system in the ceiling. My head is one giant, soaking scream.

I pass out but come to when something screams somewhere in the distance, then, and I'm screaming, too. My hands slip from the wall, choking as my knees finally buckle beneath me and I sink to the ground. My belly drops straight out of me, like it does on a roller coaster. A rush, a flash.

Screaming, screaming. The door opens. People rushing in. Men. Boots. Helmets. Voices I don't recognize, shouting, hands, lifting, lifting me up.

Silence.

"Liver, you can't stay here."

It's very dark. Stern is beside me. There is no echo and there is no weather and space does not quite exist around us. And I realize it then: "I'm dead."

"Not yet," he says. "Go now, or you'll get stuck."

"I want to stay with you." My voice sounds very far away, but I feel him beside me, and I reach for him. When we touch, we fall into each other, like separate streams meeting to become a river. We become the same thing.

"No. You don't want to be here. Here is Nowhere, Liver. The Gray Space. We won't be able to stay together here."

Snowflakes. I see his voice as tiny orbs of light, streaming through the darkness and disappearing as soon as they are born. A thousand tiny deaths in a single instant. "The Gray Space," I whisper, understanding that, before, I was only on the edge of it. Now I'm smack dab inside its heart. I am part of it.

"How long have I been here?"

"I don't know, Liver. There's no time in the Gray Space."

"I can't leave you, Stern." My voice seems to bounce for a moment between invisible walls and then get sucked clean away, into nothing. "Even to have one more minute with you, I'd take it." I feel wrapped in silk, like I'm floating through cloud-mists.

"Liv—I have to leave. And once I go, I can't come back."

"Ever?"

"I can visit you in your dreams."

"I hardly ever remember my dreams."

"You'll remember these."

"Stern—"

"Liv—"

"Lucas—"

"Olivia Jane—"

"I need you to know," I pause. It's my last chance, and so, bodiless, in the middle of Nowhere, I tell him: "I love you."

"I've loved you since we were four," he says, simply.

"But that day . . . we kissed, you said it was a mistake. You ran away. Do you even remember?"

"Of course I remember. It was never a mistake, Liv. I got confused. I didn't know how to deal with any of it; I don't think either of us did. But I always loved you. Always. And

I will love you until you come back to me. Somehow, and somewhere. In a very, very long time. You will come back to me."

"Please, Stern. Please, let's just stay here. We love each other. Let's stay." And it's all I want to do. Stay here. Here I will never be alone, because Stern and I are wrapped in each other. We are made of each other. "I belong with you."

"No, Olivia," he says, his voice soft. His voice. The voice I'll hear forever in my head, the voice I'll hear until I'm too old even to move. "You have to live. And I have to die."

"But I don't want to go back. I don't know how."

"Just," he starts—I feel his body leave my own, and then his lips, touching mine, a burning, fast, wild stroke of an instant. "Wake up."

# twenty-five

"Wake up, Livie. Livie, Livie, Livie." Wynn's voice. The beeping of monitors and wheels squeaking down a hallway. I stir, try to open my eyes—everything is very bright.

The brief imprint of Stern's lips still lingers on mine, the cold dark Nowhere space that held us. *He loves me.*

I try to sit up, but with each tiny movement, I'm struck by the sharp, rib-ripped feeling I imagine being stabbed repeatedly must also bring. A big part of my shoulder feels half-numb with stinging pain. My chest feels hot all over.

My father's voice somewhere close by: "Heather—get the nurse—she's moving. She's waking up."

Waking up—I woke up. I'm alive. *No.* I wanted to stay. I wanted to stay there with him, in that silk-wrapped warm place forever. Why didn't he want me to stay?

Heather's voice: "Just push that button by the bed, Dave. That's the call button."

"Right here?"

"Yes, honey. Right there." Their voices are soft, careful. Wynn's is not: "I wanna push it!" she shrieks. "Shhhhh," Heather says.

My lungs ache, and my eyes hurt—I struggle to open them, but everything is so bright. Stern's face breaks over me like a wave. His voice singing as he leapt over the high dunes to Oh Susannah: *It rained all night the day I left, the weather it was dryyyy. The sun so hot, I froze to death, Liver, don't you cryyyy.*

I wait. I wait for him to come as he has before. It was the last place he ever saw alive—Oh Susannah—my house. And somehow, it called him to me.

Every time except for now.

And I start to understand, finally: he is gone from me. My Stern. My love. My heart squeezes in my chest, curling into itself like a wounded animal.

I feel soft little fingers clasp over mine.

"Wynny." I croak out.

Her little fingers wrap more tightly around my right hand. A set of larger fingers are wrapped around my other hand and another set smoothing at my temple, brushing hair from my eyes. "Dad."

I turn my head and crack my eyes open further to see him smiling down at me, sunlight bright beyond his head, the ceiling wide and opened like the heavens. "What time is it? How long have I been here?"

"Liv." The corners of his mouth tremble when he says my name. He sits beside me in the bed, he kisses my cheeks, my forehead, my nose. "You've been out for almost thirty-six hours. We weren't sure—it was a very close call." He's shaking his head, tears in his eyes. "Livia, you had us so scared. I don't know what I would have done if we'd lost you. I really just don't even know." He kisses my forehead again, and I feel the wet of his face meet mine. Wynn is in Heather's arms now, and Heather is rocking her gently on the opposite side of the bed, keeping her calm. "My sweet little girl," Dad says, sweeping a strand of hair from my forehead. "Raina's been camping out here, too. Pretty much two nights not sleeping, holding your hand—she was so tired, honey—I told her she'd better go home and get some sleep about an hour ago."

The thought of Raina temporarily warms me in my middle, but then a colder reality sets in: I've been here practically two whole days. Two whole days wasted to coma. *Two days left* and then: Doomsday. "Does Mom know?" I blurt out.

Before he can answer, the door swings open. Several people come through it at once, including a short woman in doctor's scrubs, her thin, dark hair arranged in a messy bun.

"She's awake," she says, smiling encouragingly at Dad. The three people behind her—interns, I'm guessing—approach my bedside and Dad gets out of the way so they can poke and prod me.

"Hi, Olivia. I'm Dr. Carey," the short woman says, taking my wrist in her hand, checking my pulse. "I've been looking after you since you were brought in and dressing your burns. Do you remember what happened?" A tall, youngish intern—almost cute, if not for the giant mole on his left cheek—rubs a thermometer strip across my forehead.

"The fire. I was in Dad's office—and Ted—" But then the coughing starts.

She puts a hand on my chest, sits me up a bit higher to listen with her stethoscope to my lungs. "Okay. Don't push it. Just rest—your lungs took quite a beating."

Another intern—a tall, skeletal-looking woman—fiddles with the fluid bag at the end of my IV before strapping a blood pressure monitor to my bicep and squeezing. "One-twenty over eighty," she says.

Dr. Carey nods. "Good," she says. "Perfect."

My coughing subsides. I try to breath.

"On a scale of one to ten, how would you say your body feels right now?"

I think about this. My heart is on a seesaw between one and ten, but my body . . ."Four. I feel weird. My chest really hurts, and my head. And my shoulder, and above my knee." I glance briefly down myself and notice that most of the paces I've mentioned are bandaged, taped. Must be the burns she's been dressing. And then, I think about my time in Nowhere, with Stern, how our lips touched there in the darkness when we were streamed together; there, I felt fine. More than fine: perfect.

But I came back. *You have to live, and I have to die.*

"We ran some tests while you were unconscious. It looks like there won't be any permanent damage to your lungs, and your vital signs are good. But you inhaled a lot of carbon monoxide and smoke. For several months, it will be harder for you to breathe than normal. A lot like asthma. It's pretty amazing you're still with us. Maybe someone's looking out for you." She winks, her eyes wrinkling up a bit at the sides as she smiles. The interns smile, too. "You'll also feel a little out of it for a few days, a little confused. Just make sure you get a lot of rest. If everything continues to look good, though, we'll probably discharge you tomorrow."

"Tomorrow?" I reply, weakly. *I don't have that much time.* "But, what if I'm feeling fine? Isn't there a way I can leave today?"

"Probably not, Olivia, but, anything's possible. We'll keep an eye on everything and see what we can do." Dr. Carey retreats toward the door, interns in tow. "I'll be back in a bit for some blood tests. Buzz if you need anything at all." The door shuts behind them.

I turn back to Dad, and pick up where we left off. "Mom."

He looks to Heather, wipes a bead of sweat from his upper lip. "We weren't going to worry her if there was nothing to be worried about. And—thank god—the doctor thinks everything's going to be okay."

I sit further up in my hospital bed, try not to look at the IV poking out of my forearm. "Dad," I start to cry, as he squeezes my hand. I was almost dead—could have stayed in the solid center of the in-between place and then I wouldn't be here, blinking in the too-bright light of this hospital room, solid and breathing. And then I cry harder, for Stern, for the final and ultimate loss of him. "Ted—he was there—he . . ." I start wheezing then, struggling to catch my breath.

"Shh, darlin'," Dad says. Heather, Wynn still monkeyed around her neck, comes to stand beside him. "We know all about Ted."

The shock of it gets me coughing again. I wait until the fit ends, and tug the words, hoarse and painful, from my throat. "You do?"

"He's taken full responsibility."

"*Really*?"

He sighs. "I didn't believe it myself, when I heard. I really just couldn't believe it. He might have gotten away with it if the cops hadn't pulled him over. He was driving drunk." Dad puts a hand on my forehead. "They found fire starters in his trunk, matches. The whole thing was an insurance scam, start to finish. He got me hook, line, and sinker. But Liv, he had no idea you were inside. No idea. He feels just awful. And, believe me, he should." He sucks in a long swig of air. "Chances are, he'll be going to prison, possibly for a long time. We'll have to wait and see. It's a big shock."

I fight past the searing pain in my lungs. "Dad—that's not what I meant."

"Calm down, Liv. Less talk, more rest."

"No—*more* talk." I sit further up in bed and fix him with a stare. I take a deep breath. "Ted Oakley did not burn down Ghost Town for insurance money. He was trying to kill me."

He lifts his eyebrows. "Why on earth would Ted Oakley try to kill you?" he asks gently. "I think this is that confusion business coming through—you heard Doctor Carey—things are gonna be a little foggy for a few days, darlin'."

"I'm not foggy, Dad. Listen to me," I say. "He killed two other people." Dad's eyes widen; he and Heather exchange a quick glance. "He knew that I knew, and he tried to kill me. He locked me in your office and set it on fire. There was no insurance scam! You have to believe me . . . you have to—" I start coughing, again, dredging up the blackness in my lungs.

"Liv," Heather says gently, setting Wynn down, "You need to rest, okay, honey? And then we can talk all about this, in a few days, when you're feeling better."

"I'm feeling fine!" I howl, feeling completely helpless—all of them hanging around my bed, staring over me like I'm some brain-dead invalid. "You weren't *there*. I know he's Ted-fucking-Oakley"—Heather covers Wynn's ears—"and you think I'm crazy, but I'm not. He framed Mom, and I figured it out, and he tricked me. He took Austin's phone and—"

"Olivia, please—your mother *confessed*, Liv. And while Ted may have done some *very* awful things, accusing the man of *purposefully* going after you is—"

"Let her talk, David," Heather cuts in. Just for that one second, I really love the woman.

Dad leans back in his chair beside my bed and rests a hand on his forehead.

"Ted took Austin's phone. He knew that I'd asked Austin to leave the door to Ghost Town open for me. He knew I was going to be there, alone." I push on: "Just before Stern died, a girl disappeared, Tanya Leavin—you can look it up. Ted and Tanya were having an affair. He *told* me they were. Austin told me he thought Ted was cheating, but I don't think he knew anything for sure though. Tanya was going to tell, I think, and ruin Ted's life, so he killed her. He killed Stern, too, and he blamed it on Mom."

I wait for something to change in Dad and Heather's faces, some moment of realization or clarity. But they stare at me with the same mirror images of pity. Even Wynn has picked up on the mood of the room, stands beside me, stroking the top of my IV arm like she's petting a sick cat.

"I don't know what you heard from Austin, or what's going on with Ted and Clare, but none of that's about Mom and what happened. We've been over this a million times."

"She was *framed*!"

Dad looks me over and sighs. "You're tired as hell," he says, rocking forward in his chair, putting a hand over mine. "You're in total shock. But we're going to get you all fixed up." He leans over and presses the call button for the nurse. "Let's just get those tests over with already so we can take you home soon as possible and let you get some real sleep."

"Allll fixed up," Wynn chimes in, smiling at me through the gaps in her teeth.

But they don't know where I've just come back from. They don't know there is only one way to get "all fixed up" from here.

*Two days left. We have the answers, Stern,* I think to him, hoping my message might somehow reach him, wherever he is now. *Now, we just need proof.*

I spend the rest of the night in the hospital alternating between the mind-blank powers of the little overhead television and Dad's regular dismissals whenever I try to bring up Ted again. As I grow more and more emphatic, he grows less and less attentive, to the point where I think he's just tuned me out entirely, thinks I'm just ranting, delirious. Several interns come through the night to re-dress the more serious burns on my shoulder and chest and thigh, rinsing the areas that need it with cool water that stings like hell before patting me dry and applying sterile gauze, more bandages, surgical tape.

It's not until the next morning that I'm finally released. *One day. One stinking day.* Dad and Heather fawn over me, tucking me into bed, bringing me a tray with drinks and soup, and setting up my computer on a chair in front of my bed in case I want to watch something on Netflix.

"Just holler if you want anything else, okay? We're going to be right downstairs," Heather tells me, as she and Dad stand, lingering in the doorway. I decide not to bring up Ted anymore. Until I have real proof, there's just no damn point.

"I'm not crippled," I tell them. "If I want something, I'll just *come* downstairs."

"You sure are proud, Liv," Dad says, trying to joke. "If I had two and a half people at my beck and call, I'd be milking it like hell."

He shuts the door. I lie in my bed and shut my eyes because the ceiling above me is spinning. There's still one piece of this puzzle I haven't placed yet: Tanya's body. Ted threw Stern, still not quite dead, but unconscious and badly wounded, off the pier. That probably means Stern tried to run—run to Oh Susannah, where he knew he could find help. Ted must've chased him down the beach.

But Tanya's body never turned up. Stern's washed ashore—and couldn't have taken too long to do so, for there was still blood, oozing from his wound and onto Mom's hands as she cradled him. But not Tanya's body. Hers never washed up. Why? How could a body just disappear? What did he *do* with her?

I roll over to my side in bed and heave, but nothing comes up.

I roll back, trying to breathe deep, trying to think, trying not to cry.

*I can do this.*

I think back to everything that's happened since Stern first appeared. How he showed me the caramels my mom kept hidden. How we played music together in my mom's studio. The slashed tires. All the strange stuff between me and Austin that I still can't quite name. How we went on that wild goose chase to confront Marietta Jones, which lead to what? Nothing.

There's something I'm missing. Marietta Jones pops into my head again—the story Annabelle told of the classmate's inhaler that she stole, hid in her piano. The one place she would revisit again, and again, and again.

The place closest to her—so obvious. So freaking obvious.

*Of course.* Ted would do the same: hide evidence in the place closest to him, his pet project, a place he knew well. A place he had control of. The site of her death.

"Holy shit," I whisper to myself. "Ghost Town." It wasn't finished yet. It was still under construction. . . .

That's where he hid her body. I'm sure of it, more than I've ever been sure of anything. But how can I prove it?

After a few minutes, I stand up and make my way carefully to the bathroom. My chest and shoulder look red, blotchy, but my face in the bathroom mirror is ghostly, almost translucent. Maybe I brought some of that other place with me—some of Stern, in those moments when we flowed into each other, weightless and timeless and without form. *I have loved you since we were four years old.*

I think I've loved him all that time, too—it just took me until a week before he died to figure it out.

But at least I figured it out. We both did. The heart doesn't change. And I know this now. Maybe I have always known it.

I'll find a way to make this right.

I shut the bathroom door softly behind me. Heather and Dad are mid-conversation in the kitchen, and standing in the hall, I can just make out their hushed voices from downstairs. I hold my breath and listen: ". . . Yes, I agree that she's in shock, David. The way I felt, after I found Liam? The things that went through my head, the rationales I came up with to explain it . . . none of it made any sense, but I don't think it's all that uncommon."

"In a few days, she'll even out again, trust me."

"Honey, I think it's more than that—I just think that all the stress she's been under, with Miriam's final sentencing tomorrow. . . . She's making up stories because she feels she has no other choice. I mean, that is a huge weight to hold for a sixteen-year-old—for anyone."

"Well, what can I do? What am I supposed to do?"

A brief pause, and then: "Take her to talk to someone, David. Someone professional, who knows what to do in these situations. We're not equipped to handle this anymore. It's too big for us."

Another pause; I hold my breath and wait for his response. I wait for him to defend me in some way. "She—she had an awful experience with therapy a long time ago,

Heath. A doctor we found through the school system. I felt so bad about it. . . ." He trails off.

"David—you're her father."

Dad sighs. "I know. You're right," he says, weary but resolute. "She'll make a fuss, but I'm her father. I'll make her go."

"She'll understand one day, when she's a parent." I hear them kiss. It sets me shuddering.

I charge from the stairwell back into my room, buzzing with frustration, kicking a path through all the crap nesting on my carpet, throwing my book bag across the room where the books inside thud against the closet, crumpling shirts and dirty underwear into tight balls which I thud, in a similar fashion, against whatever surface I can throw them. It's satisfying in a base sort of way. My skin burns and my lungs burn but I push the burning away and keep on. I grab the pair of dirty cutoffs I wear nearly every day—the pair I wore the afternoon I spent with Austin at the Ghost Town condo, just before I was nearly burned to death—and throw them with special rage straight up into my ceiling fan. But when they hit, something flies out of one of the pockets and lands a few feet away from me on the carpet.

I go to it, crouch down. A coin. The coin Medusa gave me the day at the park, when Carlos and his dickwad cronies were beaning her with their soiled trash. I turn it over in my fingers and start scraping away at some of the dirt and sediment melded to the surface. I have to shine the coin even further before I see that it's not a coin, but a small, round silver pendant, and that there are three letters engraved in script into its surface. *M.K.T.*

My mother's initials. Miriam Kathleen Tithe.

I've seen it before: I remember it dangling from a thin chain around her neck. Her own mother gave it to her on her sixteenth birthday. I didn't even know she'd lost it. Medusa, the ever-present beach urchin, found it. Always lurking somewhere on the sidelines, waiting beneath the piers, watching for things lost and forgotten.

*Always lurking.* My breath stops for a second. That night—she might have been there that night.

*Medusa.* I relocate my favorite cutoffs and slide them carefully over my legs, ignoring my dizziness, the sharp pains in my lungs. I slip out of my room, barely remembering to grab my purse, and make my way downstairs. Dad and Heather are still in the kitchen, sipping tea out of big white mugs. I scoot past the entranceway to the kitchen, hoping they won't see me. No such luck.

"Olivia Jane." Dad stands from his chair, quick as hell, intercepting my path by the door. "You trying to sneak out?"

"No, Dad," I try to move my purse behind my back, real nonchalant, try to laugh but end up just sort of hacking instead. I poke my head into the kitchen. "Hi, Heather!" I say, very cheery.

She smiles warmly at me. "How are you feeling, Olivia?"

"A whole lot better," I say, "but I'm feeling *really* claustrophobic up there. Is it okay if I take a short little tiny drive just down the street?"

"You've got a whole house to walk around if you're claustrophobic, Liv," Dad responds, but I hear a subtle softening in his voice. "Plus, we've got to change your bandages soon, hon. You know Doctor Carey said every single day, if you want to heal up right, not get infected."

I inch my way closer to the front door, rest my hand on the knob. "Look"—I pull my cell phone from my bag, wave it a few times back and forth in Dad's sightline before grabbing the keys to his truck off the hook by the front door, shooting him the biggest, sweetest grin I can possibly muster—"if at any point you need me in the ten minutes I'm gone, just call. I'll be so safe, so don't worry *at all*, okay? And we can change the bandages when I get back. I promise it'll be fine. I'll be fine. I love you both and I'll be back with the truck so soon you won't even know we're gone. Great! See you soon!"

Dad stands there big-eyed, taking in my nonstop rush of words. I don't even give him a second to respond before I open the door and shoot right outside, leaping out of sight and into his old Chevy before he can stop me.

I clutch Mom's pendant in my hand as I drive through West Grove, past Beast Beach and the Smoothie-Kinged shopping center where I worked summer after freshman year, to the stretch of beach near Oh Susannah. The stretch of beach where Stern's life drained from him into the wicked mouth of the ocean while the moon looked on, a silent culprit. I park Dad's truck in the closest lot and make my way through the saw grass and patches of crinum lilly to the skin-soft sand, pausing every few steps to hack, my lungs searing like they're being stabbed, again and again. I feel bloody inside, raw, cut-up.

The old house rises in the distance and the sun's too bright. I'm too far to see its graffiti ruin. I wind time backward for a moment until I'm eight years old, racing home from tree-climbing with Stern, and the windows of our beautiful purple house glow gold onto the beach, and the notes Mom plays stretch the length of the beach all the way to my ears, calling me. *Dinner, Livie,* they say, *Dad's cooking us up a Texas special. You can help me ice the cake for later. Any color you like, sweetheart.* The notes laugh, crescendo, explode, and pour over me, until I'm glittering and coated all over in perfect particles of a past I would cling to forever and beyond forever if only I could.

But I cannot, and so I wind time forward, back to the present—this same beach, my dark, desecrated childhood home, searching for Medusa. There's a wind picking up over the ocean and the waves look angry as they crash and foam, taking mounds of sand back with them. Further down the beach, there's a bonfire going—the sight of it, the smell, makes my lungs cinch up even tighter—the silhouettes of several people gathered around it. They are laughing. Someone's got a guitar—starts playing a song I don't recognize.

I search the docks until I spot a shaky hovel, set up beneath one of the more wood-rotted piers further down the beach. I've seen Medusa emerge from this place before, but I've never gotten this close. It's not a big place—two big slats of wood she must have dragged from a trash heap and rested into each other, a sheet guarding part of the entrance—and it smells briny, sour.

I peer inside. Medusa's huddled in the corner—sleeping, it looks like, on a towel on her side, her back pressed up against one of the wooden boards, another towel covering her legs. The rest of the narrow, triangular space is literally stuffed with junk—piles of shells, old pizza boxes, glass bottles, a whole load of flip-flops and other shoes that don't match.

"Medusa," I say her name softly, not wanting to startle her.

Her eyes pop open. She sits up slowly, her tangle of steely gray hair blowing around her face. Her eyes are red, and the skin beneath them droops in little dark triangular folds, like her skin can't wait to crawl right off her bones and be free. She pulls the towel around her legs into her chest—I can't tell if she's suspicious or just cold. "Oleevia," she says, moistening her thin, cracked lips.

"I need to talk to you," I say. She hugs the towel tighter to her chest. "*Por favor*," I say more gently.

She watches me, silent—tilting her head, her eyes crinkling up, tongue peeking slowly out of her mouth and back in again like a lizard, testing the air.

Not sure how else to convey what I need, I open my fist to her, revealing the cleaned pendant in my hand, holding it out to her. It glints with sunlight. "My mother," I say, half of my voice lost to the thrashing of waves. "You had this pendant. You gave it to me. You knew her. You know who she is."

She nods. Slowly, she brings herself forward onto all fours, and crawls out to meet me. Stoop-backed, shaking slightly in the legs, the hands, she straightens up as much as her curved back allows, staring sadly at me.

"Si, yes, *tu madre. Yo se.* I find this." She points to the pendant in my hand. "She drop it."

I lick my lips. "A long time ago—last year—she was here, at night, and a boy was killed. Were you here? Did you see anything?"

Her head starts shaking, her whole body, curling her lips in and out, in and out, against her gums. She stoops back to the sand, digging her fingers in, as she always does. I can see that I'm already losing her.

I stoop to the ground beside her, speaking low and calm. "Medusa. I don't want anything from you. I just need to know what you saw, or, *if* you saw, anything at all. Please," I beg. "Please."

"*Si. Lo vi,*" she says, suddenly. She blinks several times, looks out over the waves. "I see it."

"What did you see? Did you see him—the boy? He was tall—black hair—"

"I see him. *Si. Sangre, cubriendo todo su cuerpo—*" she motions at her head, down her chest and arms.

"His body," I say, breathing hard. "Blood?"

"*Si*, his body. Blood. All over. . ." Her hands curl in and out of tight fists. She digs, digs, digs into the sand. "The man chase him, he hit him on the head with *un ladrillo,* and *sangre*, blood, and the boy—*se callo*." She demonstrates, falling into the sand, her eyes shutting, body shaking. "I warn you, this man. I see—The shadow man—he take the boy to the water. He run away."

The shadow man. *Ted*. I'm trying to control my body from shaking. "Did the shadow man see you?"

She shakes her head. "I hide there." She points with a dirty finger to one of the rotted piers straight ahead.

"What about my mom?" I press. "What happened?"

"She come out, *más tarde*, and the boy is back on the sand," Medusa whispers, bringing her fingers to her mouth. "*Y, entonces, todavia estava sangrando*—he still bleed—and she see him and make a loud scream and run and sit, and take his head in her lap and she put her hands on his head, on the blood, and she is crying, she is very sad—"

"She was trying to stop the bleeding," I whisper. "She must have gotten confused," I say, "she must have somehow started to believe that she was the reason he was bleeding, somehow, that she was killing him. She was just confused."

"She kiss his head. She say 'I so sorry, I so sorry.' She don't stop crying."

The image flashes bright before my eyes: my mother on the sand with Stern, as he bled all over her lap, as he finished dying. And everything bursts out of me—all the darkness in my lungs, in every organ, in my head, and I'm sobbing, big, heavy, salty tears.

"Then *la policía* come for her. All she say is 'I so sorry, I so sorry,' and she look behind her, and she say 'tell Oleevia I so sorry. Tell her I love her.'"

Her last thought was of me. I think about the words she'd repeat at night, stroking my hair in the lamplight of my bedroom, wind coming sweetly through the screen: *You're the most beautiful thing I've ever made*. More beautiful than music, she'd said, bigger than that.

*She didn't do it. Stern was real.* Is *real. I'm* sane.

"Shh, shh, *mija*," Medusa says, her hand on my head, and I hug my arms around her legs and she just keeps saying "shh" and I stay there for a long time, hugged around her.

*Tell her I love her.* No one told me. But they'd never needed to.

I always knew.

# twenty-six

I watch, poised with sketchpad on my lap, from the top of an overlooking hill as the wrecking ball arcs through the sky and crumbles the charred walls of Ghost Town to the ground.

It is a deafening, glorious event—one which Dad couldn't bear to watch, still reeling, both furious with himself for not taking my word over Ted's, and in total shock that a man he trusted so deeply turned out to be, as Dad put it earlier, a *goddamn maniac*.

Once Dad was ready to actually *listen* to the whole story, I told him—not about Stern so much as the "weird hunch" I had, based on things Austin had told me, things I'd started to figure out on my own. Since there was little more reason to avoid it at this point, I also told him about my eyes; he was concerned and fussy and asked a million questions between pulling me in for big, tight, heaving hugs, but, he didn't think I was crazy. And that's all I really needed. He said we'd go back to the doctor, that we'd figure something out. That we'd get me better. It felt good to say it, to have him know.

I reach for a tube of watercolor, squeeze out a squiggle onto a small easel, and dip my brush in. I don't care that it just looks black to me, even though the tube says *alizarin crimson*. I'm just happy to feel paint on the edge of my brush again, moving soft across a surface.

So I paint. I paint what looks like ash, sailing through the sky, paint the death of this evil place. The death that might actually make life possible again.

Amazingly, at the police station last night, Medusa didn't go cold. The police gave her blankets, and something to drink, and once she got rolling, it all slid out clear as when she told it to me. Even more amazing: they listened.

I told them the truth—about the fire, that Ted trapped me there when I'd gone to search for evidence against him. I told them about Tanya Leavin, how she and Ted must have been having an affair. They perked majorly up at her name. They'd been trying to untangle Tanya's case for the past year, and they'd suspected her involvement with Ted because of phone records and texts, but hadn't yet figured out a way to pin her disappearance on him. They warned us that even with substantial evidence, the case might be a difficult one to make against such a well-connected, well-lawyered man. But they got the DA to postpone Mom's sentencing in light of what we told them.

Finally, she's got a chance.

I watch them work, the men in muddy boots and

reflective vests, the sky thick with clouds promising impending drench. It's music, really, hearing the pieces of this structure fall, thud to the ground. Soon it will all be dust for them to sift through, piles of drywall and wood and glass from which they might decipher human remains. Bones. Teeth.

I picture a whole well full of trapped ghosts, finally released, and I picture Stern—I picture him in that time-stopped instant before everything changed—sunlight making honey of his skin, the flash of his teeth, his eyes fixed just on me inside that old shed outside of Oh Susannah. I shut my eyes amidst the crashing and the banging and the twangy jaws of monster-big machines opening and shutting and spitting and I think of his face: the square angles of his jaw, eyes that pierce through to some hidden layer of me, how even in black and white and gray, he somehow had more color than any person I'd ever seen, even when I could see the stuff full.

So I paint him, too, hovering in the corner of my wide, watercolor-smattered page, my best friend who, even in death, forced me to fight just when I started to think I had no fight left to give. I ring the brush around in my water bottle.

I still don't know if any of it was real. Maybe Stern was a way for my bruised-up brain to dissociate me from the things I already knew. Maybe it decided all that pain was too much to contain inside the walls of one body, and it had to form his image so that I could move forward in any kind of way. So that I would have a reason to keep hoping. So that I wouldn't just slink away and die, or something. So that I'd love. So that I'd fight.

Still . . . there were things. Things *only* Stern could have known about. And the feeling I had when he would come—like both of us were bridging some gap between life and death, existing in that gray space neither of us quite knew how to figure. I just don't see how all of it could have been made up.

I finish Stern and paint Medusa, too. The cops tried to set her up in a shelter, offered her a clean bed and showers and everything but she didn't want it. She likes living in the sand, searching for treasure. I paint her on a big pile of gleaming combs, the ocean rising around her feet-turned-fins. So she can dive in and escape whenever she needs to, whenever she's in danger, so, like Mom in the mermaid stories she'd tell me as a kid, she'll always know where home is.

The light is fading, the big toothy machines finally starting to clear away some of the larger bits of rubble, when I hear footsteps behind me. I turn, and my heart throbs fresh: *gu-gug-gu-gug-gu-gug*. Austin, coming up the hill. His hair is all messed up and his clothes look dirty, like he's been wearing them a couple of days. There are dark circles under his eyes like he hasn't been sleeping much lately, either.

I don't know what he knows. I don't know what he knew. I can't help but look at his face and, though there's no biology connecting them, think of Ted's. I start to pack up my paints quickly.

"Olivia—stop. Please don't leave."

"Austin, I can't talk to you."

"Just listen for a second. Please," he pleads, his voice raw, husky. "I've been looking for you for hours. Then I realized you might be here."

"Okay." I tell him, still uneasy. But I owe him this—a fair hearing, I guess. "Sit."

He sits, tentatively, beside me. "I've been trying to talk to you since I found out you were in the hospital. The police came to our house. They grilled Ted about the fire. He said it was an insurance thing, you know . . ."

"I know what he said."

He frowns, staring hard at the ground. "Olivia— I know you don't have to believe me, but, I really didn't know. Anything. Until it was already too late."

"Is that what you came here to tell me? That you figured it all out a little bit too late?" In the distance, another wall of the building crumbles.

"No." He runs a hand through his hair. "I came here to say sorry. For—for everything. For keeping that secret from you, for so long."

"Why didn't you say anything sooner? Why didn't you just come clean? I would have known so much sooner. Austin—this whole thing is so much bigger than you or me."

"Olivia. If I thought there was a *reason* he asked me to keep an eye out for you—other than the fact that he was worried—I *would* have said something." Austin says. He sucks in his lower lip. "Ted has raised me pretty much my whole life. He's been a father . . ." His voice breaks and he coughs. "I didn't know it was all a lie," he spits out.

I stare across the broken landscape, the gray sky, the stretch of highway just out of sight that leads to Broadwaithe, to Mom's cramped cell. "I know exactly what you mean."

He gulps back something thick in his throat. "That night, when you came over for dinner, and he freaked out—I told you I thought he was just upset over some business deal. But I realized after I drove you home that he really *did* freak right after you brought up the hearing."

I nod, watch the grief building on his face—on his beautiful mouth, in the twitching of his right cheek, just below the eye.

"I kept thinking about it, how strange he'd acted. And then, the other night, in the condo," he blushes, eyes flashing up at me, "after we fought, and you left, I had this really bad feeling about everything—like maybe he was messed up in something pretty bad, and—I didn't know how, or what, or why—but that you were somehow involved." He grips his knees, hard, like he needs something to hold onto. "I asked him about it. I wanted to know why he was so *obsessed* with you, and what you were doing, and everything you said. Why he wanted me to become close with you. I told him I thought it was screwed-up, and I thought he was lying about something. I told him

I thought he was messing around on my Mom. And then he . . . he exploded."

"So what did you do?"

"Well—that's when I started trying to call you—but you didn't answer. I went to sleep, hoping that when I woke up you'd have gotten in touch. When I woke up, my phone was missing from my nightstand. Which was weird, because I'd definitely set it right there before I passed out." He bites his lip, blinks, shielding his eyes from the sunlight. "I called it from Mom's landline—and that's when I heard it ringing . . . inside Ted's office. I saw the text messages."

"The ones he sent me. Pretending to be you."

He clears his throat, picks at the grass beside the blanket, his stomach muscles visibly tight, clenched beneath his crumpled polo. "Yeah. Those. Later the police showed up to talk to Ted. He was talking about the insurance scam—it didn't make any sense. And the police mentioned a girl who'd been inside, after the fire had been set. They mentioned you. He hurt you. I knew it. I—" He looks at me, starting to shake. I've never seen Austin Morse shake. I've hardly seen him ruffled at all. "I don't know why I didn't say something right then to the cops, right there—my mom, maybe—the look on her face. I just—I froze. Maybe I'm an idiot, but, I wanted to talk to you first, that's all I could think of. I called your house—over and over again. I called the hospital. They said you'd been discharged already. I let him hurt you—I never would have—I didn't know that he was going to—" His voice breaks.

"And you've been looking for me?"

"I would have looked forever. Seriously, Tithe. I don't give up easy."

Austin comes closer to me, tentatively taking my hand in his. His big warm hand. Against my will, Stern's face takes siege of my brain, sending knives through my sore lungs. I wonder if that's just how it feels to miss someone so bad—like being stabbed in the gut a little bit, each time you think of them. I bring myself back. Here. To Austin. A boy I've hated. A boy I've wanted. A boy I will forgive, for not knowing. There is so little we really know, after all.

I touch the tips of my fingers to his face because he looks so sad and there's some nurturer instinct in me that suddenly kicks in, wanting to ensure him that he's cared for. He kisses my fingers, one by one, puts my palm in his. Just holding it, on the grass, on the dirt, the clanking, thudding symphony of Ghost Town's destruction rising around us.

"Olivia?"

"Yeah?"

"I'm scared."

"I know."

"I'm scared about what's going to happen when . . . when it all goes down," he says, watching the machines devour so much brick, mortar, glass.

His jaw clenches up, his right foot digs into the ground. "My mom won't talk. She just . . . she screamed, and then she went mute. The house feels different. Like—dark, all of a sudden, even though it's not. . . ." He trails off, looks to me.

"Whatever happens, Austin: you're not alone," I tell him, kissing him softly on the cheek. "You're never going to be alone."

"That a promise, Tithe?" His voice is small and soft.

"Yeah, Morse. It's a promise." I stand, pull my blanket up from the grass, fold it up small, gather up my book bag and art supplies.

I extend my hand to lift Austin from the ground. More police cars are gathered near the rubble of Ghost Town, poking around with flashlights, saying hushed things into walkie-talkies. "Come on," I say, letting go of his hand and weaving my arm in his, shivering hard with the souls of who-knows-how-many unleashed ghosts, sidling up against my warm, fire-blotched, living skin. "Let's get the hell out of here."

Austin offers me a ride home, but I don't take it. I want to walk, to hold the speckled leaves of trees in my fingertips, let the moist air soak my skin, to sweat, to feel earth beneath my feet. I go slow, taking the long way. It takes me nearly an hour to get home.

The smells of dinner greet me as soon as I make it back—thick smells of cooking pasta, roasted garlic, olive oil, something else bubbling in a pan. I see Wynn in the living room—the light-reflections of the television against the side of her face, the yippy sounds of cartoons just loud enough that she doesn't hear me come in. Dad's sitting at the kitchen table, Heather behind him, rubbing his back, soothing him.

For a moment, I don't see Dad and Heather as parents, but as people, soothing each other. Keeping each other alive.

And then I see them as parents again and I get a little grossed out because old people aren't supposed to touch when it's possible younger people might see them touching.

I stand in the doorway; he looks up from the table as soon as he sees me. "Livie—darlin'—" I know by the sound of his voice, the bright in his eyes, that something's happened. I drop my bags in the foyer and rush in. He stands and pulls me in, hugs me so tight.

"Dad—what? What's going on?"

"The police . . ."

"I was just there. I watched the demolition." My stomach tightens up. "Did they find something?"

He hugs me tighter. "Bones."

"Tanya?" I ask, shivering, wondering if Stern's beside me right now, too invisible even to see, hugging the side Dad can't cover.

"They need to verify, of course. They need to be sure." My dad exhales. "They're going to rush it. Of course, this changes everything. It's proof—real proof that Ted was connected to another murder, that he's been in this game for a long time, that Mom was a pawn in this whole mess, someone he manipulated based on what he knew about her."

*Mom.* I want to call her, to run to her, to spread out a picnic on the sand and run through the surf with her beside me. I wonder if I'm dreaming. I feel like I'm floating, bursting, made of light and air.

"We're going to get her out of there, Liv, we're going to get her out." His voice breaks on the word. Heather comes beside us, wrapping her thin arms around my back so they connect with Dad's. There are some things you don't choose, but then, things change, and you have to. Or you will starve.

That is freedom. The choices you get to make, to move forward, to live.

I let both of their arms encircle me, pull me tight between their hearts, the smells of dinner rising, settling over our heads. "We're going to get her out."

# twenty-seven

But Mom doesn't come home.

It takes the police a week to verify that the remains buried in Ghost Town did, in fact, belong to Tanya Leavin and to arrest Ted.

At Mom's sentencing, eight days later—more of a formality now than a necessity—the single most beautiful word in the history of language leaves the prosecution's lips: *innocent*. And then, three more impossibly perfect words: *All charges dropped.*

We all cry. Dad, and Heather, and Raina, who has come, and sits beside me, and holds my hand on her lap on that smooth wooden bench, so much like a church pew. And we throw our arms around each other's necks and stay clung to each other for what feels like hours.

*Innocent.*

*All charges dropped.*

Free.

But, still, she doesn't come home.

She cannot wind time backward and erase what happened, and what she'd been through.

Ted Oakley, arrested first for arson and then released on ridiculously high bail that, of course he was able to cover, no problem, is re-arrested—not only for murder, but for his involvement in drug trafficking. Cocaine. After he was arrested the first time, Miami PD got a warrant to search his house and found a whole slew of shit with which to indict him—a shoddily concealed paper trail connecting every financial turn of Ghost Town to the drug money he was raking in.

Turned out to be some big-deal case for the Miami PD—the reason he met Tanya in the first place, the reason she died—an unlikely college-student looking to pay her way through eighty thousand dollars of tuition. So he hired her on not only as a mistress, but as a dealer, helping spread his wares like wildfire through the U of Miami campus—a regular cash cow. But then her demands for Ted's time and for his money increased. She got angry—he got desperate—the reason he had to bury her body beneath his new apartment complex, only half constructed. The reason Stern had to die, as witness.

A domino effect.

In too deep, he freaked. His whole life would have been fucked—so he fucked everyone else's instead. I doubt he ever saw himself as a killer, as someone who'd done something truly wrong.

Ted Oakley was not *that* to the world. He was wealthy, and powerful, and generous. Mom was sick, going through a divorce, and lived on the salary of a piano teacher and sometimes-composer. It was easier for everyone to believe that line of logic. Easier to believe she could snap.

But I also know that anyone can snap.

And not one of us is immutable, or predictable, or immune to the chaos out of which the entire universe spun out. Chaos is what we are made of, and we will return to it, again, and again, and again. Our hearts will beat for it while our brains will search for order, and find that, almost always, it is elusive.

"Take a right here," I tell Raina. "End of Collins Street—there should be signs." I stare at the window, searching for them—*Calyer House*. The sunlight pours in through the windshield, makes Raina's skin glow, her long dark braid shine like obsidian.

"Look. See?" I point to the building on Raina's side of the street—not a building, even, but an old Victorian-looking house with painted shutters. Big, wide lawn. Clusters of palm trees, crinum lily, a zen rock garden right, its black rake leaned up against the porch. More resort than psychiatric clinic. Mom's reward: leaving jail to deal with a different kind of incarceration—the one in her head.

Raina turns sharply into the parking lot. I lurch forward, clutching my stomach.

"You okay, girl?" Raina puts the car in park, glances over at me. I take a deep breath, nod. "Close your eyes for a second," she orders. I do, and then I feel her thumbs come to my forehead, pressing lightly in. "It's your third eye," she tells me. "Mom's new yoga-teacher boyfriend just taught me about it. It awakens your intuition or some shit."

Her hands smell like the packet of Drum tobacco she's got stashed in the little compartment beneath the radio and like her jasmine hand lotion. "What does that even mean?"

"I don't know," she admits. "Dude does that to my face pretty much every time I see him." I open my eyes and look at her and then we both start cracking up. The knot in my belly starts to unwind. "Damn," she says, softly. "I wish Stern was here."

He flashes through me, huge, as I realize: there's so much she doesn't know—so much I need to tell her.

"I—I loved him." I stare at my hands in my lap. "I never told you. We kissed, the week before he died. We loved each other." I meet her eyes, feel tears rim my own.

"Well—*duh.*" she reaches out and swipes the wet from my eyes. "That much was obvious from, like, day *one*. He always had it so bad for you, man," she says, pressing her back into her seat and turning her head to look at me. "It used to make me a little jealous, even, what you guys had." Her almond eyes grow shiny, her voice soft. "I'm glad you figured it out. And I'm glad you finally told me."

I nod, and swallow down the lump in my throat. For a second we sit in silence.

"So . . ." she starts, breaking the quiet of the hot car, "what's the deal with you and Morse? You guys doin' it yet or what?" She raises her eyebrows, grinning.

I whack her thigh with the back of my hand.

"Well . . . ?" she persists.

"I don't know Rain. He's actually . . . really cool, and cute, and I *like* being around him, but after everything that's happened . . ." I trail off.

"But he's not his stepdad, Liv."

"I know he's not. But I feel like I'd be an idiot to really trust anyone, ever again." I run my fingers loosely over the dashboard, lift off a sun-sparkled line of dust. "I never felt that way about Stern. Ever. I never wondered whether or not he was a good guy, he just was. And there's no one that can top that. Stern was the best guy I'll ever know."

She reaches out for my hand, sandwiches it between hers in her lap. "Liv, maybe it's not about finding another person who lives up to what Stern was to you. You're right, that's probably never gonna happen." Her hands are warm around mine; there's a thin, cool film of sweat forming between our fingers. "Maybe you just have to let people love you. You have to give them a chance."

"It's really hard for me to do that right now."

"I know, babygirl."

We sit in that hot car a few more seconds, just being quiet, our fingers entwined.

"I guess I should go in there," I say finally.

Raina hugs me hard, and I keep the feeling of her arms around me even as I pull away.

"Take your time with her, okay?" she tells me. "I'll be here."

* * *

"She's right at the end of the hall. Number thirty-six," the nurse says, pointing me in the direction of Mom's room. Her own room. No creepy guards standing vigilant watch.

I hug the clay-potted jade plant I've brought Mom to my chest and thank the nurse, walking down the wide-windowed hallway, light pouring in, soaking the wood floors—spider plants lining the windowsills drinking it up to grow greener and greener. My forehead is sweaty; my hands are shaking.

Thirty-six. The silver numbers glint against the door. I knock softly. Inside: the sound of things being moved, furniture scraping against the floor. I put my face in the jade, seeking its smell. I want something to latch onto right now, something concrete.

The door opens—more sunlight, backlighting Mom's face so she glows there before me. She glows—my mom.

"Livie!" She pulls me right to her and hugs me in tight—I clutch the plant in one hand behind her back. I expected the greasy sweatsuit she wore at Broadwaithe, but she's in nice black pants, a white silk button-up with round pearlescent buttons she used to wear all the time, at recitals.

Pressing my face into her neck, I'm flooded with relief: she smells like herself—plumeria, even though there's none of the stuff in sight, and even in the faintest, smallest way like the ocean—like she's somehow soaked it back into her skin in the past week. "My sweet girl," she says into my hair, and I let my nose fall into her shoulder and take even more of her in. “I love that green dress,” she says, stepping back, looking me over. “You’re too skinny, Liv, but the dress is so nice. With your red hair.” She touches her fingers lightly to my bandaged shoulder, to the scratch above my eye. “These bandages don’t go at all with your outfit, though,” she jokes, pulling me close one more time to plant a firm kiss on my forehead.

“I brought this for you,” I say, shyly, stepping back and handing her the jade. “I thought—I thought it would make you feel more at home.”

She smiles, big. She takes the jade and places it on the windowsill. “Look at that,” she says—her eyes are clear, her voice is clear. She seems normal, she seems like *her*. “Looks just like my old studio in here, now, Liv. I love it. I really love it.”

Her room isn’t big, or fancy, but it’s all hers. A twin bed in the corner, a knit rug beside it, soft-looking curtains with little flowers all over them tied back at each corner of her giant window—sans prison bars—that overlooks the back garden, a small wooden desk, and . . .“Your piano! Mom! How did you get this here?”

I walk to it—only a few steps—and run my fingers over the little bench, the lid, the smooth rectangular top.

“Your father,” she says, smiling softly. “He spoke to Meredith Calyer—she’s the owner—about finding me a room that could fit this old thing. And, she did.” She gives the piano a shaky little pat.

My heart surges a little bit—hopeful. "Dad did that?"

"He sure did."

I try to read her eyes—to piece together some kind of conclusion that matches mine: they are still in love. They are meant to be. They both know it now, more than ever, but they're too afraid to say it out loud.

"Mom—do you think . . . maybe . . ." I trail off, worried I might set her off. Even though she's on new meds now, meds that seem to be working, you never know what might do it, when she might crack again. *She's not a murderer, but that doesn't make her* well—is what Norma, Mom's doctor, said when I cried to her over the phone last week, begging for her to release Mom back to us, back to life.

*She's not ready,* she'd told us. *She needs time to heal, to come back to herself on her own terms, to be cared for, by professionals. Just come visit,* she'd said. *All she wants is to see you here, to see her getting better.*

I want to say it to her now, as she takes both my hands into hers: *come home.* Her fine-boned fingers wrap around mine and her skin is soft. My mother's skin. "We're not going to be together again, Livie," she says gently, as my heart dips. "Your father and I will always love each other, but we will never be married to each other again."

"But—if you love each other, then why? Why not?" I know it's a desperate, childish kind of logic, but I can't help it.

"Because," she sighs, moving a stray curl back behind my ear. "It's not enough. Not in the long run. We—we'd been going in our own direction, separate from each other, for a long time. We both wanted this, even if it was very painful at the time. It was the right thing to do, for your father, and for me. I mean that, Liv. I really do."

I stare at her. "I just don't get when it all changed, Mom. I mean—you guys used to be solid. You were everything to each other. How does that just go away?"

"Liv, trust me, we tried our best to make it work. We wanted it to work, for a while; we didn't want *you* to suffer at all." She pauses, eyebrows furrowed, deep lines set into her forehead. "But there was a rift, and it was getting bigger, and I wasn't happy. My meds were just awful—you remember, I couldn't even get out of bed, I couldn't compose, I couldn't do anything—so, instead of going to the doctor, as I should have, I just stopped taking them, and that turned out to be even worse. You father went through a lot. We both went through a lot. That's what our relationship started to revolve around—the mess inside my head. It wasn't good anymore. It wasn't right."

"But he still loves you, Mom."

"I know that, Liv," she says, taking my hands, her eyes shining, clear. "And because of all the love I had, and still have, for your father, I had to let him go. Let him live his life. I know it doesn't seem to make any sense when I say it out loud, but it was the only way I could start healing, too."

"But, don't you think that Heather—"

"I know all about Heather," she interrupts, sensing my instinct to say something nasty, "and everything she went through in her past. She seems like a good woman, Liv. And she seems good for your dad, and I'm happy for him. I really, truly am, because if I chose bitterness, about all of this . . . that would be the easy option. The default. Really, Liv. I get to choose, here, and I choose happiness. Okay? I choose to focus on what's good, on what I have." She squeezes my hand. "This place is good for me, where I am, the people taking care of me while I figure out how to really take care of myself again. I'm finally starting to heal, to learn how to really do that, Liv. Trust me."

"Mom." I start, turning to face the piano, lifting the lid from where I sit. "I need to know . . ."

"What's that, sweetheart?"

"Stern." Her face draws downward when I say it, and she looks haggard for a moment, freshly ashamed. But, I keep on, because I have to, I have to know. "Mom—why did you confess?"

Tears ridge up in her eyes. "I—I thought I must have done it," she says. "There was blood on my hands . . . and I'd been thinking . . . I'd been wanting—" She chokes back a little cry of pain. "I'd been off my meds for too long, and everything in my head had gone strange, Liv," she says. She inhales deep. "I didn't want to tell you this, Liv, but the truth is, I'd been thinking of killing myself. More than thinking it. At the time, I wasn't thinking about anything clearly at all. It was so dark inside my head, and I was so confused—I just thought I must have killed him. I didn't remember—anything. Just my hands. Just the blood on my hands. His head, in my lap."

"It's okay, Mom." By instinct, I move to her, ribbon my arms around her neck.

She'd blamed herself, the whole time, for Stern's death. She'd held all of that guilt in her cells, let it expand, take up every single inch of her brain so there were no parts left to play back the truth of that night.

She pulls away after a few minutes, our hands still held in the space between us, surrounded on all fronts by white. White walls. White bed. White sun. "So, Livie," she finally says, blotting at her face. "It's not too much of a dump here, is it? It's plain, I know . . . but, I bet we can fix it up. Don't you think?"

I take it in again. White walls. White bed. White sun. White walls. Blank walls. Something forms in my brain—in my fingers. I stand suddenly from the piano bench, put my hands on her shoulders. "Hold on a minute, Mom. Okay?"

"Where are you going?"

"Be right back, Mom! One minute!"

I jog down the wide, sun-drenched hallway—past the nurses station, several other patients stirring things in the common kitchen, NPR humming along on the radio, holler "coming right back!" to the short-haired woman at reception—and to the parking lot. Raina's passed out, snoring softly in the leaned-back front seat. I reach through the (mostly open) window to unlock the door, grab my book bag, lock everything up, and run back inside.

Mom's still at her piano when I get back. "Thought maybe you got freaked and decided to skip town," she cracks, leaning her elbows against the piano lid.

"No, no," I tell her. "I just remembered I brought you something."

I grab the wooden chair from her desk and start unzipping my bag.

I unload my sketchbook, my charcoals, a red pen, India ink. Mom lights up—I do, too, seeing her face.

"Artwork," I say, "for your new place. But I'm going to need some music, while I draw."

"Oh, Liv—I don't—my hands are . . . they're not back to normal yet, you know."

"Mom—it doesn't matter what you sound like." For a moment, I consider telling her about my own artistic "issues," but something stops me—some fear, maybe, that she'll blame herself. That the glow in her eyes will retreat, that all her forward-moving healing will freeze in place and shrivel to some black goo in her center that sucks her back inside of it. So I say nothing. "Just play for me."

"Well," she sighs, "just don't say I didn't warn you if it's no good." Then, slowly, she opens the lid, hovers her fingers over the keys like she's not quite sure what to do next. But when her hands touch down, they just *go*—and what starts to fill the room is sound that actually does manage, in some small way, to stop time, to reverse all its salty, vengeful effects. And when I draw her, it's as she was—as she always will be to me when she plays—young, and long-haired, and mermaid-finned, and strong, and passionate, and healthy.

Free.

I rip it gently from my sketchbook when I finish and place it in front of her.

"Liv," she says, turning to me, my sketch trembling in her hands as she stares at it. "You remembered. The mermaid story."

"Of course I remember," I tell her, feeling so full-up with joy I'm surprised my body hasn't burst from it yet. "It's my favorite story."

She lays the sketch down on the piano stool and comes to hug me. Big fat happy tears roll down both of our cheeks as we sway there, rocking foot to foot, almost dancing. In her white room, with its white curtains, white carpet, white sunlight, blue sky. *Blue sky.*

"Mom!" *Holy crap holy crap holy crap.*

She pulls back, looks at me worriedly. "What's wrong? Is something wrong? What's wrong?"

"No—it's just—the sky." We turn together to look at it. Hope brims up inside of me to bursting as I see it: *blue.*

Not gray. Blue. I'd thought *innocent* was the finest word in the entire English language, but I change my mind.

It's *blue.*

My whole body flushes with it—the most brilliant, sparkling thing I've ever seen in my life—this sky. Today. I'd forgotten what it was like, to see like this. To see *color.*

*Blue.* Every cell in my body feels lit up.

"It's really beautiful, isn't it?" she says, and I open my eyes wider because I want them to be absolutely flooded with it. *Blue*. "You should go outside and enjoy it, Liv. Too gorgeous to stay cooped up in here."

I stall, a little tug of fear in my belly—fear of all the things that might happen as soon as I leave her. "What are you going to do?"

She glances over her shoulder, at her piano. "I think I might keep playing." There's a glint in her eye that I recognize—that middle-of-the-night-adventure glint—and a flush in her cheeks that I can *see*. I never thought something that small, that simple, would send chills ripping through me—a kind of base joy I'd even forgotten I could feel.

"I'm gonna be back real soon, Mom," I promise, hugging her again. She kisses my forehead. Her lips are soft; her hair smells good. Little things—little things you don't realize until they go, and come back again, as though by magic. "Real soon."

I let myself out of Mom's room and stand by the door a minute, until I hear the notes of her piano again, wafting out her door and down the hall like a siren song, calling me back to myself, calling me to the outside.

To Raina, awake, now, and singing along to the radio, as she waits for me to emerge.

To the wild cerulean sky.

# twenty-eight

On the other side of chaos is order.

Order is what we make happen—an instinct hammered into our lizard brains to help us stay upright, even when everything around us is chaotic, tilting, trying to buck us off its back, back into bottomless Nowhere, back into the Gray Space.

People die. They die too early, sometimes. And there is grief that almost crushes everything.

Almost. But then there is the realization that it *is* worth it to be alive, even if just to smell the very particular scent of your mother one more time—the scent as she leaned over you nightly before you fell to sleep, and told you, again and again, what made a person free, and how you meant something, and how you were meant *for* something—even if it takes a long time to figure out what that thing is, even if that thing is just to remember this story and tell it, or keep it.

You remember it is important to be alive because there is love, even if you cannot touch it with your hands or your lips. There is love.

* * *

"Liv!" Heather calls from the bottom of the stairwell, Wynn in hand, bouncing back and forth on her sparkly pink flats.

"Almost ready! Almost ready!" I lean over the banister; my hair's still a wet mess, my dress tugged about halfway on, paint still caked to the parts of my forearms and elbows I forgot to scrub in the shower.

Heather looks beautiful. I, however, am full-mess: makeup not on, heels that have dug themselves into some mysterious black hole in the crumpled-up-clothes wasteland of my room (who knows what other lost things I'd find in there, if I bothered to really look), paints scattered, loose across my windowsill, the canvas I've been working on slowly, for the past month—since the day I first visited Mom—still dripping-slick with burnt sienna, olive, canary, linseed oil. Every time I finish one, I bring it right to Mom; she's started to joke that I'm just using her for the free gallery space.

"I'm heading to the church now," Heather says. "My sister's waiting in the car, and your dad's already there." She smiles, a happy, nervous smile. "We'll see you soon."

"See yoooou soon, Livieeeee," Wynn squeals.

I run down the stairs, tugging my dress just a stitch more secure before lifting Wynn up into my arms. The bandages have finally come off and I'm getting used to the scars, raised and pink and trying to find their way back to normal skin. Raina says they make me look "hardcore."

Pam, my new therapist, who's like some blissed-out, grown-up, yoga-hippie version of Rain, says that the physical body, the idea of the self, is kind of a scar: a brief puckering of time, a fleeting sewing together of energy and heart, which go beyond the physical form, on and on and on, forever.

"Mommy sandwich," I whisper into Wynn's ear, and she giggles like it's the funniest thing she's ever heard as I lean her over to Heather's right, and I lean left, and we kiss both of her cheeks at once. She smells like honeydew and hairspray.

I put Wynn down, and she resumes twirling, and admiring the stupendous glitter of her footwear with funny little coos. "Do you need any help?" I ask Heather. "With your dress, or the car, or anything?"

"How does my makeup look? Does it look okay? Is my hair—has it fallen out? Should I have left it down?" she asks, patting at her pearl-studded, tendriled blond bun as she searches my face for some sign of *uh-oh, you got this* all *wrong*.

Her sister *beeeeeep*s from outside. Heather inhales deeply. "I told her not to come in," she says. "I'm already running late, and she'd just fuss."

I'm pretty sure Dad's pacing in some back room at the chapel right now, just as nervous; he rehearsed his vows to me for an hour last night after dinner. "You look perfect," I tell her, understanding this is what she wants. Perfection. Order. And there's nothing wrong with that.

"I didn't expect to feel this nervous." She laughs, exhaling, shaking herself out. She hugs the plastic-encased mass of dress into her chest with one hand and grabs Wynn's hand with the other. "Okay, then." She starts to shut the door behind her and then turns back, panicked again. "You'll be there by four?"

I nod. "Deep breaths."

Only a few minutes later, back up in my room stepping into my heels and putting on the final touches of lipgloss, I hear the *diiiing-dong* of the bell. I straighten Mom's pendant necklace against my collarbone, and rush downstairs to open the door.

"Olivia Tithe," he says, leaning against the door frame in his tux. He runs one hand through his thick blond hair, a piece of it coming to fall over his eye as he looks me up and down. He swallows hard before he says anything. And all he can say is: "Wow . . . I mean. Wow."

For some reason, all I can think at that moment is of Wynn, that thing she repeats when she's uber excited: *wowwowowowowowowowowow.* This sets me giggling. Giggling hard, smiling stupidly, embarrassingly big as I say his name, and step right up close to him.

"Austin Morse." He puts his hands on the waist of my silky cobalt blue gown and draws me to him—into the spice of his skin and his warm chest and his fast-beating heart—and I keep my eyes open as we make out there in the doorway, squares of sunlight reflecting against his face so it looks gold. And we keep making out, there in the doorway until my phone buzzes.

Raina. *Get yer hand out of Morse's pants and come get me!*

"It's time," I tell him, trying to pull away but finding it very, very difficult right at this moment because, though I still don't quite know what Austin is to me or even what I want him to be, it's just so goddamn fun to kiss someone. I kiss his lips, the dimple in his right cheek, the shine of his cheekbone. "Then again . . . what *is* time, anyway? Just a human invention . . . clocks . . ."

He laughs. "I think it starts to matter when you have a wedding to go to."

"Oh. Right . . . a *wedding*." I stare at him funny. "I was wondering why you were wearing that tuxedo."

Austin climbs into the backseat of my perfect, rusty junker of a car when Raina gets in—two braids today, flowing down the back of her emerald green dress—only a little past four o'clock.

The three of us drive—windows all the way down even if it totally messes up our hair, late-September wind flowing in—plumeria, sweet acacia, honeyed lilt of palm and fresh-cut grass—and Blonde on Blonde blaring from the radio. My hair is wind-wild, whipping behind us. However it ends up looking when we get out of this car, it doesn't matter. It's perfect, far as I'm concerned. Nothing matters right now but this.

We pass Dovedale Park on the way. The carousel slides past in a shock of color—the ponies and their pastel manes and wide green eyes, the glow of bulbs overhead, pulsing through all that velvety red. I'd forgotten how beautiful it was, how I used to ride it for what felt like hours, amazed, as a little girl in Mom's lap.

And then, from the rearview mirror, I see him again—the memory of him, full-color, fully alive, sitting in the backseat beside Austin. And, for a moment, it's the four of us, stuffed together in my car—like some funny double date no one knows about but us. Me and Stern. My Stern. And, right now, in the car—I see him as he was—Stern—leaning his face out the window to let the wind whap him as he always did, his ink black hair, hazel eyes squinted into the falling sun.

For a second—a second that lasts infinite seconds—he turns his face away from the wind to meet my eye. He smiles, he smiles without worrying about the gap in his teeth, he smiles in a way that I know: he is free.

And then he goes. He does not shiver away this time. He glows, he glows so bright, and then I can't see him anymore. But when I blink, I see the brightness of him for a whole minute, like after staring into the sun. And I realize, right now and forever, maybe: so what if I am a little crazy, if ghosts are real, or if they're not. I got to tell him I loved him. I got to say it. Who knows if it was real for him, if he felt it, if we were there together in some other place entirely. It was real for me, real as anything else, a thing that burned inside of me and found release.

Raina leans forward to turn up "Fourth Time Around," and our mouths—hers and mine and even Austin's (who is messing up all the words because he's just starting to figure out Bob Dylan)—open to take the music in and release it: a loud, fearless, whole-hog singing, which is the only way to sing as you drive to your father's wedding with a person you love deep, and another you might love—one day—and another you will always love, forever, and who is gone.

But you are here. And the sky is four different colors right now, at least. And you are free.

So you sing. You sing whole-hog, fearless loud. You sing the whole way.

E N D

# acknowledgments

First and foremost, I owe thanks the length and weight of thirty-to-forty full-grown elephants to Lexa Hillyer, Lauren Oliver, and Rhoda Belleza, for always pushing me further, and better; for trust, patience, ideas, insights; for always being on the other end of whatever line's around to keep me calm and writing; for making all of this seem manageable even when it feels glaring and mountainous; for making every sentence better; for being teachers, and beacons, and wild party animals, when the time is right.

Stephen Barbara, for agenting wonderment and delight, and Greg Ferguson, for giving another book the kindest home its rearer could imagine, for superior, thoughtful editing finesse, for making many parts of this book make any sense at all, and, mainly, for always being ready, willing, and more-than-able to quote *Wayne's World*, whenever possible.

The Hatz: Danielle DuGuay, Landon Newton, Annie Raife, Grace Lowman, Camila "Poodle" Danger, and to all my friends (I'm naming you in my head right now, and will soon tattoo your names in a neat list down my spine, I promise) for being the dreamiest human beings a girl could wish to have by her side. Thank you thank you thank you, for it all. You keep my heart working right.

All the folks I met in Miami—and especially Barbara (and a very cool dog named Dmitri)—who were among the kindest, most generous people I've met, and who took me in and cooked me meals and showed me how amazing and weird and truly unique your city is. (But no thanks to the very aggressive mosquitos, who showed absolutely zero restraint and drank my blood in swarms at every possible opportunity (shame on you).)

S—for love, and for heartache. Any responsible writer, and human, probably needs to learn both.

Finally, to my family: for endless support, and endless love, and endless a-million-other-things it's difficult to write succinctly about. I'm more lucky than I even really understand, I think. But I'm trying. I'm trying.